Mothy Knickers

Are We Having Fun Yet?

Jo Milanne

PAPERBACK

ISBN: 978-1-7644452-0-7

Copyright © 2025 by Jo Milanne

All rights reserved.

No portion of this book may be reproduced in any form without written permission from the publisher or author, except as permitted by U.S. copyright law.

Contents

1

Tim & Three Girls

The Bridcombe Sisters

A pair of screaming girls clutched at firm hands dragging them through a doorway by their ponytails. They feared the rough handling could pull some hair out by the roots.

Detective Timothy Funicular, better known as Tim Fun, rarely lost his cool, but in this case, he did. The girls had trespassed on his property, invaded his privacy and put his honour in jeopardy.

"Our dad is going to kill you." Kinta yelled.

"He will break you in two." Lirah roared.

Their captor knew that to be possible and highly probable. Nevertheless, he forced the identical fifteen-year-old twins out of his ground floor flat and towed them towards his car. There, he met another problem, he couldn't manage to open the car door with both hands full.

"Behave yourselves or this is going to get a lot worse. Just be quiet and get in the car. Please." Tim puffed.

The twin's older sister, Xanthe Bridcombe, ran up the footpath towards them. Her own shiny brown pony tail swung in time with her fast gait.

"It will get worse for you, that's for sure Tim Fun." Xanthe shouted. "Let my sisters go. I've already phoned Dad and he is on his way. So you are in for it now!"

The girls' father, Sergeant Angus Bridcombe, a giant of a man, came to a screeching halt in a police squad car. Gravel sprayed over the tableau of Tim and the three sisters, lit by a single streetlight surrounded by moths. The big policeman leapt from his vehicle leaving the door bouncing open on its hinges.

"Alright. This better be good. I want you ALL down at the station."

"But Daddy…"

"Don't *Daddy* me. NOW! You girls come with me. TIM FUN! YOU better be right behind me. OR ELSE!"

Shaking with rage, Bridcombe pointed an accusing finger at the slender younger man. Tim Fun twigged to whatever *or else* meant did not bode well for his health. The twins tried to preempt their father's dreaded interrogation during a riotous drive back to the police station.

"It was just a joke." Kinta cried.

"He thought we were Xanthe." Lirah added.

"What? What did you two do?" Xanthe screamed at her younger sisters.

"SHUT UP all of you. Or I'll bring your mother into this."

That threat hit home. The girls' mother, Opal Bridcombe, ruled the roost. Her hulking husband Angus, descendant of Vikings, rarely crossed his little woman and nor did anyone else.

DC Anwei Timothy Funicular, better known as Tim Fun, obediently followed the squad car in his own trusty old Fiat.

Adding to the young detective's angst, he had deliberately opted out of attending a public beach party to avoid trouble with Xanthe Bridcombe. Yet, his plan for an early night at home had already gone pear shaped before 9pm.

Tim Fun reached his twenty-ninth year without mishap until the Bridcombe teenagers threw a spanner in the works. An ambush at the local surf beach first embroiled the shy bachelor with sixteen-year-old Xanthe.

He'd done his utmost to behave properly but the Bridcombe sisters had other ideas.

Several years ago, three ambitions owned by the new police recruit coincided: Tim Fun found a cheap flat near the beach, he joined the local surf club, and his budding detective career kicked off.

Training alongside experienced officers, DI Dougall Grimslade and DS Dulcy Vestige boosted Tim's success in the investigative field of police work.

DS Dulcy Vestige's first husband, David Dubois, became Tim's landlord.

In the past, as a married couple, policewoman Dulcy and army regular David, both worked in The Northern Territory. The soldier applied to be at Robertson Barracks in the NT and talked his detective wife into transferring to Darwin as well.

The Dubois/Vestige marriage fell apart when David's sneaking reason for moving out of Queensland came to light; Dulcy discovered her husband went behind her back to buy a beach house for his former girlfriend, Zelia Wild and their illegitimate child, young Davy.

Zelia died as a result of domestic violence, at the hands of a lover who believed himself to be duped. DI Grimslade and DC Tim Fun undermined the killer's false tale blaming Dulcy's ex, and the real culprit ultimately went to prison. *[cite The Whodunit Thing by Jo Milanne.]*

David Dubois moved into his beach house to finally become a proper father to his six-year-old son, Davy.

A humble bedsit built-in underneath Dubois' beach house proved ideal for Tim. The small accommodation fitted his simple needs, being cheap, near work and close to the surf. Tim could store his surfboard overnight at the surf club, and walk down to the nearby shore. In time, the stigma of murder attached to the beach house faded.

Landlord, David Dubois eventually teamed up with Chantel Cheron. The couple each had sons from previous relationships. Those boys, Davy Dubois and Dominic Cheron, had been six years old when Tim first came to live at the address as a tenant.

As a trusted tenant, Tim would be called upon to mind the young boys when David and Chantel went out. Tim watched kids movies or played video games with Davy and Dominic upstairs in the main house at those times. The lonely young detective enjoyed the youngsters' company and appreciated having his rent reduced for babysitting.

Mostly, Tim Fun enjoyed a carefree bachelor existence, working and training with experienced mentors and surfing in his spare time.

Although the reserved young man longed for female company, he took each day as it came and been happy enough.

When he qualified as a detective constable, friends and colleagues gave him t-shirts emblazoned with jokey captions. The humorous gifts made the shy young man feel part of a team, as intended. Tim collected more of the same type of t-shirt to wear over his board shorts. In the back of his mind, he imagined sign-posting himself as a police detective with a witty sense of humour, would attract bikini girls.

It didn't.

Slim part Asian Tim Fun invited various girls out to dinner. None ever lined up for seconds and his polite generosity never earned so much as a goodnight kiss. Overshadowed by strapping blonde and bronzed Aussie lifeguards, he failed to gain even a taste of romance from the bevy of beach belles who hung around the surf club.

Considered an oddity for the way he spoke, nastier females back-stabbed him with snide remarks:

"He's too posh. Always putting on the dog with the way he talks."

"He thinks he is better than us. But he's good for a free meal anyway."

"I ordered lobster. He can afford it. Then he tries for a goodnight kiss. As if."

"No! He tried it on? How did he lead up to it?"

"He begins by saying *if I may be so bold*. I nearly peed myself laughing."

"All the free bubbly you drank wouldn't help."

"I know. That too."

Tim's old fashioned phraseology evolved out of his studious and bookish childhood. While other pubescent kids in high school flirted and explored an overload of hormones, Tim had his nose stuck in classic literature.

Forever absorbed in heavy old tomes, Tim was dubbed Mothy Knickers, a corruption of Timothy Funicular. The hated nickname forged the young man's insistence on simply being known as Tim Fun. He dropped his first given name of Anwei since it attracted racist comments.

Made painfully aware a free meal to be the only incentive to any date with him, Tim resolved to go it alone. His solo state sufficed until the pretty teenager Xanthe Bridcombe busted his resolution.

Tim had been lazing on his surfboard out beyond the breakers when Xanthe popped up virtually out of the blue. She used the tried and true method of getting close to a lifesaver, swimming the last several metres underwater to catch him by surprise.

"Ooh Timmy. I'm feeling terribly breathless. Could you please paddle me back to shore on your surfboard?"

Timmy? No one ever called him that. It seemed rather familiar from a young girl he barely knew.

Tim helped her scramble onto his surfboard, glad to be of assistance. Back on the beach the maiden in distress threw her arms around the surprised man and kissed him soundly on the mouth. Seemed Xanthe Bridcombe had caught her breath by then.

"You're my hero Timmy," she exclaimed, "how can I ever thank you?"

Embarrassed, Tim's smooth tanned complexion did not disguise his deep blush. He positioned his board between himself and the girl as a barrier, hoping no one noticed her over-eager embrace.

"No worries. It's part of my lifeguard duty. Which one are you?"

"I'm Xanthe."

"You three sisters are so alike, you could be triplets."

"I know. Everyone says that, but I am the eldest by a year. I've turned sixteen now. That's the age of consent you know."

"Yes. It is. That is correct."

Xanthe smiled coquettishly.

"So, there must be something nice I can do for you Timmy. Just ask me for anything. I'll do it."

Taken aback by the teenager's forthright manner and suggestive offer, Tim suspected a set-up.

He looked about the surf club and the beach to see who observed the peculiar exchange. As far as he could make out, nothing seemed out of the ordinary. His 'rescue' of the brazen sixteen-year-old had apparently not made a ripple in the normal everyday scheme of things. Nevertheless, Tim remained sceptical.

"I'm glad you're feeling better. Perhaps don't swim so far out in future Xanthe."

"Can I at least buy you an ice-cream Timmy?"

Tim tried to put the brash teenager off kindly.

"Maybe another time. But thanks for the offer."

"Come on Timmy. Please. You're not actually on lifeguard duty today are you?"

Xanthe had previously checked that he wasn't on the days roster posted on the surf club notice board. It had encouraged her approach plan.

"I'm on call for work."

"A policeman's work is never done hey Timmy? I know because my Dad is in the force too."

"Yes I know your father well. Sergeant Bridcombe is an excellent officer."

"Mum says his jumbo size is a huge deterrent to crooks."

"For sure. Unlike mine." Tim was sure his physical appearance drove the suspected set-up.

"I reckon you'd outwit them anyway Timmy. You're so smart."

Xanthe's smile struck Tim as genuine. At just sixteen, she seemed too young to be as conniving as some of the older girls at the surf club. He warmed to the compliment coming from such a pretty lass. It made his day.

Tim knew Xanthe's attention might still be a set-up, but it so happened he had not tasted ice-cream in a long time. Sweets were only partaken as a rare treat since he kept himself fit. Temptation nudged the lonely bachelor. It seemed ungracious not to accept the girl's well-meant thanks. *She's just being friendly. I could do her that small favour. Why not?*

"Ice-cream hey? I suppose one won't ruin my physique." Tim joked.

"I wouldn't want that to happen Timmy. You've got such a gorgeous athletic body, much sexier than those muscle bound apes at the club. Everyone says so."

"Really?" Tim laughed. "Who's everyone?"

"My sisters Lirah and Kinta think you're really cute Timmy. So do I. You're our top pick out of all the life guards."

Cute?

The unlikely couple ate their ice-creams while ambling bare footed along the esplanade, still in their swimsuits. The pattern on Tim's colourful Hawaiian board shorts almost matched Xanthe's brief bikini.

Tim tried to keep from ogling her attractive figure. The girl clocked whenever his gaze fleetingly flicked over her body. Tim was sure she sucked her tummy in and stuck her chest out to whet his interest.

The sixteen-year-old's flirtation awoke some basic needs Tim had put on hold. Their thirteen year age difference did not sit well with his innate sense of propriety, yet he entertained private thoughts, and began to daydream. He told himself he'd never act on his fantasies, so no harm done. Xanthe prattled on:

"I know you have that flat where Davy and Dominic used to live."

"So, you know those two boys?"

"Sure. We went to the same school. I'm only a few years younger. I've danced with both Davy and Dominic at our formals. But I wasn't allowed to go out on dates with the likes of them."

Tim still thought of Davy and Dominic as kids since he used to babysit the pair. It brought home the wide age gap between himself and Xanthe. He briefly wondered why she referred to those lads as *'the likes of them'*.

Before long, one of the reasons put Tim's own good reputation in jeopardy, yet he did not suspect anything yet.

Xanthe bit the end off her ice-cream cone and sucked out the last creamy sip, slurping and licking her lips. Fascinated, Tim had to drag his gaze away. She walked to a bin to dispose of the wrapper, swaying her hips, then spun around to catch him admiring her performance.

Tim covered his ogling by pretending to have sand in his eye. He then made an attempt at innocuous conversation.

"A shame the lads moved out of home. I guess they were ready to be independent."

"Yep. Davy and Dominic wanted to party and have sex with girls which would be awkward living with the oldies."

Xanthe's ribald response confirmed Tim's opinion of why those lads left home, yet knowing the girl aimed to shock, he did not react. His air of detachment only made her redouble her efforts.

"Now that I'm sixteen and of legal age, I want to try everything too. You could be my first lover Timmy. Okay?"

Aghast, Tim broke a sweat and blushed more deeply than ever before.

"Good grief Xanthe! That is a highly inappropriate suggestion. I am sure you realise it too. I strongly suspect to being set up for a laugh by people at the surf club."

"Nope. It's my own idea. Don't worry our close friendship would be our secret Timmy. For one thing, I don't want my parents to find out of course. Mum and Dad would kill me, and then you. Or maybe kill you first. Anyway murder would be done."

"You should mind your parents' wishes and not disappoint them. But look, I am happy to be friends with you Xanthe and I will leave it at that. Now I have to go. Take care. See you around."

Tim felt he clearly dismissed the precocious girl and foiled the probable set-up. Xanthe did not see his response in the same way. His acceptance of friendship and saying he would see her around, encouraged her. Aware Tim had to in his late twenties, the sixteen-year-old year old preened for successfully luring an older guy. She and her sisters assessed all the lifeguards and Tim Fun truly topped the list. The teenagers loved his boyish good looks and smooth athletic body. He didn't seem to have any steady girlfriend either, so the girls tagged him ripe for the picking.

Later, Xanthe made an announcement to her sisters:

"Timmy likes me and says he wants to be friends. So I'm going all out to get him."

"Are you going to do it with him?" Kinta asked wide-eyed.

"Of course. First chance I get. That's the whole idea."

"I can't wait until I'm sixteen." Lirah sighed.

In the fresh new break of another day, Tim paddled his surfboard out early into the chilly ocean. Xanthe Bridcombe had haunted his dreams inappropriately and he strove to dispel what he'd imagined. Needing to douse himself in cold water, he wore board shorts again, instead of a wet suit. The icy conditions did little to stem his recollection of yesterdays encounter. *I have to stop thinking of her. This is so not right.*

Tim could not forget Xanthe saying she wanted him as her first. If it happened, it would also be his first time. He imagined another virgin would have no idea of his fumbling ineptitude and that made a nice extra incentive.

Tim took a tentative step into forbidden territory by daring to consider taking Xanthe up on her offer. After all, if he didn't accept someone else would. Although he berated himself for this thought, one small step became one huge leap onto a slippery slope for the shy bachelor. Tim Fun would teeter on the brink for many a day.

"Boo."

Xanthe emerged beside his board. As Tim shivered, startled, she tipped him off into the sea.

Laughing, the delinquent girl groped his private parts. No one had ever done such a rude thing to Tim. The shock made him almost choke on a mouthful of salt water. He no longer registered the cold as instant heat suffused his entire body.

"NO. Xanthe you can't do that." he gasped.

"No one can see what we're doing underwater Timmy. You can feel me if you want to."

Tim floundered for seconds before regaining his board. He had to escape. Fortunately a half decent swell rolled up and he rode it to shore. Xanthe ably body-surfed in on the same wave. Squeezing salt water from her ponytail, she sashayed up the beach beside her conquest as he doggedly toted his board back to the surf club.

"I meant what I said yesterday Xanthe. Just friends. Okay?"

"Sure. Just good friends. I won't tell if you don't." she smiled. "There's a beach party tonight. A bonfire too. Mum and Dad say we can go but have to be home before ten."

"We?"

"Me and the twins. We hope you'll be there Timmy. Will you?"

"Nope. Early night for me. Work tomorrow." he replied shortly.

Tim very looked forward to the surf club bonfire parties. Yet he wouldn't encourage Xanthe or cater to any set-up by going this time. He decided the best course of action would indeed be in his own bed in the dark.

Despite best intent, Tim's imminent fall from grace began that night. No sooner had he switched off his bedside lamp, then he had a visitor in the nubile form of Xanthe. She had crept in silently and slipped into bed beside him.

"Geez!" Tim leapt out, shielding his nakedness with a pillow. "How in blazes

did you get in?"

"Everyone knows you hide your back door key in the peg basket."

"Everyone? Who's everyone?"

"Davy and Dominic bragged about using it to sneak girls into your flat when you were working away." she laughed.

That news upset Tim. He did not expect such a betrayal from the boys he used to babysit. He regrouped in the face of his compromised situation.

"You have to go Xanthe. I will not be a party to this. Go back to the bonfire or I will call your parents myself."

"Don't you want me?"

"No. I do not want you," he lied, "are you leaving or do I call your father? I have the police station on speed dial, and I know Angus is on duty tonight."

Tim did indeed have the number on speed dial. He went for the cell phone on his bedside table, but Xanthe palmed it first and held it behind her back.

"That phone is police property Xanthe so give it back. Listen, I'll watch you run back down the lane until you reach the surf club lights. That's my best offer."

"Spoilsport." Xanthe pouted. "Anyway, if you call my father I'll just say you brought me back here yourself."

"Don't you dare." he replied crossly.

"Oh, don't be mad Timmy. I just want you so much."

She stroked his arm with the phone. Tim wrestled it from her hand, dropping the pillow in the process.

"Ooh. Timmy. I think you must want me too." Xanthe said as she eyed the evidence.

Tim panted against an onrush of desire, hastily grabbing the pillow again.

"On the other hand, you can go outside and get in my car. I will drive you home right away."

"Naked?" Xanthe giggled.

"I'll get dressed in the bathroom."

"Don't bother. I want to go back to the bonfire anyway." she sulked.

Xanthe left as quietly as she'd arrived. The perturbed man threw on a pair of shorts and watched her jog back to safety at the surf club.

Tim dragged himself back inside and collapsed on his bed feeling very let down. All the teenagers wronged him. Davy and Dominic went behind his back and Xanthe misused his key to sneak in. He could only guess at how many were amused knowing where he hid the key.

The whole ordeal of disappointments exhausted Tim. If only Xanthe was older or he were younger, and if only he didn't feel set-up for the amusement of others. Yet Tim ached to have what the sixteen-year-old offered so generously. He fell into a deep sleep that conjured up taunting dreams.

Later that same night, Tim experienced an illusion of a warm female body sneaking into his bed. He welcomed her exploring hands. His ensuing reaction erupted like Vesuvius. In his dream the hand maiden exited with a whisper.

"I'll be back soon."

Tim roused half-awake believing he'd experienced a colossal wet dream generated by his fever for Xanthe. Not wanting to relinquish the dream, he chased sleep again to relive the thrill. His reward came as a replay of a warm body slipping into the bed beside him. Gripped by the hallucination he rose to the occasion entrapped by the irresistible sensation.

"Xanthe." he murmured.

It felt so good, but it turned out to be so very bad.

A little giggle came from the girl in his bed. Another girl entered the room and got in on his other side, making it a very crowded threesome in the narrow bunk. He had inadvertently entertained the fifteen-year-old Bridcombe twins, Lirah and Kinta.

When Xanthe returned to the bonfire she couldn't see her sisters amongst the other party goers. Earlier the twins were observed engaged in some private whispering. With an idea they were up to some mischief involving Tim Fun, the eldest sister retraced her steps back to his flat.

Tim sprung up in alarm at the twin invasion. His wonderful dream morphed into a nightmare. He snapped the light on and hastily tried to don a pair of jeans. That's when he grabbed both girls by their long ponytails and dragged them outside.

Xanthe approached Tim's flat as he pulled the twins by their hair and tried to get them into his Fiat.

Seeing her younger sisters roughly manhandled, Xanthe riled up. Without waiting for explanations, she phoned her dad, Sergeant Angus Bridcombe.

With the arrival of the girls' father, the unassuming shy and reserved young detective faced a major disgrace. Tim Fun cringed to imagine what everyone would think of him. If the Bridcombe sisters implicated him in misconduct, it was three against one.

Since the twins were underage, he would be accused of being a paedophile. It was just too awful. He would lose his career and become an outcast, a veritable leper to society.

Tim could not deny befriending Xanthe and obviously she kept her sisters well informed. No doubt that hook-up had been noted by others. Despite reaching the age of consent, sweet sixteen made Xanthe far too young for himself. It would appear he took wrongful advantage.

To be fair, the precocious girl instigated the flirtation, but that excuse would not hold water since Tim held a position of trust as a member of the police force.

Tim sought help from his supervising officer, Dougall Grimslade, in a quick phone call before following Bridcombe's squad car back to the police station.

Fortunate to have been mentored by DI Dougall Grimslade and DS Dulcy Grimslade (nee Vestige) Tim Fun earned their respect as a diligent and clever addition to their investigative team. He'd been among the first to congratulate the Grimslade couple when Dougall proposed to Dulcy publicly at The Whodunit Thing, a police club charity ball.

Tim sincerely hoped the Grimslades would see his side of the current debacle.

2

Accused

At The Cop Shop

Married for twelve years, Detective couple Dougall and Dulcy Grimslade remained totally enamoured with each other.

Their usual Saturday night at home included wee drams of whisky enjoyed outside on the broad patio overlooking the sea. Background music from Dougall's extensive collection always set the mood.

On the particular night of Tim Fun's dilemma, Dougall chose a classic Paul Anka song *Put Your Head On My Shoulder* as he slow-danced his adoring wife under the stars.

The raucous jangle of Dougall's phone broke the magic spell of romance.

"Oh no." Dulcy moaned. "What dreadful timing."

"It's Tim. He wouldn't call for no good reason." Dougall answered.

Dulcy watched her husband's face change from concern to complete surprise. She only heard his side of the conversation.

"So where are you now? Alright. Listen Tim. Bridcombe might be riled up and unpredictable. Stay in your locked car until I get there."

Dougall ended the call.

"What's wrong?"

"Tim says he is accused of being a paedophile by Angus."

"No way! How did that happen?"

"Apparently all three of the Bridcombe girls found their way into his bedroom and compromised his integrity."

"Compromised his integrity?"

"That's how Tim put it."

"That will take some explaining. I better come with you. Cripes. Opal will kill him if Angus doesn't."

"That's why I said to stay in his car until I get there. They're all heading for the cop shop."

Dulcy and Dougall shed their pyjamas and dressed quickly before speeding down to the police station. Tim had parked beside Angus's squad car in the backyard behind the station. The Grimslades drove in, Dougall behind the wheel.

"Park close behind the squad car Dougall."

"Yep. My thoughts exactly."

As usual the Grimslade's minds meshed. Parking behind the squad car prevented Angus following Tim out, if it came to a crunch. They arrived just as Sergeant Bridcombe pounded a ham fist on the roof of Tim's Fiat while at the same time rattling the door handle.

"Open up!" Angus roared.

Angus Bridcombe had a reputation for being a gentle giant, yet his behaviour at this juncture belied that. Tim had never been so relieved in his life to see friendly faces in the form of his detective colleagues.

"Settle down Angus mate," Dougall placated, "we will talk this out reasonably inside."

"I'll kill the little prick." Angus seethed.

"No Angus. You will do no such thing. Act sensibly or I will call Opal." Dulcy added.

Opal and Dulcy had been best friends since childhood. They told each other everything. At the risk of damaging their friendship, Opal had pointed Dulcy in the right direction about her first husband's deceptions. The strong bond between the two women endured, although they hadn't always seen eye to eye.

Dulcy preferred not to involve Opal with the current trouble, but she knew the threat to be the greatest advantage with handling Angus in this fraught situation. Angus felt Dougall's advisory hand on his shoulder and took a few steps back.

Feeling to be a total chicken, Tim unlocked his car door and gingerly stepped out. In the heat of the moment, he had left home bare chested, wearing only a pair of torn and faded hipster blue jeans he'd hastily pulled on without underwear.

Half naked, Tim's well-defined six pack abs and toned muscles drew envy, anger or admiration depending on the observer.

"Do you have a shirt or a jacket?" Dulcy asked.

Tim found a t-shirt in his car. Printing emblazoned on the shirt front: *Detectives Cop A Feel* did little to amuse Angus Bridcombe.

Dougall ushered them all towards the rear of the station where the three saucy Bridcombe brats waited within. Angus had only heard a snippet of the incident. The twins saying *'he thought we were Xanthe'* supplied ample fuel to his temper.

Almost indoors, Angus suddenly wheeled on Tim and threw a punch. Dougall half expected it and managed to deflect the sudden blow with a strong forearm. Dougall rubbed his arm, knowing if that strike connected with Tim's face the younger man would have been king-hit out cold. Or worse.

Dougall Grimslade and Angus Bridcombe had been good friends for years. Both very determined men neared middle age and neither tolerated nonsense from anyone.

"That's it Bridcombe!" Dougall snarled. "Get inside and sit yourself in a cell or I'm charging you with assault."

"You could at least let me get one in Grimslade. Sorry you took the brunt though that was your own fault. Mate."

"Shut the feck up and put yourself in the feckin' cage Bridcombe."

Dulcy raised her eyebrows towards her husband because he never used coarse language. To do so now underlined the severity of his emotion. Bridcombe decided not to become a victim of his own rage and deigned to obey the order. Fuming with the indignity, Angus went to sit in the lock-up.

The prison cells usually held drunks overnight. No matter how much disinfectant got splashed about, a lingering odour of stale urine permeated the space. Fortunately, there had been no other inmates at the time to witness the police sergeant's humiliation.

Despite the unpleasant accommodation, Dulcy made Angus's three daughters join their father on the hard bunks in the same cell. She locked the four Bridcombes in to protect her beloved Dougall from receiving or delivering further violence. At that point Dulcy feared her husband could become the instigator himself.

"Why are we in jail?" Xanthe cried.

"You are not actually in jail. Just in protective custody." Dulcy ad libbed.

"Protective custody? Why? So Tim Fun doesn't drag us by our hair again?" Lirah yelled.

"WHAT! Did he drag you by the hair into his flat?" Angus roared.

"No Daddy." Xanthe intervened. "He was dragging them out of his flat when I got there."

"So! He'd already had his way?"

"NO." Tim spoke up despite an intention to politely wait his turn. "I was sound asleep when they crept in."

"He thought we were Xanthe." Kinta repeated Lirah's earlier ill-advised comment.

"Xanthe? Why would he think that? Xanthe what do you have to say?" Angus bellowed.

Everyone garbled at once. Grimslade let them get the allegations out of their systems before he attempted reasonable interviews. He raised an enquiring eyebrow to his wife. She got the drift.

"I'm making coffee." Dulcy said. "Who wants one?"

Everyone opted for coffee albeit of the bitter brew from the office machine. Dulcy handed it through the prison bars in paper cups. She avoided using china mugs for the potential of becoming hard missiles.

The coffee break gave time for all their marbles to fall somewhat back into place. In the interim, before further questions, Angus's phone rang. He answered a call from his wife, Opal. Everyone heard his meek reply.

"Yes dear. The girls are with me. We're just having coffee. We'll be home soon. Don't wait up."

He rung off. Xanthe smirked.

"Well Daddy that is the truth even if not the whole truth and nothing but the truth."

"Just keep your smart-mouth comments to yourself Xanthe. This is not over by a long shot and you have a lot of explaining to do."

"Yes Daddy."

"And don't *Daddy* me Xanthe. I'm your father."

His daughters fell about laughing. It seemed useless trying to get sense out of the unruly Bridcombes, so Grimslade addressed Tim Fun first.

"Tim, tell us your side of it."

"I retired before eight o'clock. I'd just turned the light out when Xanthe visited."

"Xanthe, why did you visit Tim at his flat?"

"I wanted to talk about something."

Xanthe's look to Tim begged him not to expand on what she had tried. Tim didn't want to explain that anyway.

"So Tim, you invited Xanthe into your flat."

"NO I did not." Tim replied.

"I let myself in." Xanthe admitted.

"How did you do that? Was the door unlocked?"

"Everybody knows Tim hides his back door key in the peg basket."

"Define everybody." Grimslade ventured.

"Dominic Cheron and Davy Dubois boasted about taking girls there while Tim was away. They used to laugh about the key being hidden in the peg basket."

Tim shook his head and groaned. He had always thought it an ideal hiding place.

"Tim, is that right?"

"I knew nothing about Davy and Dominic misusing my flat and I would never have condoned it. In fact, I feel betrayed by those boys because I expected better of them both. I used to babysit them as youngsters. There is no way I wanted every Tom, Dick and Harry making a convenience of my private rooms."

"So, you never noticed anything amiss when you returned home at any time?"

"Can't say I did. But then I didn't suspect anything."

Lirah and Kinta broke out laughing again. Xanthe thought better of it.

"Call yourself a detective." the twins chortled.

Angus waved a chiding finger towards his wayward teenagers. Dulcy waded in.

"So Xanthe. You let yourself into Tim's flat in the dark. Why?"

"Because...well...he said he wanted to be my friend. I just wanted to talk about it." she blushed.

"Xanthe!" Tim exclaimed. "I said I was happy to be your friend. I meant just a friend."

Xanthe began to cry. Tim attempted to explain.

"Xanthe formed an attachment to me. I tried to discourage her."

"How did that happen?" Dulcy asked.

"Xanthe had swum a long way out beyond the breakers. She felt out of breath and wanted a lift back to shore. So I paddled her back in on my surfboard."

"He did. He saved me. I felt like I might drown." Xanthe fibbed.

"Then what."

"Then he said he'd have an ice-cream with me." Xanthe sobbed.

"Xanthe offered to buy me an ice-cream as thanks." Tim amended.

It seemed judicious not to divulge the eager kiss she had planted on his mouth.

"So you took her up on the offer. Who paid?" Angus growled.

"It was Dutch Treat. We paid for our own." Tim replied.

"I wanted to pay for us both but I didn't have enough money. Daddy, now that I'm sixteen I think I should get more of an allowance."

"What? You think this is the perfect time to ask for a raise Xanthe? You're lucky I don't suspend your allowances indefinitely. For all of you."

"Not fair!" the twins chorused.

"We weren't in on the surfboard ambush." Lirah added.

"Ambush?"

Xanthe shrugged. Dulcy continued an attempt to get to the truth.

"So Tim, the extent of your connection with Xanthe is you helped her back to shore and had ice-creams afterwards."

"More or less. Apart from when Xanthe playfully tipped me off my board the next day."

"Didn't you see her swimming towards you?"

"No. I'd been half asleep waiting for a swell."

"That sounds flirtatious Xanthe." Dulcy remarked.

"It was just a bit of fun."

Xanthe's look defied Tim to say what swell bit of Fun she had groped underwater. Confident he would never tell, she delivered him a cheeky wink. Dulcy, Dougall and Tim all caught the wink. Fortunately Angus did not. Grimslade put the interrogation back on track.

"How did you handle Xanthe's surprise visit to you flat, Tim?"

"I told her to leave or I would call her father."

"Xanthe, is that true?"

"Yes. He chickened out. He said he'd drive me home right then, but I wanted to go back to the beach party."

"He chickened out of what Xanthe?" her father demanded.

"Of having me in his flat. You know. At night. And all that. He thought it was improper."

"Improper doesn't begin to describe it." Angus shouted.

Dulcy waited for tempers to cool before continuing with the fact it was only a short walk down to the surf club.

"So Xanthe you went back to the beach party alone?"

"Yes I did. I met my sisters back there again."

"Can you twins confirm that?"

"Yep. We knew nothing happened because she was back so soon. She said Tim chickened out."

"Thanks a heap Lirah." Xanthe looked daggers at her motor-mouth sister.

Xanthe was so like her mother Opal. Dulcy had a fair idea of what the girl hoped to get with Tim, and what he chickened out of giving her.

Dulcy and Opal had shared the rundown of their first sexual experiences during schoolies week holidays when they'd both been seventeen. At the time, Angus had been in his early twenties but Opal said he'd been a complete pushover. The women still enjoyed that story whenever they drank wine and reminisced over old times together.

Dulcy summarised:

"Alright. Nothing untoward happened except Xanthe trespassed on Tim's privacy."

"I have Angus on speed dial and said I was prepared to call him." Tim added in his own defence.

"You should have." Angus grouched.

"Anyway Xanthe ran outside and down the street. I watched until she gained the lights of the surf club to make sure she got back safely."

"Why didn't you escort her back?"

"She ran out before I got dressed."

"You were in pyjamas?"

"He was stark naked." Xanthe smiled coyly.

"Naked!" Angus shouted.

"I sleep naked. It isn't a crime. Obviously I didn't expect visitors." Tim retorted.

"How did the twins feature in this?"

"I went back to bed and fell asleep. Then the twins played a trick on me pretending they were Xanthe returning."

"Is that so?" Angus glared at his younger daughters.

"How did you get in?" Dulcy asked.

"The door was still unlocked." Kinta replied.

"Why didn't you lock the door Tim?"

"I felt so unnerved I didn't even think of it. I wish I had locked it but I never had any security problems before. Well, at least not that I knew of." he replied with the truth.

"I understand why you'd be unnerved, Tim." Dougall said.

Angus glared at his younger daughters.

"Okay you two, what exactly happened?"

"He erupted like a volcano." Lirah's smile looked cheeky.

"What?" Angus roared.

"He sprang out of the bed like he was jet propelled." Kinta added with wide-eyed innocence.

Both twins stared at Tim defying him to say they'd had their wicked way with his private person. His deep blush indicated he would avoid telling on them at any cost. He supplied an edited version in a partial truth.

"They jumped on the bed and giggled a lot."

"Do you agree with that?" Dulcy asked the twins for confirmation.

"Yes. Sorry but we just thought it would be really amusing. Like a blooper. Only we didn't video it."

"Shoot. We should have thought of videoing."

"It would've been too dark anyway."

"Oh yeah. It was dark. Until he turned the light on."

Dougall interrupted, naming Tim as their victim rather than the other way around.

"What did your victim do then?"

"He didn't see the funny side. But we thought he would because of the jokey t-shirts he wears. Like the one he has on now."

Tim regretted wearing *Detectives Cop A Feel*. He sought to shorten the narrative before the twins landed him in worse hot water.

"I dragged them outside by their pony tails. I planned to drive them home but I couldn't make them get into my car. Then Xanthe ran back, got angry, and called Angus."

The adults shared pointed looks. Angus compromised.

"I'm NOT sorry I defended my girls."

Angus escaped further censure for his furious reaction.

"Understandable." Dulcy said.

"A parent's worst nightmare." Grimslade agreed.

In the past DI Grimslade committed a major crime to defend his own daughter. Dulcy would never let on she knew what he'd done, not even to Dougall himself. Angus declared punishment on his daughters.

"You are all grounded until further notice."

"NO! That means Mum will find out."

"Unavoidable. And thanks to you lot, I'll probably be up all night trying to explain to your mother."

The girls were in deep trouble once Opal became involved. Xanthe tearfully tried to mitigate her actions.

"Timmy. You did say you wanted to be my friend. I really thought you liked me."

"Xanthe. I do like you. I am sorry you took anything I said or did to heart. It was never my intention to mislead you."

Tim's own heart shattered seeing Xanthe's beautiful liquid brown eyes brim over with tears. If only he could take her in his arms and kiss those tears away. He mentally admonished himself. *That thinking won't get me over this mess.*

Angus remembered how Opal had been at a similar age. He realised Xanthe took after her mother in more ways than one. His daughter was not only very beautiful but extremely forward. He put himself in Tim's shoes and knew the struggle.

"Tim. I am sorry I got the wrong impression and blamed you automatically." Angus apologised. "And Dougall, sorry I hurt your arm. And Dulcy, sorry I subjected you to my brutish side."

"I've seen worse. Good luck with Opal."

Dulcy knew Angus would be in for the type of inquisition his wife excelled at.

"Thank you." Tim breathed a sigh of relief.

"No drama. We all need to turn in. Tomorrow's another day." Dougall replied.

Tim returned to his flat, took his back door key out of the keyhole and vowed to fit a slide bolt to the inside. He'd keep the key on his personal key-ring in future instead of hiding it outside.

The Grimslades went home, Dulcy applied a cold pack to Dougall's arm before bed.

"Well that was a different Saturday night." Dougall yawned.

"Now I can put my head on your shoulder at last." Dulcy snuggled in.

It seemed a long time since they danced to the Paul Anka tune earlier. Dougall sang a line from the song.

"Just a kiss goodnight baby."

Dulcy picked up what she recalled of the other lyrics.

"And maybe we will fall in love? No maybe about it. I fell for you long ago Dougall."

"How long ago?"

"Forever ago."

"I think we were on the same page with that." Dougall replied.

"How's your arm now?"

"My arm is feeling better thanks. But something else has started throbbing."

"I'll get the cold pack." Dulcy teased.

"I've got a better idea."

Angus arrived home with the three girls well past their ten o'clock curfew. Opal had waited up and greeted them at the door.

"You had me worried. This is a later night than usual. You girls go clean your teeth and get straight to bed. Goodnight. See you in the morning."

"Goodnight Mummy. Night-night Mummy." The twins echoed Xanthe's choice of address.

Mummy? Opal twigged to a problem. The girls rarely called her *Mummy* unless they'd been up to mischief.

"Angus. Why do I suspect some misbehaviour?"

"Opal dearest, I'm bushed. Can it wait until morning?"

Dearest? Coming from Angus that term increased Opal's scepticism.

"No Angus. I'm not going to sleep with whatever happened tonight hanging over my head."

Angus sighed. This was never going to be easy.

"It was nothing really. Just a little misunderstanding. A silly prank."

"And? You claimed to be having coffee with the girls."

"We were having coffee. Your best friend Dulcy made it for us."

"Dulcy did? Were you at the Grimslade's place?"

"Um. No. We were all down at the cop shop."

"Dulcy was at the cop shop late on a Saturday night? Where was Dougall?"

"Dougall was there as well."

"Anyone else?"

"Tim Fun."

"Angus! Stop hedging and just spill what happened. I'm waiting."

Opal stood tapping a foot clad in fluffy cat slippers. Hands on her hips, the small woman managed to look forbidding even in the frilly floral nightdress she wore. Angus toned it down as best he could.

"Seems our Xanthe formed an attachment to Tim Fun and she went after him."

"At the beach party?"

"Nope. In his flat. She knew where the key would be hidden and let herself in. She actually trespassed illegally."

"Has she BEEN with him?"

"NO. Thank goodness he rejected her. I believe she is heartbroken. So Opal, I hope you don't make a big deal of it."

"Don't tell me what to do Angus. She is my daughter as well as yours."

"Yes, she is actually more your daughter than mine in this case."

"What do you mean by that?"

"Remember how you chased me when you were about Xanthe's age?"

"So? That has nothing to do with this."

Angus believed it had a lot to do with it. However, self preservation stilled his argument.

"Anyway. Tim sent her packing back to the surf club. But the twins decided to play a joke. They went to his flat and also trespassed. Apparently he'd been asleep when they jumped on him in bed."

"How did that go?"

"Xanthe thought they might be up to something so she went back and caught Tim pulling them out of his flat by their pony tails."

"You're saying Tim dragged them by their hair like a bloody cave man?"

"Opal, as it turns out, the twins put him on the spot in a compromising situation. Anyway, Xanthe phoned me because the girls were screaming blue murder. You can imagine what I thought."

"What did you do?"

"I ordered Detective Fun to follow me to the station. He must have phoned Dougall on the way because both the Grimslades turned up within a few minutes."

"I will be checking this with Dulcy tomorrow." Opal fumed.

"You can. So I might as well tell you what I did before she does."

"Fire away. I'm all ears."

"I accused Tim of being a paedophile. Then I threw a punch that landed on Dougall instead."

"Is that it?"

"Isn't that enough? I'm the one ending up with egg on my face. Our darling daughters were completely in the wrong. Tim could have taken advantage but he did what he could to oust two of them together out of his flat. I had to apologise to Tim, to Dougall and to Dulcy."

"Ouch. Well you learn something new every day."

"Don't be flippant Opal. I might never live this down and I have to work with all of them."

"What did Dougall and Dulcy say?"

"They said it was understandable. A parent's worst nightmare."

"So they were sensible about it. Lucky for you."

"I might have over-reacted but what else could I do? In my shoes you'd probably have screamed blue murder yourself."

"I know. I feel like pulling those naughty girls out of bed right now. But I'll wait for the morning."

Opal kissed Angus's mournful face. "Nevermind. It could be worse."

"I've told them they are grounded. We should suspend their allowances as well."

"We'll see. Your hand looks swollen. Did you hit your poor old mate hard?"

"Pretty hard. Luckily Dougall deflected it. Surprised he still has such quick reflexes to be honest. Anyway, he didn't cop the full force. The blow just glanced off his arm. He made a song and dance about it of course and put me in the slammer."

"No doubt you deserved that."

"I also pounded on Tim Fun's car when he first got there. That did more damage to my hand than anything else."

"Idiot."

Xanthe, Kinta and Lirah shared a bedroom. After going to bed that night they spent time talking, too excited to go straight to sleep. Xanthe berated the twins in a stage whisper.

"See what your stupid joke did? You got Tim into deep trouble. He could have lost his job and so could Dad if those Grimslades hadn't turned up. Plus we are definitely grounded and our allowances might be cut off."

"Let's not forget who called Dad." Lirah reminded.

"I reckon Tim might've let us go back to the bonfire party if we'd apologised and begged to be forgiven." Kinta said.

"I was protecting you. I should have known Timmy wasn't to blame."

"At least now you know how Tim feels about you Xanthe."

"You've wrecked all my chances with him. Thanks for nothing."

"No way Xanthe. We saw how he looked at you."

"Bunging on the tears was a really cunning stunt."

"It was not bunged on. I really felt very upset. I'm still upset if you want to know."

"But Xanthe, the look on his face when you cried said it all."

"I didn't want his pity."

"He looked more kind of caring." Lirah said.

"He did Xanthe. And sort of in love too. You were crying too much to notice his face." Kinta added.

"You think so? I might still be in with a chance? How's that going to happen now that you've gotten me grounded. Plus Mum and Dad will be watching me like hawks."

"We'll find a way, Xanthe."

"You both can stay out of it thanks. I don't want more of your *help*."

Lirah and Kinta formed their lips into identical pouts.

"Anyway. He lived up to his name. Tim Fun was lots of fun."

"What exactly did you two do to him?"

"Well, we gave him time to fall asleep after he turned the light off. Then we snuck in the back door. Thanks for leaving it unlocked."

"I didn't leave it unlocked on purpose."

"Whatever. Anyway, Kinta waited in the bathroom and I got under the sheet with him. He was on his back and his willy was sticking up like a flagpole. I always wondered what one felt like. I mean a willy not a flagpole. So I put my hand on it and felt around. It seemed sort of hard and soft at the same time. I tried to be gentle but it threw up."

"Oh shoot. That means you wanked him. I haven't even done that yet and I'm the eldest. Though I did give Timmy a good grope underwater." Xanthe admitted.

"Did he like it?"

"Hard to say. He nearly drowned."

A scandalous triple snicker came out louder than intended. Opal heard it and called out:

"Do I have to come in there?"

"Sorry Mummy."

There was that childish M word again. Opal nudged her husband and said:

"Those young devils. I don't know where they get it from."

"It's a mystery." Angus replied.

After an interval waiting for their parents to fall asleep, the sisters continued their whispering.

"Anyway, Lirah crept back to the bathroom so I could have my turn," Kinta said, "I got to do what Lirah did."

"Did he explode again?"

"He sure did. This time he groaned *'Xanthe'* – then Lirah came back in and we let him know it was only us. We know he wanted it to be you because he said your name."

"He must have thought he was seeing double." Lirah giggled.

"You're under the age of consent so I bet he was shocked."

"Yep. He jumped out of bed like one of those Jack-In-The-Box toys. Then he turned the light on."

"Everyone knows he sleeps naked now. He gawked at us while he pulled his jeans on in a mad hurry. Almost caught his boy wonder in the zip too."

"It was so funny. We fell about laughing - until he got hold of our hair."

"Yeah. That hurt. He is a lot stronger than he looks. My scalp is still sore."

Xanthe didn't care to hear the incidental details except the one that gave her goosebumps:

"He groaned my name? Did he sound sort of yearning?"

"He did. And really desperate for you too."

"Like how?"

Kinta mimicked Tim's voice, dramatising with her own embellishments.

"He went, oh Xanthe, Xanthe, oh Xanthe."

"He must really love you." Lirah said dreamily.

Xanthe hugged the fond notion to her heart. The sisters fell asleep with satisfied smiles on their impish faces.

3

David & Chantel

Tim's Landlord & Landlady

Tim Fun's landlord, David Dubois and his partner Chantel Cheron, shared the main house where they raised their sons, Davy and Dominic as brothers.

David and Chantel pretended faithfulness, but both played around. Due to David's army duties and Chantel's job on holiday cruise liners, the couple often spent weeks apart.

In the distant past, David declined to tell Chantel of his divorce from Dulcy. He enjoyed Chantel as a convenience and avoided pressure to re-marry.

Privy to hot gossip back then, Chantel knew all about David's impending divorce from Dulcy even before he did.

David's estranged wife had vowed to want nothing except to be free of her first marriage.

Chantel kept the prior knowledge to herself. She felt secure living comfortably in David Dubois' beach house since Dulcy would not contest any assets.

In a poetic twist, Chantel valued her own freedom and never wanted ties to marriage. Yet, she resented David withholding the information.

The naughty Bridcombe sisters weren't the only females with designs on the youngest detective in Grimslade's team.

When home alone with time on her hands, Tim's landlady toyed with the idea of seducing him. Chantel found it difficult to ignore such a cute sitting duck just downstairs so conveniently placed and available.

As his name implied, Tim seemed likely to be a fun candidate. The woman's exploratory sojourns went over Tim's head. Naively, he misconstrued her blatant proposition.

"Tim. With David away I could use a hand."

"Of course. What can I do for you?"

"Perhaps a hand is an understatement. I need a bit more."

Her smile had been leery but Tim took it as self-deprecation for being a helpless female.

"I'm the first to admit to not being much of a handy man. But if you need something else I might be able to help out."

"If you could gird your loins Tim, I could use some manpower in the bedroom."

Chantel felt her broad hint with its lascivious message had been crystal clear. Tim imagined she needed help with moving heavy furniture or perhaps turning the mattress. He had a foot on the bottom stair about to follow the schemer upstairs when an urgent demand to attend a crime scene waylaid him.

"Sorry Chantel. I must rush. Orders are to drop everything and go immediately."

"Bummer." she replied.

The incident kept the detective busily engaged for a few days. By the time Tim found himself free to help Chantel, his landlord had just returned from a tour of duty. David Dubois shut the door of his Jeep and threw a duffel bag over his broad shoulder. Having arrived home at the same time, Tim exited his Fiat sedan.

"Hi David. It's good to be home again, hey? A few days ago your missus asked me to help with moving something in your bedroom. I think she might have been trying to turn the mattress."

"Oh yeah? That king-size mattress is a heavy sucker. Chantel asked for your help, did she?"

"Yes and I was happy to oblige, but as luck would have it, I got called away urgently and didn't get around to it. Anyway now you're home she won't need me."

The returned soldier twigged immediately to Chantel's ploy. The woman had always owned a roving eye, and he knew her well. It had been how he became inveigled with her in the first place, helped by the fact their kids were best friends.

The Dubois/Cheron union fired up twelve years ago when their six-year-old sons asked for a sleepover. Also desperate for sleepovers, David and Chantel jumped at the excuse. There had been a *Bob the Builder* TV game, pizza and popsicles. The sleepovers became permanent, and they formed a family of four.

The couple continued to use *popsicles* as a euphemism for sex. Hearing Tim Fun's greeting when he returned from duty, David had no doubt Chantel lobbied to share a popsicle with the tenant.

In Dubois' estimation, infidelity went hand in hand with being male and therefore warranted, yet he regarded similar behaviour by females to be shamelessly promiscuous.

Ms Cheron did indeed make the most of her weeks working away. Despite strict employment rules to the contrary, staff cabins on the cruise liners were commonly used for casual trysts.

Many employees rode more than just the high seas and harboured no guilt. Fleeting bumps with tourists and other crew were considered perks of working on the holiday ships.

On gaining diplomas in hospitality and cookery, Chantel imagined herself creating fabulous recipes, baking masterpieces or decorating wedding cakes. Reality differed. Tasks in the galleys were limited to cleaning benches and floors, scraping dirty plates and loading or unloading dishwashers.

Although Chantel's kitchen tasks on the ships proved tedious, the job provided broad scope for other variety.

David Dubois also indulged in temporary adventures while away on assignments, but that didn't mean he could be easy going over Chantel making sexual overtures to the tenant. *The bloody puny ten-*

ant no less. And another one in Grimslade's band of merry bloody gum shoes.

The homeowner held no logical grudge towards Tim Fun except that he worked closely with Dulcy and Grimslade.

In Dubois' jealous mind, Tim Fun held a taint by association of being in cahoots with the despised interloper on his marriage to Dulcy.

Bitterness eroded David Dubois' guts like acid, just thinking of that old man Grimslade being with *his* Dulcy.

David Dubois first met Dulcy Vestige during her schoolies week holiday. She shared a beach cottage with girlfriends, and he camped with surfer mates nearby.

At seventeen, the naïve school leaver was seduced and helplessly smitten by the experienced twenty-three-year-old. Two weeks of steamy nights on the beach captivated the pair to fall in love.

Typically, David failed to mention he already had a steady girlfriend, Zelia, back home.

When Zelia made a surprise appearance at a gathering of friends, Dulcy had been horribly humiliated. Everyone in their holiday group knew David and Dulcy had become an item.

Caught on the spot, luckily not with his pants down, David took the path of least resistance. He played along with Zelia's romantic expectations hoping to iron it out with the younger girl later.

However, David did not get another chance with Dulcy until very much later.

Heartbroken, Dulcy had run for home. Her girlfriends closed ranks and would not help David in his quest to find the teenager he'd fallen for.

Dulcy threw herself into her career to put the heartache on hold, but she could not forget her handsome first lover. It took David three years to find Dulcy again and convince her to marry him.

Unfortunately, just prior to marriage, David made Zelia pregnant in a bout of goodbye sex. He strove to keep his illegitimate child secret because he truly loved Dulcy and didn't want to lose her.

Side-stepping blackmail, David secretly acquired the beach house and allowed it to Zelia rent-free. He excused his subterfuge as a way of keeping everyone happy. It kept Zelia off his back, provided accommodation for the child he had never held, and Dulcy need never know.

Flack hit the fan after Dulcy got a hint that her husband bought a beach house without her knowledge.

Dulcy's mentor, senior detective DI Dougall Grimslade in Queensland investigated at her request. He phoned the news to his favourite protege in Darwin.

"Dulcy. I'm afraid this is not what you wanted to hear."

"Just say it."

"The deed to the beach house is in the name of a David Dubois."

"It has to be him."

"Maybe he bought it as a surprise investment for your future Dulcy. I sent the new recruit on a little surveillance exercise. Tim Fun says a couple called William and Zelia Kirby appear to be living there."

"Zelia! That's the name of David's old flame. It isn't a common name."

"Now now Dulcy. That name might be purely coincidental."

"You know this stinks to high heaven Dougall."

Dougall placated his friend yet smelt a rat. Quite sure her nearest and dearest deceived her, he advised treading lightly.

"Cool down before you confront him Dulcy. Think like the clever tactician I know you are. You'll need a clear head."

"Yes. I should wait and get my thoughts in order. Thanks for your help and advice Dougall."

Yet the wronged wife did not heed best advice. Overwrought after a hard days work, burdened by doubts, just wanting it out in the open, Dulcy took the bull by the horns. She turned on David in their kitchen when he tried for a kiss and cuddle.

The accusation caught David off guard. Half tanked from drinks with mates after work, he confessed to siring a child with Zelia and to keeping them in a house he bought.

Never before suspecting her erstwhile brave soldier's weak character, Dulcy could not abide his cowardice and lack of integrity. Stepping away from the kitchen knife rack, she stopped just short of committing grievous bodily harm.

Dulcy packed two suitcases and never returned to the marital home for anything else. David Dubois no longer seemed worth her upset. She did not even bother with immediate divorce.

Zelia had been found dead at the beach house one day after David visited, making him one of two obvious suspects. The other, a man who apparently found her body, called ambulance and police.

Despite David's failings, Dulcy never believed her errant husband capable of murder. Focused on finding the truth, she worked undercover to help absolve him. A confession obtained under intense grilling by Grimslade and the new recruit, Tim Fun, sent the true killer to prison.

In the ensuing aftermath, both David and Dulcy relocated separately back to Queensland from the far north. David took over his beach house to become a proper father to his motherless son, Davy. Dulcy boarded with her best friend Opal and regained her former position working in Grimslade's team.

Dulcy finally divorced David Dubois after acting on a desire to be with the most trusted and admired man she knew: The widower Dougall Grimslade. *[cite The Whodunit Thing]*

Despite the divorce, David Dubois remained certain his ex-wife must want him back. Dulcy had so loved his touch and his lovemaking. He would forever consider her to be his and the love of his life.

The handsome soldier could not stomach that his adored Dulcy preferred a rugged old goat like Grimslade to himself. It stuck in David's craw. *She had to marry the mongrel.*

David had always envied Grimslade's working association with his wife. It formed the base of many arguments. Dulcy knew what really nettled David, but she would not cater to his jealousy.

Her eventual decision to wed the very source of his discontent seemed calculated and catty to David. He was sure Dulcy aimed to hit him where it most hurt.

Even twelve years on, David held onto a fantasy of Dulcy begging to come back, thinking he would forgive her and call it even. Although he weighed her cruel retaliation with Grimslade as far greater than his own discrepancies, he told himself he'd be magnanimous.

Getting Dulcy back would be worth sacrificing his pride and he'd see Grimslade humiliated at the same time. Win win.

The embarrassing incident with the Bridcombe sisters did not end there for Tim Fun. He had to explain to his landlord what happened. The quiet tenant had never before caused the slightest trouble but David Dubois exercised his right to know why a police car had been seen visiting his address.

"What went on here that night Tim? I'm told there had been lots of screaming, yelling and a police car."

"Sorry about that David. I had a home intrusion. I'd been asleep in the dark. Long story."

"I'm listening."

"I got pranked by three young girls. They gained entry and tried to shock me by surprise. It was just some silly teenager high jinx. Apparently the girls all thought it would be highly amusing."

"Did you know them?"

"Not well but I know they are the Bridcombe sisters. Their father took a dim view."

"That would be my old surfing buddy, the big copper Angus."

"Yep. And Angus might have killed me. Luckily I could call on other colleagues. Anyway, we all congregated at the police station. Eventually it got sorted."

"Don't you lock your doors? How did they get in?"

"They knew where I hid the back door key."

"How did they know that?"

Tim saw no way out of telling.

"Um. You mightn't like this. Davy and Dominic bragged about gaining access to my flat at times when I was away."

"What? Davy and Dominic did that? What for?"

"Girls. You know what for."

"Those bloody little buggers!" David actually smiled fondly.

"I had no idea. Obviously I am not happy about them using my place. Those Bridcombe girls made me look a prize mug for what went on behind my back. They even said 'call yourself a detective' because I never suspected anything."

"You're kidding. That's hilarious."

David laughed uproariously. How good having one of Grimslade's team made to look a fool by three little girls.

"I wish I'd been a fly on the wall to see that."

"Yeah. Thanks a lot. Glad you see a lighter side. Will you be talking to Davy and Dominic in the near future?"

"Maybe. Suppose I should say something." David sobered somewhat.

Tim suspected David would congratulate the boys rather than berate them.

David asked the lads to come home for a meal when Chantel returned from her latest cruise job. Chantel had been less amused by their sons' misbehaviour.

"Thankfully Tim is too nice to press charges." she said.

"Yeah. Tim is a nice guy and it was wrong of us. But see, we never thought he'd find out, and no harm was done. We always cleaned up after ourselves." Davy said.

"How could he press charges now anyway? There's no proof," Dominic grinned shamelessly, "but I guess we should level with him."

"You at least owe him a proper apology. Tim might have been in deep trouble after those schoolgirls got into his flat."

Chantel chided and David waded in.

"That is true boys. If Bridcombe made a paedophile case stick, Tim would be kicked off the force."

That thought put an unworthy idea into David's head. How good would it be to actually get Tim Fun disgraced and disbarred. The scandal would reflect on Grimslade's cosy little operation.

Tim had been trusted to babysit Davy and Dominic when they were young. Dubois wondered if he could twist that to serve his purpose. He ventured an opinion.

"Somehow Tim must have got those young girls interested in himself. Otherwise why would they do what they did?"

"Probably just took a dare. They're all dumb enough to do it." his son Davy replied.

Chantel nodded, Davy's explanation seemed entirely plausible. David pursued his idea.

"Tim minded you boys when you were kids. So did he ever do or say anything to suggest he had an unhealthy interest?"

"What? Don't be ridiculous David!" Chantel burred up.

"No way Dad." Davy cried.

"Never." Dominic added. "Not in a million years."

David saw that line of speculation would never float. In any case, he preferred not to involve the lads. He would think on it further. There could be some other way to discredit Grimslade's team and have mud stick.

When Davy and Dominic dutifully apologised for misusing the flat, Tim only nodded without a word. Both boys felt shamed that it cut Tim more deeply than he could say. They much preferred he told them off in anger, rather than seeing the hurt in his eyes. The lesson would be remembered.

4

No Glamour

Curse of the Raven

Soon after the Bridcombe sisters' debacle, David Dubois departed ostensibly for an army exercise camp, and Chantel took another stab at seducing Tim Fun.

The tenant had removed his key from the peg basket and duly purchased slide chains for the inside of the two external doors of the flat. Only after returning home, Tim realised he did not possess even the most basic tools to fix them on. He called on Chantel to borrow what he needed.

"Chantel. Sorry to bother you but could I possibly borrow a drill and a screwdriver? As I've admitted before, I am no handyman but I think I can fix safety chains to my doors with the right tools."

"Sure Tim. Come on up. David keeps a toolkit under the sink. Help yourself."

Satisfied no one could take him by surprise in his flat again, Tim returned the tools after ably installing the slide chains. Chantel cursed the lost advantage to her own schemes. She had been tempted to use the peg basket key herself.

On the bright side, David said he would be away for the long weekend. With only a few days of freedom, Chantel did not waste time.

Tim squatted in front of the sink cupboard while he neatly replaced the tools in the kit box. Chantel admired his cute backside straining against the faded blue denim of his jeans.

"Ow!"

Tim banged his head on the underside of the sink when Chantel lovingly squeezed his tight buns with both her strong hands. Appalled, Tim stood up and spun about to face his landlord's promiscuous woman. He rubbed his head.

"That's going to be a b-big b-bump." he stuttered.

"Ooh. I wouldn't mind a b-big b-bump." she leered.

Chantel's prior innuendo about girding his loins and needing manpower in the bedroom fell horribly into place. Tim cringed recalling how he'd innocently told David. The man had given him an odd look at the time, but Tim supposed turning the heavy mattress hadn't been high on David's to-do list after just returning from an arduous army task.

Caught with his back against the cabinet, Chantel trapped Tim with an arm either side of his slender body. Tim's every instinct urged him to push her away and run. Yet such a move could be construed as violent. He'd witnessed enough domestic violence cases to avoid any suggestion in regards to his own conduct.

"Come on Tim. It will be our little secret. No strings. I promise." Chantel crooned.

Tim took refuge in a lie, he'd recently seen something similar in a TV sitcom.

"Um. I am bound to admit that I b-bat for the other side." he gasped.

Chantel saw her embarrassing faux pas reflected in Tim's startled expression.

"Oh no. My god Tim. You don't mean what I think you do?"

"Yes. Sorry. Your interest is flattering, but my sexual persuasion preclude females. In fact I have never been in a physical relationship with a member of the opposite gender."

At least Tim's last sentence was true. Thwarted, Chantel tasted abject humiliation even stronger than her disappointment.

"Hell. I should have known. I mean you are so neat and nicely spoken, plus you rejected those nubile young girls who threw themselves at you. I hope you can forgive and forget my mistake."

"No harm done. But please, I'd rather not have my predilections made public, you understand."

"Of course. Less said the better."

Tim's recent popularity with the opposite sex taunted him. After years of virtual drought when it came to females, suddenly no less than four sought his sexual favours. The irony mocked him that he could take none honourably.

Later, Chantel's face burned with regret over her blunder. She wondered how she'd never cottoned on to the tenant being gay. Then her angst turned on Tim. She had to admit, he had not misled her, yet he might have been up front with his status to save her making such a fool of herself.

Though no rational fault emerged and Tim Fun did not owe her his life story, Chantel never appreciated having information withheld.

A call from the cruise ship recruitment agency asked if she might fill in on instant short notice. One of the scheduled staff had fallen and broken a leg. Chantel jumped at the chance to escape for a fortnight and gratefully agreed to do it.

The particular cruise line reserved limited parking for staff but it was not free. Chantel always got David or someone else to give her a lift to avoid the hefty parking fee. She decided to ask Tim, feeling he owed her a favour anyway.

Tim utilised his front door slide chain for the first time when Chantel knocked. After what she'd tried on him, Tim did not welcome the landlady's visit, though he managed to behave as if nothing had happened.

"Tim. There's some crisis where I work so I'm needed to fill in on short notice. I don't like leaving my car in their parking lot. Could you possibly come for the drive and bring my car back here?"

"Sure. Okay. I'll just grab my phone and wallet."

Tim could hardly get out of doing it, and he felt relieved the woman would be away for a while. He quickly took a precooked dinner out of his freezer to thaw for later, left his own car keys on his bedside table, and joined Chantel in her car.

Chantel drove into the quayside parking lot, taking a space reserved for staff. Tim helped lift her luggage from the boot and wheel it to the boarding ramp. Impressed by the size of the cruise ship, Tim exclaimed:

"Wow. These liners are massive. It looks huge up close. What a dream job you have Chantel."

"Actually Tim, it's far from exciting. The decks are out of bounds to lowly kitchen staff like me. Our cabins are in what used to be called steerage and don't even have portholes. Plus, the tiny space has to be shared with one or two others. Your own work as a police detective would be far more glamorous."

"Not at all. It can be interesting but never glamorous. The unrelenting research gets boring and some crime scenes are the stuff of nightmares."

"At least each day would be different."

"Same horse, different jockey. Anyway, I'd love a quick tour of the ship. Is that allowed?"

"Not usually. Perhaps if you flashed your police ID you might get by."

However, security did not allow the visit. The guard explained that police were only given special passes to attend if a crime occurred on board.

"Nevermind. I might go on a cruise myself someday."

Chantel handed her car keys over to Tim. She felt well disposed towards him again since he'd been so helpful. She bid him farewell with a peck to his cheek and a pat to his back. Tim blushed and quickly extricated himself from any further embrace.

"Bon voyage."

"See you in a couple of weeks." she smiled.

Chantel decided she rather liked having a gay man as a friend.

After seeing Chantel off, Tim detoured to take a loo break in a public convenience before heading back to the car park. Distracted, daydreaming of taking a cruise, Tim fell easy prey to an opportunist thief.

The aggressor waited for his target to wash his hands. A practised move bashed Tim Fun's forehead down onto the sink. Crumpling to the floor, stunned, Tim's phone, wallet and Chantel's car keys were stolen.

Avoiding CCTV, the mugger wore a Covid mask and had the hood of his lightweight parka pulled up as an effective disguise. He sauntered away. To run would only draw attention.

Tim's wallet held about a hundred dollars in cash. The mugger-thief quaked seeing the police ID in the victim's wallet. *Shit I rolled a fuckin' lawman.* He decided to pocket the cash and ditch the rest in a rubbish skip. It wouldn't do to be caught with any of it in his possession.

Tim remained bloodied and dazed on the hard tiled floor. Within an hour, a gang of no-good youths on a rampage, came across him.

"Ha ha. We got a volunteer by the looks." one lout laughed.

"Nah. Stupid prick has already been done over."

Finding no loot when they rifled his pockets, they gave the barely conscious sufferer a swift kicking to go on with. Then one of them noticed the black shorts Tim wore bore the orange police logo depicting a badge and U2.

"Hey. Aren't those police training duds?"

"Anyone can get them."

"But what's the odds he's a copper. They'll be out in force to nab someone for this."

Adding to that concern, a gang member posted as a lookout appeared in the doorway and hissed a warning:

"Look out Scuzza. That witch doctor is coming down the path. He's slow as a wet week but he'll be here soon."

The victim began to moan at the same time.

"We gotta go anyway, we don't want this twat recognising us. Lucky we sprayed those security cameras out last night."

That vandalism allowed the first mugger to escape Scot-free as well. The half dozen in the criminal cult scarpered in all directions with a plan to meet up later.

Tim fought to regain control of his limbs. He rolled over painfully onto his knees and managed to pull himself upright by the rim of the sink. He splashed his face and noted the bloodstained water swirl down the plughole.

Exploring inside his mouth with his tongue, Tim found no broken teeth. Vaguely aware of a sense of relief, he sat down again on the floor and leaned against the wall. No one else entered the facility before an old homeless man shambled in.

"Looks like you got trounced by those bad boys." the old bloke said.

Tim had no idea what had happened, only that it wasn't anything good. He couldn't remember where he was or how he came to be there.

"You better come with me and rest up a while, son. I got a camp down by the river under a bridge. Don't worry, old Warragul got those bad boys bluffed. That's me, Warragul. Wild Dog. They think I put a spell on them. What's your name?"

Tim couldn't remember his own name nor where he came from.

"Nevermind. It will come to you." his rescuer said.

The hobo helped Tim along to his squat. Tim collapsed onto a pile of flattened cardboard cartons while his host stoked up a fire with driftwood and put a battered old billy can on to boil.

Tim accepted a tin can of black tea with sugar and a few ants floating on top. His saviour known as Warragul or Wild Dog wrapped paper around the makeshift cup and made sure the young man had a safe grip with two hands.

"Careful little brother, it's hot."

The old man scrounged up some stale bread and slapped cold baked beans into a sandwich. Tim felt parched, he drank the tea, ants and all. Warragul gave him a refill.

To be polite, the guest ate some of the food served on a fairly clean piece of newspaper. The repast constituted foreign cuisine to Tim, or at least he could not recall ever dining on anything like it.

The old man ate the leftovers when Tim seemed to want no more.

Old Warragul worried that those bad gang boys would be looking for the lad, afraid he might recognise them and dob them into the police. Their victim wouldn't be the first ever to end in the swirling brown waters of the river, swept out to sea, never to be seen again.

With best intentions, the homeless man decided to keep the *poor little bugger* safe and hidden in his camp until he recovered.

The refugee reminded him of one of his own kids back in the bush.

Through a series of mishaps, Warragul long ago lost touch with his family. A favourite son had gone to the city and changed his surname to Smith to get a white boy job. A message via bush telegraph took a while to reach the old man. His boy sent directions clearly printed with street names and numbers, so his dad could come down and share the good fortune his steady employment provided.

Warragul hitchhiked in cattle trucks, helping the road drovers along the way. He walked the final miles in off the highway and tried to make sense of the maze of roads and streets. Illiteracy limited him to matching patterns of the characters in the printed signs, to instructions his son sent.

Confused and exhausted, Warragul looked for somewhere to rest. Finally finding a shady park, he drank thirstily from a water fountain and reclined on a park bench for a snooze. He did not notice a broken wine bottle, streaked with blood, under that bench. It had been used in a fracas the night before.

Police on duty, found the indigenous man sleeping above the jagged bottle. The officers put two and two together and came up with six. Warragul tried to explain but no one listened. He'd been handcuffed, loaded into a paddy wagon and taken to the watch house.

When Warragul riled up in exasperation, he'd been shoved into a cell and his face slammed against the concrete wall. When viewed by a magistrate the next day, the facial injuries condemned the fearful man as being involved in the park riot.

Wild Dog had been incarcerated for months before social workers found him a bed in a shabby half-way house. He absconded as soon as possible, afraid authorities would keep tabs on his whereabouts and blame him for something else. He followed the river, as the only landmark he trusted, to continue his quest to find his son.

After leaving the boarding house, Warragul wandered the riverside path at night, ducking into bushes to avoid other people when necessary. Traversing the deeper darkness underneath a bridge, he spied wavering torch lights in the distance, coming towards him. In a panic, he crawled up further under the bridge, and crouched behind some big boulders.

By chance, the fugitive came across his current good hiding place, a cave-like space, high above the pathway, and hidden from view by the large rocks. Like his namesake of a wild dog, the man holed up where he felt safe and unseen.

Warragul had the idea to lay low until he thought of a way to find his son.

He covertly watched other homeless people seen in a park across the river. Finding where they went to get food at soup kitchens he followed their lead. By the grace of charity workers, scant supplies and a blanket were carried back and hidden in the man's secret hideout.

During his lonely time in retreat, Warragul befriended a raven. He had chased away a marauding cat and found the black bird on its back with its sharp clawed feet sticking up, but still alive. He'd carried the bird back to his cave, given it water and food scraps, though he did not try to confine it.

Within a short time, the raven recovered and flew up into the trees. Warragul imitated the bird's cawing whenever he heard it, and the raven watched him. Smart enough recognise the human face and voice, the raven often visited for more morsels of food, coming to the man's call.

Warragul also watched everything that went on around the area. He observed the unruly youth gang accosting lone walkers and regretted being powerless to help. He couldn't help himself, let alone anyone else.

The aggressive teenagers picked on any vulnerable person. Caught out collecting wood for his fire, Warragul had been taunted by them. His stolid silence and non-reaction gave them little joy. Nonetheless, he feared being tossed into the raging river as entertainment for the yobbos.

Afraid of the gang, the old man kept a chicken leg bone found in a trash can. The next time the bad boys bothered him, he pointed the bone at them, stomped his feet and chanted in a language other than the Queen's English.

Surrounded by threatening bullies, the theatrics had been the old man's only defence. He dramatised the act with wild-eyed glaring, strictly off the top of his own creativity. Warragul finished his concert by cawing to the raven.

The jet black bird flew to sit on the backrest of a nearby park bench. Wild Dog abruptly stopped chanting and intoned a threat as he pointed the bone:

"Curse of the raven on you." he rasped.

The bullies slapped each other on the back and laughed for triggering the comical display by the homeless man. One of the gang known as Wozza, palmed a stone and hurled it at the raven. The bird deftly evaded the missile and flew up into the branches.

Looking for richer pickings, the group slouched slowly across a busy road to the tune of tyres screeching and car horns blasting in protest. Full of camaraderie and bravado they dared drivers to hit the brakes.

In a last second decision, an angry bus driver chose not to endanger her full load of passengers by a panic jump on the brake pedal. Two of the foolhardy jaywalkers glanced off the oncoming bus but one fell. Their mate Wozza was crushed to death under the wheels.

While Wozza's flattened body was being scraped off the bitumen, the gang leader spoke to his distraught living minions. He told them blackfella witch doctors could dreamtime people to death.

"Them boongs kill ya by bone pointing. What's a bet he can't even drive a bus, but he got it to charge us like a wounded fuckin' bull."

They fell for every word of the gang leader's *expertise*.

"Shit. The old git is a witch doctor. He put the raven curse on us."

"We oughta kill that bird."

"There are hundreds of them black birds. You ever see that old Hitchcock movie called *The Birds*?"

"Yeah, I remember that. The birds swarm on ya and pick ya eyes out."

"Stupid old fool. He's got nothing to steal anyway."

Rattled by superstition, the pimply band of young crooks steered clear of the witch doctor and any black birds ever after.

Kurdaitcha Man and Feather Foot were among various tribal names for the bone pointing executioner. Wild Dog couldn't care less what he was called as long as it kept the hoodlums at bay.

Greatly amused since the bone pointing act had been pure theatre, Warragul enjoyed his newfound notoriety. The raven echoed his thoughts with its jeering caw.

While remaining wary of any police presence, fooling the gang meant the old man could brave going out more freely in sunlight and make use of various public amenities during his wanderings.

So, Warragul came across his unknown guest after the criminal youths scarpered, in fear of the witch doctor.

Suffering the hard beatings and losing his memory was sadly far removed from Tim Fun's forgotten dream of taking a glamorous cruise. At least he'd been fortunate that the old man scared the gang off.

5

Missing Person

No Clue

Two days later when Tim hadn't shown up for work, Dougall Grimslade tried phoning him.

"Dulcy, did Tim mention he'd be away? I can't reach his mobile."

"No, he didn't say anything like that. I remember he said he'd see us Monday. I hope he isn't sick."

Dougall phoned David Dubois asking him to check on his tenant.

"Dubois says Tim's car is in the carport but he doesn't answer his door. He says Tim usually walks down to the beach every morning because he leaves his surfboard at the lifeguards' club."

"We better look into it...if he's missing in the surf..." Dulcy didn't dare mention shark attack.

Tim's colleagues split up. Grimslade went to the surf club immediately. He'd been relieved to be told Tim's surfboard was still on the club premises.

"Does he always go out on the board? Never just for a swim?"

The lifeguards present at the time included a trustworthy source, Ethan Birdwhistle. Dougall addressed questions to Ethan since they were related. Dougall's daughter, Isla, had married Ethan's brother, Aiden.

"He only surfs on his board as far as I know, Dougall. I've never seen him just go in for a dip. Anyway, Isla is always out early, so she might be able to confirm that."

"That's true."

Meanwhile, Dulcy visited Tim Fun's address. His car remained parked where he'd left it under the tenant carport attached to his flat. She rapped on the door and called his name. No answer. Dulcy's ex-husband David Dubois emerged from upstairs.

"Hello Dulcy. Of all people, fancy seeing you here." David said, tongue in cheek.

"I'm looking for Tim. Can you access his flat for me?"

"Sure Sweetheart. I keep spare keys to the flat in my glove box."

David had never knowingly allowed Chantel access to the spare keys. He only recently found out Tim had been hiding his back door key in the peg basket out near the backyard clothesline.

"Thank you. And don't call me that." Dulcy added.

Her ex-husband hid a smirk. He felt sure Dulcy actually liked the Sweetheart endearment. At least she had done when they'd been happily married to each other.

He did a pretend yawn as an excuse to flex his rippling muscles. Chantel always said it made him look sexy when he did that. He gave his ex-wife an eyeful for free to remind her of what she was missing. Dulcy recognised his vain ploy and ignored it.

Dulcy half-expected Tim might have been dreadfully ill in bed or fallen over in the shower. There could be any number of reasons for being indisposed. His bed was neatly made. She noted a newly ironed shirt and pair of trousers on hangers in the bathroom, beside fresh underwear and socks. It looked as if the clothing had been set out for a new day at work.

A once frozen meal thawed wetly in the fridge. She smelt the contents and decided it should be thrown out. The state of the food suggested he had not been home for two or more days.

David had followed her inside. Dulcy felt he breathed down her neck. She shot a crisp question to him to maintain a business-like attitude.

"When did you last see Tim?"

"Um...Friday morning I think it was. But I had to go on duty. I only got back late last night."

"Would your partner have been home?"

Dulcy declined calling Chantel by name. It wouldn't do to let David know she took any interest in his live-in lover.

"Chantel left Saturday for two weeks. She works on a cruise ship."

"Can you supply the details please?"

"Why?"

"It's just standard procedure for information checks. If it isn't too much trouble."

"No worries."

Back at the office, Dulcy duly confirmed Chantel Cheron had indeed boarded the cruise ship for her job. Dougall phoned his daughter. Isla confirmed what Ethan said.

"It seems Tim did not go surfing on the weekend. His board is where he left it at the surf club. Ethan thinks he hasn't used it since last week."

"That seems curious. Tim always looks forward to the surf club weekends. You had the better subject with Ethan; I had to ask David to open Tim's flat. He made a meal of that, flexing his muscles in a pretend yawn. He is so transparent."

Dougall kicked himself. He should have done the flat inspection to save Dulcy having to deal with her ex.

"What did you find?"

"The place appeared clean and neat. No sign of any struggle. A meal had thawed in the fridge, supposedly ready to heat, but it was past its prime. It looked like Tim prepared clothes for work. His car keys were on his bedside table. I didn't find his wallet or phone. David thinks he last saw him Friday morning. Mind you, his recollection probably isn't reliable anyway. And his partner is away on a cruise."

"Nice."

"No. She actually works on the cruise ship. I've already confirmed she went on the roster and boarded Saturday morning. She would be miles out to sea by now."

"No one remembers seeing him since last Friday, so Tim is officially a missing person. Your inspection of his flat indicates he did not plan to go anywhere voluntarily."

"Tim's next of kin will have to be notified."

"I recall that is his aunt, Francis Funicular the wedding celebrant. We met her at Isla's wedding remember?"

Beside herself with worry, Ms Funicular confirmed she hadn't heard from her nephew for at least a week. Dulcy attempted to ease the news, saying it would likely be a false alarm. It was not what she really thought.

"All points bulletin Dougall?"

"Definitely. The Coast Guard chopper too. In case he did go for a swim."

"Knowing Tim, he might dive in to save a dog or something like that."

"That is a concern and a logical explanation. However, in view of recent events, I want to re-interview the Bridcombes."

"Tim could be a victim of foul play. Who knows what enemies we make in the course of doing our jobs. But I can't see any of the Bridcombes being involved in that kind of thing." Dulcy said.

"I agree. But something might come to light if the girls remember anything said amongst their peers. We've cracked cases with far less to go on, and as it stands we don't have a clue."

6

Official Interview

David Dubois

The Coast Guard helicopter scoured the coastline. A dead shark washed up on the beach triggered a false alarm, but no sign of human or canine remains were found. No one reported any missing dog either. Grimslade and Grimslade faced their friend, Sergeant Angus Bridcombe, for an informal interview.

"Angus. Seems our young team member, Tim Fun has gone missing."

"Gone AWOL has he?"

"It looks highly suspicious Angus. Our investigations indicate he did not plan an absence."

"I haven't been near him if that's what you imagine. And my daughters were grounded over the whole weekend. If you think living with that is easy..."

Dulcy had an unsettling thought. Opal was like a tigress where her children were concerned.

"Ahem. Angus. I have to ask, did Opal go out over the weekend?"

"No she did not Dulcy. She hasn't let the kids out of her sight. I've had to do all the grocery shopping myself. I tell you, that damn supermarket is like a war zone. There are kids in there who are as bad as ours. One of them grabbed the last crusty wholemeal loaf from right under my nose! I almost had it in my hand! The treacherous trolleys don't go where you aim them, then you cop abuse for ramming someone. And don't start me on the senior citizens using their walking frames like weapons. And those motorised scooters! I feared for my safety. Then the bloody checkout idiot put all the heavy tins in one bag and it burst." Angus sounded hard done by. Dulcy stemmed his litany.

"Opal manages it."

"Who'd pick on her though?"

"True." Dulcy smiled.

Dougall had another idea:

"Angus, would you be aware if Tim visited your home?"

"I can't see any of the females in my house keeping that a secret, if he did."

"No. I see. I'm pretty sure he would rather put that embarrassing scenario behind him anyway."

"Opal and I rarely punish the girls, but they've been grounded for a month and have their allowances suspended as well. The grounding probably hurts them the most since they get everything they need from us anyway."

"Could you ask your daughters if they've heard any bad mouthing about Tim? We just want to know of any grudges."

"I've heard them say Tim gets ridiculed."

"Ridiculed? Why?"

"Some sheilas reckon he bungs on a posh way of talking to impress them. They laugh behind his back saying he's a soft touch for a free meal anyway."

"How unkind! Tim's old fashioned mode of speech is natural given his education. Those surf club floozies probably have vocabularies limited to four letter words." Dulcy retorted.

"There's definitely some alley cats at that surf club." Dougall replied.

"For sure. Anyway, I'll ask my girls and let you know."

They thanked Angus and let him get back to work.

Dulcy remembered to mention another observation.

"That reminds me Dougall, something else I noticed in Tim's flat. It looked like new safety chains had been fitted to his doors."

"Really? I might have a look at that." Dougall mused.

Later he visited Tim's flat on his own. Dubois let him in. Dougall saw that the safety chains appeared new. Fine traces of sawdust remained along the edges of the decorative door panels. He went through Tim's kitchen tidy bin and found hardware receipts for the chains, dated Friday. A search of Tim's cupboards and vehicle found no handyman tools, not even a screwdriver.

Dougall questioned Dubois.

"Did you install safety chains in the flat?"

"No. He must have done it himself. It's not a big job. Even someone like Tim could manage it."

Dougall clocked Dubois disparagement of Tim Fun. He let it ride for the moment.

"Would he have borrowed your tools to do it?"

"Not from me. I'd have done the job myself if he'd asked. But I'd probably gone away by then. Maybe Chantel lent them to him. I don't know."

"Just for the record, where did you go?"

"Army camp long weekend. Basic fitness exercises."

"So you left Friday morning and returned Sunday night."

"That's right."

Grimslade changed tack.

"Where do you keep your tools?"

"Under the sink upstairs."

"Can you show me where?"

David complied with a sour face. Dougall followed him into the kitchen and took a look in the toolkit. Minute traces of sawdust on a drill bit looked like it had been used recently. He wondered whether Tim would have gone up into the house, or would the lady of the house bring the bag down to him. The bag held hammers and other heavy objects and the woman might not know what he needed. It seemed more likely Tim came upstairs and chose a drill and screwdriver.

"Tim has been your tenant for many years now. Has he ever caused trouble?"

"Nope. At least not until those Bridcombes played their trick on him. Anyway, it seems Angus sorted that out. Pity he didn't give the little twerp a good walloping."

"Why? What do you mean?"

"Well. His three pretty young girls somehow got sucked in. How did a nondescript older guy manage that I wonder. Tim Fun can't be completely innocent."

Dubois' critique amounted to pure speculation. Grimslade knew Tim had been blameless. Angus Bridcombe who had the most at stake, accepted the outcome as well.

"Didn't you get Tim to babysit your own children when they were youngsters?"

"Yes. He often minded Davy and Chantel's boy when we went out."

"So you obviously trusted Tim."

"I did back then. But they say still waters run deep."

"Are you suggesting Tim ever acted improperly?"

"I did think of it after Angus's daughters gate crashed. I even questioned Davy and Dominic about that."

"What did they say?"

"They claim Tim never did anything wrong. But you know, if he just sounded them out with hints it could have gone over their heads."

Dubois rubbed his nose and looked away. Grimslade realised the man clutched at straws to disparage Tim.

"I get the impression you don't hold Tim Fun in high regard."

"Well. No. Just that, I've noticed him eyeing off Chantel at times." David lied.

"Hmm. Boys will be boys."

Grimslade replied generically without committing to any opinion. It irked hearing Tim maligned by someone he classed as a prize dickhead. Reading between the lines of Dubois' rant, he surmised old grievances fuelled those attempts.

Dulcy dumped David, a good-looking well-bodied soldier, for good reason. Subsequently she chose himself, an older man with a persistent scowl etched on his rugged face. That would be a hard blow to Dubois' pride. Smug didn't begin to describe Dougall's inner thoughts as he blandly regarded his wife's macho ex husband.

Grimslade's scowl disguised his pleasant face. He wore the face Dulcy loved when he held her close crooning love songs, and when his eyes adored her in bed. Even in a work situation, if their eyes met in a fleeting moment and he smiled, her desire for him ignited instantly. Confident in Dulcy's love, Dougall did not envy David Dubois. *I win you lose. Dickhead.*

Back at HQ Dougall began a cryptic pattern on a clean white page of paper, it included times, ticks, crosses and random words. Dulcy respected his pedantic method and let him get on with it. Subsequently, he discussed his hypothetical re-enactment of Tim's movements Friday evening.

"My theory is, Tim borrowed tools to fit those safety chains. Most likely he went upstairs in the main house to access the toolkit kept under the kitchen sink. David wasn't home so his partner must have okayed that."

Dulcy could never let go of an ingrained mistrust of her ex-husband.

"We should confirm when and where David went."

"Alright. It's not likely to be a classified secret."

However, several yards of red tape needed to be unknotted before army administrators supplied useful intelligence. Eventually Dougall received a result.

"Aha. You hit the nail on the head Dulcy. Apparently no army camp was scheduled during the specified time frame. Dubois was on recreation leave."

"He probably pulled some two-timing act on his partner. That's his style."

"But she left home on the Saturday and her cruise duty has been confirmed."

"Hmm."

"Another thing Dulcy, Dubois made a meal of trying to discredit Tim. He reckoned Angus should have given him a hiding."

"So he has it in for Tim."

"Seems so. He also said he caught Tim eyeing off his woman, Chantel."

"Not impossible but that doesn't seem like Tim to me."

The Grimslade's exchanged tacit possibilities that David Dubois had something to do with Tim Fun's disappearance.

"Your ex will have to occupy the hot seat. I'll have him brought in." Grimslade frowned.

"Could Angus sit in instead of me?" Dulcy asked.

"Good idea. If you want to, you can observe from the viewing room."

"I will."

David Dubois faced his most hated adversary in the official interview room. Sergeant Angus Bridcombe entered the room and stood at attention against a wall.

"Take a seat Angus. No need to stand on ceremony."

"Thanks Dougall."

"Why am I here?" Dubois demanded.

"Clarifying your movements last weekend, for the record."

David realised they must have checked and already knew he lied about the army camp.

"As I said. I was away from home. I went camping."

"Were you on an army training camp?"

"Everything amounts to training when you're in the army." he parried.

"Were you on recreation leave?"

"Yes. So what?"

"Can you confirm when you left home and when you returned?"

"I left Friday and returned Saturday night."

"Originally you said you returned Sunday night."

"Saturday, Sunday, what's the big deal?"

"So you were only away overnight Friday."

"Well done. No wonder you're a detective." David's smirk reeked of sarcasm.

He earned a warning from his old friend, Sergeant Bridcombe.

"Watch your manners sport." Angus said.

"When did you last see your tenant, Tim Fun?"

"I don't remember."

Grimslade referred to his notes although he didn't need to.

"I can jog your memory. You said you saw him on Friday morning."

"Did I? Well that must be when I last saw him. Geez."

"Mr. Dubois, our colleague, your tenant DC Tim Fun is officially a missing person. We believe his disappearance to be suspicious. You have changed your statement regarding your movements and whereabouts for the time in question."

"This is a fit up." David shouted. "You've got it in for me Grimslade and I know why."

"Really. Perhaps you'll enlighten us for the record." Grimslade did his best crocodile smile.

"You're pissed off knowing Dulcy only took up with you to get back at me." David retorted.

Angus offered a mild remark: "Well Mrs. Grimslade has kept up that charade for a good ten years."

"Twelve years!" David shouted.

"So you've kept count." Grimslade could not suppress a satisfied smile.

David appealed to the sergeant, his long time surfing friend.

"Angus mate. You know how it was when I first met Dulcy. You were there. You even helped me find her again."

Angus Bridcombe had reason to squirm. Back then, Dulcy's girl-friends banded together blocking David's attempts to find her. Opal Bridcombe vehemently forbade her husband to help his mate. Three years on, Angus went against his wife's order by giving David a broad hint that Dulcy would be at a local cricket match.

Grimslade avoided the personal aspect. It hit him too close to home. He continued questions:

"Histrionics aside. Why have you mislead the investigation?"

"I was not even aware of it being an investigation, was I? And I didn't know Tim Fun was missing either." David huffed.

"It has been widely aired in the media with his photo."

"Well I didn't see it."

"What reason can you give for lying about the army camp?"

"I did camp. I stayed up the coast."

"Can anyone corroborate that?"

"I paid a camping fee. The receipt might still be in my ute some-where. Or I might have chucked it away. I don't know. I had no reason to keep the bloody thing."

"Why would you bother to camp and pay a fee when you have access to miles of coast at your doorstep?"

"Alright. If you must know. I told Chantel I'd be away all weekend so I could come home early and catch her in bed with the tenant."

"You thought you'd catch your partner in bed with Tim Fun?" Angus marvelled at the odd notion.

"But apparently Chantel had to go to work." Grimslade said.

"That must have been a last minute thing. She wrote a quick message like she was in a rush. It's still on the bathroom mirror. In lipstick. Feel free to check."

"We will. So you believed your tenant Tim Fun misbehaved with your partner behind your back?"

"Yes. The sneaking little prick. Why wouldn't he?"

"That gives you motive to want him gone."

"I didn't do anything to him."

"What did you do when you got home and found your house empty?"

"I had a shit a shower and a shave. Then I grilled a steak and had a beer. Before you ask, I don't have any proof."

David Dubois' weekend camp had indeed been a ruse. He arrived home early in a plan to ambush Chantel in bed with the tenant. He'd watched Chantel's limpid gaze wander over Tim Fun often enough, he guessed where her latest desires lay.

The vengeful man imagined he might even turn it around to say Chantel had been raped. She might just agree to that falsehood to keep her sweet deal with himself in the beach house. If not, that would be her loss. A hope hovered in the back of David's mind. Dulcy might be more inclined to come back to him if he lived alone. However unlikely, the possibility appealed to him.

Apart from anything else, David most wanted to disgrace Grimslade's aide. By extension, muck would stick and discredit the entire detective team, including Dulcy. *It will serve her right for pretending to want old Grimslade.* He imagined himself adopting an understanding attitude, impressing Dulcy with his generous spirit.

Dubois' planned ambush disintegrated on finding the scrawled message in lipstick on the bathroom mirror: *David I got called into work - home in a fortnight. C. Xxx*

Certain there would be a next time to catch her and Tim Fun together, David huffed aloud to the empty room.

"Oh well. I'll wait."

After David left, Angus returned to his normal duty and Dulcy convened with Dougall. The Grimslade couple analysed the outcome.

"I can't see David doing anything to Tim. For one thing, he'd be a prime suspect, and he would know that. His explanation sounds plausible. Setting up a trap to catch them *in flagrante* delicto is exactly what he'd do. We have to consider some other reason for Tim missing."

"I'm forced to agree...so Angus was behind David finding you again? I imagine Opal would not be happy if she knew."

"She is unaware and best she never finds out."

They shared a wry smile.

"So Mrs. Grimslade, you only took up with me to get revenge on your ex. How's that going?"

"Worked a treat so far."

"You wouldn't rather still be with that handsome super-hero shaped he-man bastard?"

"Sounds like you're fishing for compliments."

"I am. How about a kind word or three."

"I'll show. Not tell. Later." she winked and mimed throwing a kiss.

Dougall made a mental note to pick up another bottle of Johnny Walker on the way home. The Grimslades grinned together and keenly anticipated the night ahead.

7

Wild Dog

& The Pram Lady

Warragul took care of his refugee as best he could. He bathed Tim's facial wounds with salt water, kept him fed, and safe from further harm. However, Tim went unwashed and unshaven.

Apart from blood stains, Tim's initial loss of his faculties soiled his clothing by incontinence. While the young man slept deeply, almost comatose, Wild Dog undressed him in the dark and carefully tucked his one blanket around the slender body.

In the dead of night, Warragul made his way across the bridge, keeping to the shadows. He bundled Tim's dirty clothes into a park rubbish bin on the opposite riverbank. The old man did not know the logo on the t-shirt named a regional surf club, nor that the shorts were standard police issue.

Op Shop donation bins became full to overflowing on Sundays, and some bags of clothes were invariably left on the footpath. Warragul found a pair of crumpled brown linen trousers, way too big but at least clean. He kept a piece of tattered rope in case it became useful. Now it served as a belt. A plaid long sleeved shirt completed Tim's new ensemble. The erstwhile neat young detective took on the appearance of another derelict, down on his luck.

Daily, the old man asked Tim if he remembered anything, to no avail. Mistreatment Warragul suffered in the past, prevented him handing the young man in to police. He thought of taking him to a hospital, but that would also involve the constabulary. Wild Dog feared being captured on security cameras. 'They' would hunt him down. He imagined being blamed for what had befallen the lad. Likely he'd be accused of stealing his money. He couldn't bear being shut up in jail again.

Tim knew enough to appreciate the old man's help, while in the shady gloom of his mind, fragments of memories sparked and faded. In anguish, he tried to make sense of images that flashed inside his head but disappeared all too soon. Tim tried explaining what he saw to Wild Dog.

"Mostly I see the ocean. Sometimes there are faces. Names are on the tip of my tongue, but they dissolve too soon."

"I found you in that bog near the big holiday boats. Might be you come off one of them. That be why you remember the ocean."

"Maybe. I remember being in the ocean too. The waves lifting me up and the taste of salty water."

"Could be you come from some beach place?"

Another lost soul habitually did her rounds pushing an old pram.

The hagged old lady came from a women's shelter. Since being beaten senseless by her husband years ago, she'd become a permanent resident of the safe house.

No one knew her real name. She gave various versions on different days, depending on her mood. Sybil, Beryl or Elizabeth were her favourites. On the days she chose Elizabeth she'd exercise a trill soprano singing the national anthem *God Save The Queen* for hours on end.

The old woman's concerts were not best loved by others in the house, so they'd tell her it's time to walk her babies. The pram lady would load her stroller with a bunch of broken old dolls rescued from trash cans. Part of her habitual routine involved checking bins for more cast offs.

One particular Elizabeth day, the wanderer spied a good leather wallet in the bottom of a big rubbish skip. She told her children to behave themselves while she scrambled over the thick metal rim to retrieve the interesting find.

Smart enough to realise any cash had been stolen, she withdrew the ID of a police officer. Hadn't something been on TV about a missing person? From memory, the photo looked like it could be that young man. In her walks of life and experience, the significance of a missing police officer pointed to a worse crime. He might have been murdered! Elizabeth of the day covered her mouth in awe.

The pram lady didn't want to get involved. Maybe they'd question her for hours, give her cups of tea but not offer any toilet breaks. These days, tea went right through her. She almost had to be seated on the throne as she drank. Also, no one else would take care of her babies.

Handing the wallet in had too many problems, yet the senior citizen still had enough sense to know it would be wrong not to. In a brilliant epiphany, a good idea of what to do with the find presented itself.

Elizabeth began warbling *God Save The Queen* again after pushing the wallet with its contents into the slot of a Royal Mailbox bearing the initials ER for Elizabeth Regina. That seemed a mighty good omen. The pram lady decided it was *meant to be*.

The Australia Post worker who cleared the postbox often found odd items, sometimes disgusting ones. Tim's wallet and his police ID triggered alarm bells.

Local officers took possession and duly informed DI Grimslade, who barely received the news before it became public knowledge.

Chuffed with his part in the drama, the postal worker informed TV News Services. He hoped in vain to sell his 'story' for a good sum. He'd been disappointed when he wasn't even mentioned by name in the bulletin.

The Grimslades mourned the meaning behind Tim Fun's looted wallet being dumped.

"Obviously Tim's fallen foul of a crime."

"He's been robbed of any cash. Yet his plastic cards and police ID are intact."

"Whoever did it avoided taking anything traceable."

"Since he is still missing, we have to face facts."

"I know. I'm afraid worse has happened to him."

"That is now our arduous duty to uncover."

8

Worst Case Scenario

Chantel's Car

Just before Chantel Chiron disembarked at the end of her fort-nights cruise job, she phoned David to come pick her up.

"I thought you drove in. Your car isn't here."

"Are you sure? Tim was supposed to drive it back home."

"Tim? Don't you know he has been flagged as a missing person?"

"What? How would I know that? I've been slogging away for the past two weeks in a sweat box. So where is my car?"

"Have you checked if it's still in the parking lot?"

Chantel found her hatchback parked exactly where she'd left it.

"It is here, but I gave my keys to Tim. Shit."

"Don't you keep spare keys in your bag?"

Chantel rummaged around and found the spare car key in a zippered pocket of her handbag. She loaded her luggage, and been greatly relieved when the vehicle started first go. She messaged David:

"On my way home. See you soon."

Dubois knew he should contact police with the important information of Tim Fun's last known whereabouts. Yet he fumed over the ordeal with Grimslade and did not want to be helpful. *No rush anyway since the little creep is probably dead.*

He'd have to get Chantel on side. Preparing for a difficult conversation, David organised a meal and poured a large glass of wine for her. Chantel returned home, dead tired after dealing with peak hour traffic.

"Oh thanks honey. Just what I need." she accepted the wine and quaffed a good swig.

"So you hadn't heard the drama about our tenant?"

"Actually, I heard a news report on the car radio saying there's been a breakthrough. I didn't catch all of it because of the static going through the tunnel."

David flicked the TV onto a news channel. They both sat on the edge of the sofa while updates refreshed including photos of Tim Fun.

"They say his wallet has been found. That means he was robbed and possibly worse."

"Chantel, I might as well tell you, I have been grilled by the detectives. They suspect I have something to do with Tim's disappearance."

"You? Why you David?"

"Because...they checked my whereabouts and found I hadn't been on an army camp. And I wasn't away the whole weekend like I said. Bloody old Grimslade took great delight in that too."

"Alright. So where were you David?"

"I only took rec. leave for a few days fishing. But then I decided to come back early to be with you Chantel," he lied, "except I found you'd left on that cruise job."

"I was under the impression you were on an army exercise too. Why make it up?"

"That's what they've grilled me about. So I told Grimslade I suspected Tim might hit on you, Chantel...and so I came back early to...you know...check if you were okay."

"Aha! You lied. You thought you'd catch me out is what you really mean." she exclaimed angrily.

"Don't come the innocent with me Chantel." he yelled back.

"That's insulting coming from you. Did you imagine I'd try to turn Tim Fun from gay to straight?"

"Gay? What makes you think he's gay?"

"Everyone knows Tim Fun is gay. It's as obvious as the nose on your face."

Dubois stared at his partner. *Shit. Tim Fun is a pansy. No wonder Grimslade smirked at me.*

"Suppose that's why he ousted those girls from his flat." David snorted.

"Perhaps they tried to convert him," Chantel put on her thoughtful face, "of course you'll have to get back in touch with Grimslade now." she said sweetly.

Chantel felt David deserved to be grilled after he shouted the insult at her.

"No. Chantel. I don't think we should get involved any further."

"We? I have to report that Tim went to the quay two weeks ago, but he didn't drive my car back as arranged."

"Do you really want them to grill you as well? They might try to pin something on you Chantel.'

"Me? What could they possibly blame me for?"

"Who knows? Bloody Grimslade can twist anything. Dulcy always said it was his main talent."

"Seems he has other talents for your dear Dulcy now."

That hit a raw nerve with Dubois. He gritted his teeth on a reply laden with a veiled threat.

"I'm telling you not to go to the police Chantel. It will only cause trouble."

Smart enough to know which side her bread was buttered, Chantel didn't want to lose the good deal she had living with David. Stuffing up her own life wouldn't help the dead, and evidently poor Tim Fun had met his final fate.

Angus explained to his family that finding Tim's wallet did not necessarily mean he'd been murdered. Yet the policeman felt the worst case scenario to be the most likely.

"His car is still parked at his flat, so he couldn't have gone far. Dulcy says it looked like he prepared a meal and had clothes ready for work."

The Bridcombe household took the latest news badly.

"Oh Mum. He has to be found alive. I love him." Xanthe cried and paced the floor in anguish.

"Now, now Xanthe. Tim would be terribly missed by everyone if he isn't found. But he might be okay. Let's try to remain positive." Opal cajoled.

"I'm positive he's been murdered." Lirah moaned tactlessly.

"And we all played horrible pranks on him." Xanthe wailed.

"It might've been the last thing he thought of." Kinta sobbed.

"Oh no. I can't stand how he might have suffered."

"Or that we'll never see his lovely friendly face again."

The three sisters bawled in unison. Their parents attempts at comfort fell on deaf ears.

"Angus. Where does it go from here?"

"They'll bring in dogs." Angus did not say cadaver dogs though Opal knew what he meant.

"Are there any clues to narrow down the search area?"

"Not really. The wallet was stuffed into a suburban mailbox, but the location might be a red herring to throw us off the scent."

Xanthe tried to make sense of what might have happened.

"Could he be kidnapped? Maybe he opened his door to someone or got in their car."

"Unless he got tricked, he'd have to know the person. Like someone from the surf club or from work." Opal said.

"The lifeguards say no one saw him over the weekend and seemed as if he hadn't taken his board out. I've already been questioned and so has Tim's landlord." Angus frowned.

"I guess they had to question you Angus after what our darling daughters caused."

The three Bridcombe sisters hung their heads in shame.

"I'll never forgive myself for causing Tim so much trouble." Xanthe wept.

9

Jarrah & Warragul

Three Flat Stones

On high alert, a police dog handler investigated a park rubbish bin when her canine displayed an avid interest in the contents.

The officer pulled a bundle of soiled clothing out, identified the significance of the find, and radioed it in. Wasting no time, Dougall spoke to the officer by phone.

"What have you got?"

"A blood stained surf club t-shirt, black police issue shorts with the orange U2 logo and a pair of soiled underpants encrusted with dried faeces."

"Good work." Dougall's reply had been automatic. It did not reflect his deep sadness.

Every indication pointed to the clothing being from the missing detective. More dogs were deployed to the area to cast around for possible trails. Unfortunately, mowing, fertilising, and sprinkling the lawn combined with a myriad of scents crisscrossing the park to befuddle the diligent sniffers.

Warragul observed the activity taking place on the opposite riverbank 200 metres across the water from his squat. He wondered what all those police were on about. Maybe after some bank robber. It did not occur to him that the dirty old clothes he trashed would spark so much interest.

The Grimslades discussed the latest turn of events.

"Dulcy. Tim has been robbed and stripped. By the state of the clothes found, he's been badly injured. You can guess what this means."

"Oh no. I feared the worst but hoped for the best. It's still a terrible shock."

"The location makes it feasible that he ended up in the river. Best we can do is try to find his body. It might reveal a clue to who did it, although I have my doubts."

"I know it is doubtful. We have to try because it's all we can do. This is just so horrible. Now what?"

"A drag of the river will begin immediately. Police divers are ready on standby."

Abreast of the latest news, Angus Bridcombe sadly informed his wife of proceedings.

"Tragic news Opal. I don't know whether to tell the girls or not."

"It will be better coming from us. They're bound to see it on the news."

Opal and Angus sat their daughters on the sofa and advised them to prepare for some bad news.

"Sorry girls. On top of Tim's wallet being found, now his clothes have been located. Assuming he was robbed and stripped, it doesn't look like being a good outcome."

"Timmy, my Timmy. How could this happen to such a good person?"

Xanthe broke down and could not be consoled.

"She really loved Tim." Kinta explained.

"And he loved her." Lirah said.

"How did you arrive at that idea when you all admit to scarcely knowing him?" Opal asked gently but she had to know.

"It was the loving way he looked at her. We could just tell."

Opal and Angus silently read each other's thoughts. It had been like that with themselves when they first met. Although four years older than Opal, it had been Angus's first love affair too. Besotted at seventeen, Opal declared she would marry Angus and let him think it was his own idea. She did and he did.

"Xanthe. We don't know exactly what happened. There's a chance he survived it all." Opal soothed.

"Slim chance." Lirah muttered.

"But still a chance." Kinta counter-acted her twin's pessimism.

Xanthe came to a decision; "I want to go to that park where his clothes were binned."

"Darling, what good will that do?"

"We could ask random people if they remember seeing him."

"I'm sure the police are doing that, and they are using sniffer dogs as well." Angus replied.

"But...having extra people looking can't hurt. Can it?"

That night, in the privacy of their bedroom, the Bridcombe parents discussed what to do for the best.

"Going there might help Xanthe with closure. At least she'll know she tried to help."

"True. They're all suffering remorse for playing that stupid trick on the poor bloke."

"They all imagine Xanthe and Tim were in love. Probably they just like to dramatize it because they read so many romance novels."

"Opal, you always claimed I had been love at first sight for you. And you had me on the hook from the first time you asked to feel my pecks. That was what...within about an hour of meeting me at that beach barbecue?"

"I chased you for sure. But you didn't offer much resistance." Opal reminded.

"The resistance Tim put up is the main reason I believed in his innocence."

"Okay. I agree. I suppose we could make a day of it with the girls and walk around the area for a while. Maybe take a picnic."

By the time the Bridcombe family arrived at the park, police had employed experts to re-direct the river drag further downstream, according to tides and currents. Yet nothing found amongst the river sludge could be linked to the missing man.

The five family members wandered about the riverside park before sitting on the lawn to eat their corned beef and pickle sandwiches. No one they asked remembered seeing anything of interest to do with Tim's clothes being binned. The park was said to be frequented by homeless people at times, though they were considered harmless.

"Dumping his clothes here could be another red herring to put the search off the scent." Angus reminded them all.

Crestfallen, the three sisters realised the enormity of the task. Opal tried to cheer them up.

"Why don't we walk across the bridge and see if we can get an ice-cream somewhere on the other side."

At the same time, Wild Dog and his guest sipped tea on the opposite river bank. The raggedy person Tim Fun had become, usually regarded the view blankly. A sudden distinct change in his attitude made Warragul sit up and take notice.

"What are you looking at?" he asked.

His young charge pointed a shaky finger towards the family group of five, in the distance.

"Those people...something about them. I don't know..." he said.

Despite advanced years, Wild Dog's vision remained sharp. He discerned the five who interested his poorly friend. The elder deduced Opal's indigenous roots by the fluid way she moved. The loose limbed ease in which she sat on the ground, cross legged, evoked memories of his own family.

"That one, the woman, she look like one of my mob," he said, "she might help me find my son."

When the group entered the walking lane to cross the bridge, the homeless pair retreated out of sight. Tim trusted Wild Dog's judgement and followed his lead in hiding out.

"You stay here," Warragul said quietly, "I got an idea to speak to that woman."

Warragul entered the pedestrian lane from the opposite end of the bridge and waited for the five to approach. The Bridcombes perceived a grubby old derelict they imagined must be a wino who would beg for a handout.

Wild Dog took his beat-up felt hat in his hand to be polite.

"Excuse me Missus." he addressed Opal.

Angus stuffed a ten in the hat to get rid of the 'wino' and been surprised to have the money handed back. Opal respected the elder.

"What is it Uncle?"

"I been looking for one of my sons for a few years now. Maybe you know him?"

"What name old man?"

"Jarrah. He go by name of Smith to get a white boy job. He sent for me to join him. But...I fell on hard times. Can't find him."

"Hey. I knew a Jarrah Smith." Angus exclaimed.

Jarrah and Angus had shared the surfside camps with some other mates during their younger years.

"One of my girlfriends went out with a young man named Jarrah. That was years ago now when we all first met on holidays at the beach." Opal said.

"She was the English girl wasn't she?" Angus recalled.

"Yes, Keziah. A redhead with frizzy hair. She was in our childhood club. We used to meet in Dulcy's tree house."

"I lost touch with the old surfing group. Maybe Keziah knows where Jarrah is now." Angus said.

"I doubt it. She took a trip to England and married a Pom. I wonder if the Jarrah we remember could be the one. Angus, maybe you can find him through your workplace."

The three young sisters stood back and watched in awe of the fact that their parents held a conversation with a person who looked like a dirty old hobo. They were even more surprised when Opal introduced them all.

"I am called Opal. This is my husband Angus and our girls Xanthe, Lirah and Kinta. What's your name old father?"

"Warragul."

"Wild Dog." Opal smiled because the name seemed to fit his appearance.

"Yes that's me. You say you met this Jarrah at a beach?"

"Jarrah was in my surfing group. Six of us used to camp together on holidays." Angus replied.

Ever forward, Lirah spoke up:

"Our Dad is a policeman you know. I bet he can find your son."

A bloody policeman. Opal caught a shade of alarm cross Warragul's features.

"Don't worry old man. I will see you right." she soothed.

Warragul relaxed realising his countrywoman had his back, since this policeman was her husband.

"Where can we contact you if we find Jarrah is your kin?" she asked.

Being of no fixed abode, Warragul resorted to a bush method. He indicated a cavity created where a metal strut met the bridge railing.

"You leave a sign inside here, three flat stones. I check every day. Sunrise and sunset."

Xanthe braved speaking, using the same term of respect as her mother did.

"Uncle. We are also looking for someone. Name of Tim Fun. He is also a policeman."

"What does this policeman Tim Fun look like?"

"He is very handsome and strong." Xanthe said.

"Part Asian, average height, aged twenty-nine, dark hair." Angus provided the basic missing person description.

"He has a wiry build. Trim and muscular. Very athletic." Opal added.

Warragul did not equate the description with his refugee, who he considered to be a sickly teenager in need of a good feed of meat. A jet black raven perched nearby watching them, cawed its opinion.

"I will keep an eye out." Wild Dog said.

"It might take a while. But if we find anything helpful, the three stones will be placed here, as you say." Opal promised.

Wild Dog bowed his thanks. Put the battered hat back on his head and shambled away in the opposite direction to his hideout. He didn't want them discovering that safe place. When he finally returned to the squat he had news for his weak companion.

"Little brother. The family spoke of a beach. Might be you seen them there some time. That is why you remember something."

"I can't quite grasp why but I just feel like those people are connected to a beach. Racking my brain has made my head ache worse."

"You need a cuppa tea again."

"Yes tea helps. If you're boiling the billy again I'd welcome it. Thanks Wild Dog."

Tim understand feeling thirsty but not why he badly needed to keep hydrating. Warragul went out to a garden tap in the park to refill the billy, and to gather sticks and bark off the ground. A few puffs of air blown into the warm campfire ash soon coaxed a flame. While the billy boiled, Warragul continued his conversation:

"The man is a bloody copper. Be buggered hey? Says he might help find Jarrah. Mind you, those people looking for someone too. If police can't even find their own, I got Buckley's he can find my son."

Wild Dog raved on. He couldn't get over his mistrust of the constabulary.

"You spoke to a policeman?"

"I didn't know until one of his kids said it."

Mention of police rang some distant bell that tolled a rise in Tim's blood pressure. Information overload worsened Tim's headache with a pounding that marched through his head like an enemy army. He could hardly take in the rest of what Warragul added.

"Yes a dang policeman, but his wife has her say. She a good woman. Gave two of her kids old time names. The other one spoke to me. Called me Uncle. That girl seem alright too. Forget her name. Something like Xanadu. But not that."

Xanthe had been named after Angus's mother, so Opal chose the traditional names of Lirah and Kinta for the twins. Wild Dog scratched his head trying to recall the girl's name that escaped him.

"It will come to me. I'm getting as bad as you Little Brother trying to remember things."

10

Father & Son

Little Brother

Sergeant Angus Bridcombe ably sourced Jarrah Smith's information through police search engines. His friend wasn't difficult to find, as he'd stayed in the same job and in the same house for years.

"Jarrah! It's Angus. Long time no see mate."

"Wow. Good to hear from you. Long time *no sea* for me as well. I haven't been surfing for yonks."

"I met up with someone says he's been looking for you. Or at least looking for someone with your name."

"What? Who?"

"Old bloke calls himself Wild Dog."

"MY DAD! I can't believe it! The whole family been looking for him for years now. Is he alright? Where is he?"

"Well. He says he fell on hard times, Jarrah. Definitely been living rough by the looks. He's in the city area. I'm guessing no fixed address. I reckon your dad is a bit leery of policemen and we let it slip that I am one."

"Well. You know. Goes with the territory. I have to go find him!" Jarrah exclaimed.

"Opal got him to agree to us leaving a message if we found you. Three stones."

"Three flat stones. That was always our sign."

Rather than return to the city themselves, Angus tasked Jarrah with the mission to place the stones. He detailed exactly where they should be put in the cavity between a strut and the hand rail. Wild Dog's son would wait nearby for his old father to check the sign. That night, Angus told Opal what he'd arranged.

"Jarrah is dropping everything and going to the city first thing tomorrow."

"What a wonderful surprise it will be for the old man to have his son greet him," Opal smiled, "maybe we can catch up with them some day. All go out for a meal perhaps."

"Yes. At least one happy ending in the making. No news on Tim Fun though."

"I felt proud of Xanthe speaking up to ask about Tim. And calling the old man Uncle too, she followed my lead to do that, so she does listen to me when it counts. I doubt that old man will ever come up with a clue to Tim though, not when the entire force is stumped."

"No. He didn't react to the name or seem aware of any search for a missing person."

"He wouldn't have access to mainstream media apart from old newspapers, if he is even able to read."

Warragul saved any clean newspapers he found, but never leafed through them apart from looking at football photos on sports pages.

"Surely he'd be able to read in this day and age?" Angus remarked.

"Not necessarily. Why not ask Jarrah? He should know."

Angus phoned Jarrah to confirm the plan, and ask to be kept in the loop.

"Jarrah, we wondered how your father became lost for so long. It occurred to us that perhaps he has trouble reading?"

"I never thought of that! Bloody hell! Dad always seemed able to read car ads. Like he knew if it said Ford or Holden or Toyota. Poor old bugger. He'd have a hard time of it trying to follow my street directions. I could kick myself."

"I hope you find him tomorrow and enjoy the reunion. Best of luck, mate."

Jarrah drove in to the city at daybreak the next day. He parked in a paid lot and began to stride across the bridge. Three flat stones borrowed from his fish tank, rattled in his pocket. Before he reached the other side to place the sign, he spied a raggedy old bloke leaning into the railing to check the site.

It's him! My Dad!

Jarrah accelerated swiftly sending a couple of speeding cyclists off kilter. They swore loudly and obscenely at the runner. The racing bike riders could not arrest their falls since their feet were clipped into the pedals. They crash landed in a tangle of metal frames. The mishap didn't stem their streams of angry invective.

"Sorry. Emergency." Jarrah called back over his shoulder.

Old Wild Dog heard the commotion and decided to make himself scarce. He didn't want to get involved as a witness to whatever sparked the uproar. He nimbly slid down a muddy track beside the bridge ramparts into some mangroves and edge growth.

"DAD." Jarrah shouted. "DAD. Don't go! It's me Jarrah."

Warragul couldn't believe his ears. He could barely voice a reply.

"JARRAH! My boy." he coughed out his answer.

Warragul's downward escape route had been easier than getting back up the slippery slide.

"DAD. Where are you?"

"Down here. Wait."

"I'm not going anywhere."

Jarrah could see nothing amongst the foliage but discerned some movement as Wild Dog used roots and grass tufts to regain the top of the bank. He'd almost reached solid ground before Jarrah held out a helping hand and hauled him up into a bear hug.

"Jeez Dad. It's really you! I can't believe I found you at last. Where the hell have you been?"

"Here and there. In the clink too. I been holed up."

"You're a right bloody mess old fella. You been sleeping rough?"

"Not too bad. I got a place." Wild Dog tried to play down his crude accommodation.

"Well tonight you'll sleep in a proper bed. I got a good house now. Inside bog and all."

Warragul's eyes glistened with tears. The turn of fate overwhelmed him. After a while, both father and son settled their emotions.

"Son, I can't leave without a brother I been taking care of. He has to come too."

"A brother? What brother? You mean some old mate?"

"This fella not that old. Poor little bugger got bashed up a while ago."

"Where is he?"

"In my safe place. You come with me Jarrah."

By habit, Warragul made a roundabout circuit back to his squat, in case anyone watched where he went. Jarrah got that he did this and felt saddened by his father's insecurity. Tim Fun startled in alarm at the appearance of another person entering the camp.

"Don't worry little brother. My boy Jarrah come to save us."

Jarrah saw another grubby hobo, looking every bit as decrepit as his father.

"What's your name?" Jarrah asked.

"He don't know nothing." Warragul replied shaking his head.

Tim only gaped back dumbly. He had not met another person since Wild Dog took him in.

Jarrah realised he couldn't just leave without his father's dependent friend. He hadn't expected to be saddled with some retard, yet there was nothing for it but to bring the unfortunate being along. Warragul began to gather his meagre belongings, his blanket, a billy can and few items of foodstuffs.

"Leave it old man. You don't need any of that any more."

"Yeah. Someone else will need this food and the blanket. I will leave it on a bench."

Warragul was loath to part with his few treasured possessions, especially the billy can. Finding the dented receptacle washed up on the river bank had changed his life for the better. Paramount to survival, the billy enabled a useful amount of water to be boiled. A stick through its handle allowed removal from the fire without burning his hands.

Wild Dog called the raven for the last time and been pleased to see the bird was accompanied by another of its species. *Now we both got family.*

Jarrah noticed his father bid the birds goodbye, and asked if he had named them. Warragul replied shortly, turning away to hide his sorrow for leaving his feathered friend.

"No names. They belong to the wild, not to me."

The two able bodied men helped *the retard* make a slow journey across the bridge and up to the car park. Both Wild Dog and Tim Fun sank into the relative comfort of the car seats and were safely buckled into the unaccustomed luxury.

During the drive home, Jarrah told of his good job with a landscaping company. In return, Warragul explained how he came to be wrongly imprisoned. His son understood why he chose to go it alone with a hope police would not notice him.

Jarrah laughed at how his wily old father shammed a death ceremony pointing the bone at the criminal gang of bullies. The ritual was not even a cultural custom of their tribal group.

"Calling the raven was a master stroke." Jarrah chortled.

"My good luck that one got hit by a bus right off. Not lucky for him. They're all bloody shit scared of me after that."

"Did that gang bash your little mate?"

"Reckon had to be them."

"Gutless hey. A bunch of them going for a poor bloke who's not the full quid."

"Yeah. They only pick easy fights. Might be they saw me coming or this little brother would be eaten by bull sharks."

"I can see why you took him in."

"He's a good listener, don't talk much. All the same, glad to have a mate. I been missing the family something awful."

Jarrah felt shame for his initial unworthy attitude. After all, apart from some scavenging blackbirds, this young disabled bloke represented his father's only friend throughout his lonely ordeal.

Stopped on the way home at a fish and chip shop, Jarrah bought three heaping servings of hot chips and batter fried mullet. The salty meal, wrapped in newspaper, was wolfed down at a picnic table in a roadside rest area. Lemon wedges within the parcel, were squeezed over the lot.

Warragul noted his young friend avidly ripped the last shreds of lemon flesh from all the rinds they discarded. He guessed the boy had been used to fresh fruit wherever he came from.

Jarrah tried to divine information from his father's *little brother* to no avail.

"He don't know any of that stuff." Warragul repeated.

Father and son assessed Tim to be in his late teens, rather than his true age of ten years older.

Warragul marvelled at the neat suburban bungalow his son called home. Tim Fun wandered in staying close to his trusted saviour, all the while staring about the rooms. Somehow he knew this type of place, not this one but something like it.

The night before, Jarrah had made up a double bed in his spare room in hopeful readiness for his dad. A smaller room used for storing camping gear and paraphernalia, he now designated for the spare guest. The host quickly unfolded a camp stretcher, topped it with its dense foam mattress, and found sheets and bedding.

Head pounding, Tim gratefully sank onto the bunk, glad of relative darkness in the confined space, lit only by a narrow horizontal window, up close to the ceiling.

Jarrah put the electric kettle on. For want of another name, he also called Tim 'Little Brother'.

"Would Little Brother like a cuppa tea?"

"He never turned one down." Warragul said.

The old man took a mug of sweet milky tea into where Tim drowsed in the dim room. He carefully set it on a sturdy carton beside the bunk.

"Here you go Little Brother. A nice mug of tea with a proper handle. Sugar and milk in this brew. Put hair on your chest." he said.

"Thank you." Tim groaned.

Back in the kitchen, Warragul said his friend was plagued with headaches. Jarrah found paracetamol he kept for times he overdid his strenuous physical work.

"Make him swallow two of these. When he finishes the tea, show him to the bathroom. Dad, you both need a bloody good scrub."

Jarrah made a production of holding his nose and fanning the air in the room.

"Been a while between me and a cake of soap." Wild Dog nodded.

"Been a while for both of you, I reckon."

Their smelly clothes, shirts and trousers, were thrown out the back door towards the laundry lean-to. It was no surprise that neither of them had underwear. Jarrah found clean t-shirts and shorts for his new occupants. Rather than tax his washing machine, Jarrah decided he'd get rid of the filthy garments and look for new duds at an Op Shop when he had time. In the meantime, he had enough pairs of old jeans and football jerseys to share.

Tim puzzled over his own reflection in the bathroom mirror. Logically, the stranger staring back had to be himself. He couldn't place the gaunt face, though it looked like someone he might have once known.

Stepping under the shower, Tim remembered the experience of running water and knew he'd done this before. The soap in his hand felt familiar as well. He sighed as the warm shower jet on the back of his neck soothed his chronic pain.

Aglow after thoroughly cleansing his body and hair with soap, wearing clean clothes, and having the pain killers kick in, Tim felt the best he had since his mugging. Wild Dog also partook of a long over-due steaming hot shower and made use of shaving gear in the cabinet.

"Ah that's better." Wild Dog said, emerging from the bathroom like a different man. He smiled at Little Brother sitting up all squeaky clean too, and made a joke.

"Jeez. He's a blinkin' white boy!"

To be polite, the white boy laughed along with the father and son. He hadn't given a thought to the darker skins of Wild Dog and Jarrah. Remembering the pale face in the bathroom mirror, he realised his difference.

Tim added the information to his scant list of self knowledge: He felt tentative links to the beach, the ocean, the police and he now knew himself to be a white boy.

Jarrah dished up a favourite dessert he cooked the night before; baked rice pudding with custard and stewed prunes. They got stuck in while sitting in the living room listening to country music CDs.

The house, sparsely furnished out of second hand shops lacked a television. Jarrah regretted he hadn't afforded one yet. Now, buying a set would be put further on hold. Finances would be tight in the wake of taking extra family under his wing.

The good son thought about asking a mate in the legal profession, Thaddeus Maekris, how to go about getting Warragul on the old age pension. Thaddeus and Jarrah socialised in different circles now, but in the past, they camped with other mates at the beach on surfing holidays.

Among other surfers who shared the campsite were Angus Bridcombe who joined the police force, and David Dubois who joined the army and married a policewoman, Dulcy Vestige.

Jarrah hoped his father accepted that he had close associations with friends in the police force. He couldn't sidestep it but nevertheless, talked around the issue.

"So Dad. You were given good reason to dislike the police. But in the long run a copper's wife led me to find you at last."

"Yeah. Funny that. But she's one of our mob. Her man seemed alright though."

"We've been mates for a long time. I was there when he first met his wife. It didn't take them long to make three kids." Jarrah laughed. "She had him at hello."

"That kid they called Xanadu or something, she called me Uncle too."

"I reckon they'd be nice kids." Jarrah remarked.

Tim sat quietly listening to the father and son discuss recent events. Again, a feeling niggled that the police subject seriously pertained to himself. Yet, try as he might, he could not grasp the thread.

During the following week, Jarrah phoned Thaddeus Maekris at his law office. Both were buoyed at touching base again after so long.

"Poppy and I have five kids now and another on the way." Thaddeus boasted.

"Congratulations. You never lost your mojo then."

The mojo topic had been a standing gag since Thaddeus dipped out a couple of times with girls he'd pursued, before he met Poppy.

"How about you?"

"Still footloose and fancy free."

"Really? You were always the popular one. A girl on each arm and a different one each week."

"Yeah. I spread myself around, that's where I went wrong, Thad. Got me banned from the local pub when a couple of girls started a proper cat fight, scratching faces, ripping hair out. The lot."

"Where were you?"

"On stage singing karaoke, so you might say I got a birds eye view."

"You're saying two girls fought over you Jarrah?"

"More than two. A couple of other sheilas joined in. My good name got screeched a few times. Other blokes cheered them on when they saw ripped clothes and bare boobs."

"How did it end?"

"Lots of damage. Broken glasses. Ambulances. Police. The lot."

"Good gracious. What on earth had you been singing?"

"Some old Elvis thing about being lonesome. Even if I wasn't. But I truly never made promises to any of those ladies. Seems like females don't always see things the same way as males do."

"That's the truth." Thaddeus agreed. "So you're avoiding further commitments now?"

"Treading on eggshells around women. Too busy now anyway. But I am committed to taking care of my old father. Finally found him after he went missing for years. Long story. I could use your advice, mate."

Jarrah filled Thaddeus in on what had befallen Warragul causing him to go underground, almost literally. The old man's mistrust of authority had him abandon the social security links he'd previously been given in prison. Homeless, Warragul lived by his wits and on charity handouts.

"No worries. I'll set the cogs in motion to have your father's age pension reinstated. It isn't a huge income but after surviving on the streets with nothing it will be a boon. He might be eligible for back payment too. I will look into it, mate."

Thaddeus assured the pension benefits were a foregone conclusion for Warragul.

Afraid of seeming a backward blackfella for taking in an unknown mentally challenged person, Jarrah did not mention his younger dependant at this stage.

Certain Thaddeus would only charge mates rates; he did not want to overload the favour either. Between his own pay and his father's pension they'd keep the sickly little brother okay. He didn't eat much or ask for anything.

11

A Blast from the Past

Tools

Back at headquarters, Angus Bridcombe shared his latest news with Dulcy Grimslade.

"Here's a blast from the past Dulcy. Remember Jarrah from years ago? Opal and I caught up with him recently."

"Really? How's he doing now? I know Keziah didn't continue going out with him after schoolies week."

"Doing really well. Still single. He's kept the same landscaping job for years and has his own house now."

"Wow. Maybe Keziah should have given him more of a chance." Dulcy laughed.

"He did come across as the least responsible out of all of us, which is saying a lot, but he is taking care of his old dad now."

"Some men mature. Some don't." Dulcy's ex-husband came to her mind.

Angus expanded on how he and Opal had taken their daughters to the park where the police dog sniffed out Tim Fun's clothes.

"The girls thought they'd try to help by asking people if they'd seen anything. No use at all of course. We hoped just making an effort might assist towards closure. Xanthe particularly wanted to go, sadly she thinks she's lost the love of her life. Anyway, no doubt Opal will fill you in with the girls' romantic notions better than I can. Losing Tim isn't easy to come to terms with for any of us."

"I can't come to terms with him being gone either. I still feel like raking over every scant fragment in case we missed something."

"What does Dougall say?"

"He says, we have to face facts. Tim has been missing going on ten weeks now."

"True. But why not go over old ground. It can't hurt." Angus mused.

"Exactly my thoughts Angus."

With the dilemma prominent in their collective minds, Dulcy canvassed the chief officer in charge of the investigation. He called it nagging. Having no new leads, her husband readily agreed to re-visit every angle for the umpteenth time. It meant re-checking David Dubois' account and perhaps questioning his partner Chantel Cheron.

Deemed a crime scene to the open case, Tim Fun's flat remained off limits. Forensics had gone over the interior and checked Tim's vehicle. Nothing helpful came to light. Subsequently Tim's car was secured in the police pound.

As it turned out, David Dubois contacted Dulcy himself. His call went via a switchboard. Avoiding Grimslade, David specifically asked to speak to his ex-wife.

"Look Dulcy Sweetheart. I know Tim Fun is, or was, your cherished colleague and all that. But the flat is still taped off. I need to know when I can rent it out again."

Dulcy replied sharply without saying what she thought of David's request.

"I'll get back to you. And don't call me that."

Dougall overheard his wife's side of the conversation.

"Was that Dubois?"

"Yes and talk about tactless. He is griping about Tim's flat being vacant and not bringing him any rent. As if they'd rely on it with both of them working. I know David's army pay is good."

"Why did you say 'don't call me that'...what did he call you?"

"He only said Sweetheart. David sees himself as God's gift to women. He doesn't realise some women actually see that type of tag as diminutive. Like a put down. Sweetheart."

"Double standards Sweetheart."

"I know Sweetheart." Dulcy smiled.

Incensed at Dubois' familiarity with his wife, Dougall's own smile turned upside down.

"Your ex is a piece of work alright. Maybe I'll pay him another visit and lean on him."

"You know Dougall, we could pay Tim's rent up to date ourselves, in hopes he is found."

"Yes. I hadn't thought of that."

"I really think we should."

"Alright. Never say die. I agree we cover Tim's rent until...or for a year anyway if he isn't found."

"If you're questioning David again, you might mention it."

"See what happens Dulcy. He can't force this issue."

Grimslade visited Dubois' beach house unannounced early the next evening, Friday. He found Chantel Cheron at home, but Dubois had not yet returned from work.

"Miss Cheron. May I take this opportunity to ask for your assistance?"

"How can I help?"

"Regarding the last know movements of my missing colleague, Tim Fun. I theorised he may have borrowed tools to fix security chains to his doors."

"Yes. He did. I told him to help himself to David's toolkit."

Chantel felt safe saying that much but not offering more, hoping her guilt didn't show. She had an idea withholding the fact Tim had gone to the quay before he disappeared equated to obstruction. *Bloody David and his hang-ups!*

"Did Tim enter your premises to access the tools?"

"Yes. I showed him where to find the kit under the sink. Then he returned them later."

"Assuming you shared some conversation at the time?"

"Probably did. Just pleasantries. You know."

Discomfort prickled Chantel for the inappropriate move she made on Tim when he returned the tools.

"He didn't mention his plans for the rest of the day?"

"Not that I recall."

"Did your partner have any problem with you lending his tools out?"

"No. It saved David having to do the job himself, as the landlord."

Grimslade observed small but telling signs of evasive body language emanating from Chantel. Noting his scrutiny, she turned on the charm to earn his approval.

"I was just making coffee Inspector. Would you like a cup?"

Dougall took her up on the offer in order to glean more. Carrying a tray laden with coffee cups and a plate of Iced Vovos to the living room, the lady of the house invited him to sit on the sofa. Engaged in polite small talk, they didn't hear David's Jeep drive in.

Grimslade's vehicle parked out front caused David to creep in quietly. He leapt into the room to find the pair engaged in what he saw as an overly friendly chat.

"This is fuckin' cosy," he roared, "chatting up another of MY women Grimslade?"

"I am. Yes." Grimslade replied smoothly. He couldn't help needling Dubois.

Already on edge, Chantel startled, causing some coffee to slop over into her saucer.

"Don't be ridiculous honey." she quavered.

"Chantel. Did you invite him here?"

"No. Why would I do that?" she riled at David's accusing tone of voice.

"Typical of the way you wrap yourself around men. Even an old codger like this one."

"How dare you say that to me David. After everything I've done for you."

Sometimes it paid to sit back, watch and listen. Dougall's silence fed them plenty of rope, he hoped there'd be enough to trip them up somehow.

"I apologise for David's rudeness Inspector. He even accused me of hitting on Tim Fun."

Stick that up your sneaky arse David, and smoke it. Chantel mixed a couple of metaphors and glared at her partner with the unspoken portion of her comment. Grimslade formed a reasonable question.

"In the interests of accuracy, Miss Cheron, did grounds exist to support that accusation?"

Chantel's fingers splayed over her bosom in a parody of innocence implying *Moi?*

In David's assessment, she didn't quite pull off the innocent act. His anger towards Grimslade boiled over. In a knee jerk reaction, he spat out an inadvisable retort.

"Our personal life is none of your business you bloody pervert. Frustrated are you? Suppose at your age you can't keep it up long enough to get any satisfaction. Hey? You just need to get your rocks off on what others do."

"David!" Chantel admonished him. *The idiot.*

Dubois' outburst could land her in deep bother if he taunted the detective to delve deeper. The three faced off each thinking their own thoughts. Despite past failures, Dubois' modus operandi had always been *when in doubt attack.*

"I demand to know when I can rent my flat out again." he snarled.

Dougall adopted a supercilious expression, knowing he held all the cards. He stooped to an irresistible urge to get Dubois' goat while offering to pay Tim's rent at the same time.

"Demand all you like Dubois. But if it helps you out with the groceries, I'm happy to cover Tim's rent. Since that makes me a paying tenant, I'll christen the bed springs now and then with my wife. Dulcy gets an extra thrill when I'm inventive with different locations. Don't worry, I'll try to keep the noise down, though she does get quite vocal at the height of her passion with me."

Dubois looked fit to explode. Chantel had hardly ever put her foot down in all the time she raised two boys. With two grown men spoiling for a fight, she reached the end of her tether. David's ex as the bone of contention flaunted in her own presence, added fuel to her vexation.

"That's enough! I know you two share a history but really this is beyond decent. David you should know better than let yourself be teased into stupid comments. And Inspector Grimslade, I find your behaviour to be highly unprofessional. Have some dignity both of you! You're behaving like a pair of tools."

Neither man took much notice of Chantel. Grimslade enjoyed getting under Dubois' skin too much and David never bothered about her opinion. Dougall stood up to leave, firing off a farewell barb.

"Well, this has been grand. Thanks for the coffee and *civilised* chat Miss Cheron. Unfortunately, I must take my leave. My wife eagerly looks forward to another romantic evening with me."

Dubois strode out of the room before an impulse to deck the detective overwhelmed his critical thinking. It wouldn't pay to give Grimslade any reason to arrest him. David had slammed the bathroom door so Chantel took the chance to follow Dougall out to his car.

"I'd prefer you send someone other than yourself or your wife, if there is a next time. You and David are just itching to land yourselves in court."

"My apologies Miss Cheron. I was way out of order. I have embarrassed myself."

Dougall bowed slightly and graced the woman with his best twinkly eyed smile that transformed his grumpy face. Forever a sucker for a good-looking man, Chantel felt somewhat appeased. She tried to explain away David's anger, hoping the detective would stop bothering them.

"David gets so emotional. I'm afraid losing his wife to you obsesses him. You'd never tell by his appearance but he isn't a very secure person. Believe it or not. I mean, imagining me with the young tenant when everyone knows Tim is gay. Or was. Whatever."

Gay?

"I understand completely Miss Cheron." although he didn't understand her final disclosure.

Dougall drove back to the office deep in thought. Dulcy wanted an update.

"Learn anything?"

"Learnt a few things about myself. Had words with your charming ex. Admit my fault for taking his bait. But more to the point, his woman claims Tim Fun is gay. Or, as she put it; was."

"Tim gay? She's wrong about that. He chased girls all the time. Took them out to dinner. Legend has it he never got to first base. Just ask Isla or Ethan. Poor Tim was a bit of a joke at the surf club. He was known as an easy meal ticket behind his back."

"Hmm. Betting Tim claimed to be gay to ward off unwanted attentions from Dubois' woman."

"That seems feasible. Proves she had a go at him. Poor little Tim. Couldn't win for losing."

"Yep. By the way. I said I'd cover Tim's rent on the flat."

"Did David agree?"

"Can't say he did."

Dougall busily shuffled some paperwork to avoid meeting her eye. Dulcy wasn't fooled.

"What are you NOT saying?"

Dougall changed the subject.

"Darn it! I meant to pick up another bottle of Johnny Walker. I'll get it on the way home. We still on for tonight? Chinese takeaway? A little moonlight and romance? Do you want to pick the tune this time?"

"Are you avoiding my question?"

"Is this the Spanish Inquisition?"

"I have ways of making you talk." she threatened.

"Bring it on. Can't wait."

Dougall's cheeky grin fanned the embers. Dulcy put the matter of Tim's rent on hold, in anticipation of getting her sexy man home that Friday evening.

By hook or by crook Dougall's wife intended to find out what really went on between him and her ex. All in good time. First things first.

12

Girls Will Be Girls

It's A Jungle

Saturday morning, Dulcy and Opal ran into each other at the supermarket. They chatted across their trolleys, and were upbraided by a bossy woman for holding up traffic in the aisle. Since they'd left ample room for another shopping cart to pass, Dulcy flashed her badge and shot the whiner down with a sharp order.

"Police business. Move along."

Dulcy and Opal enjoyed seeing the annoying woman off with a flea in her ear.

"You silly cow. You'll get in trouble doing that one day." Opal warned.

"I should stop it. But that was worth it."

They shared a giggle.

"Hey Dulcy. I was thinking of a girl's night out tonight. Trying to cheer up my kids while Angus is on duty. But I know it's your big Saturday night thing with Dougall. Would he mind?"

"Actually Opal, we did the big Saturday night thing last night. I can hardly walk."

"Geez. The man has hidden talents."

Their sex lives had always been hot topics of private conversation, with few holds barred.

"Dougall might welcome a reprieve. Though he'd never let on."

"Wouldn't want to wear him out."

"Tried. Failed." Dulcy grinned.

"Anyway, I was thinking maybe pizza and then ice-creams at the roller rink?"

"Sure. As long as I don't have to skate."

"I want to avoid that killing field too. We'll just watch my bawdy family do their thing."

Dulcy and Opal managed some conversation over the loud music and noise of the skating rink.

"Dougall and I want to pay Tim's rent at least for a year if he isn't found by then. We cling to a slim chance he isn't...you know."

"Wow. That's a good idea. But I won't tell the girls in case it gives them false hope."

"Only, I'm not sure David agreed. Dougall was supposed to handle it during a follow up question session. Apparently he had *words* with David."

"What sort of words? Guessing a few four letter ones. Bet it involved you Dulcy."

"Had to. Dougall won't say. He just veers off the subject."

"Hmm. Wonder if David's sheila knows they argue over you. It would peeve me if I were in the same boat."

"She does know. Dougall questioned her too. He found out she tried it on with Tim."

"How? Surely she didn't confess to that?"

"No, but she believes Tim is gay."

"He isn't gay though. Is he?"

"Reckon he just said it to put her off, but it means she must have hit on him."

"Right. I see. No reason to mention that to the girls. They're already feeling delicate."

They watched the three delicate Bridcombe girls traverse the rink at speed. Sparks flew off their skates when they scraped the walls in passing.

"They look very adept at roller skating." Dulcy remarked.

"Yes. It's been a while since we've been but they've always been good at it."

"You must have brought them here many times."

"Mmm. I did until they got banned for a few months over some piffling misunderstanding."

"Oh?"

"Ridiculous really. Anyway their suspension period is up now."

They watched Xanthe fend off a big boy who skated too close to her. In a deft move she managed to elbow him and send him flying onto his knees.

"He should have worn knee pads." Opal remarked mildly.

"It's a jungle out there."

The twins made a show of helping the chubby boy regain his feet, with sly winks to Xanthe. The boy sprawled on the surface and appeared to utter a few choice sentences. Lirah accidentally stood on his hand and Kinta lost her balance and sat down hard on his back.

"Ouch. That had to hurt." Dulcy commented blandly.

"At least my girls are apologising."

"You've raised them well Opal. They'd do the *Poked Club* proud."

The awful name bestowed on their own childhood club had been made up of the first initials of five schoolgirl friends; Pepper, Opal, Keziah, Eden and Dulcy. At the time, the children meant the name to poked up their efforts for worthy projects, like finding lost dogs. Their respective parents vetoed the name. The girls only realised another connotation in later years. To the current day, the original members still facetiously referred to *The Poked Club* in certain situations.

"They don't back down Dulcy."

"Nope. It's not in their genes, Opal."

The Poked Club girlfriends shared satisfied smiles. While the Bridcombe sisters took care of each other in the arena, Opal considered Dulcy's problem. There had to be some intriguing reason Dougall declined to elaborate on the flat rental outcome.

"I have an idea Dulcy. You should get on the friendly side with David's partner. What's her name?"

"Chantel Cheron. You'd know her by sight. She's been in the surf club forever. Have to say she's attractive, but in a slutty obvious way."

"You ever jealous?"

"Never. I'm actually glad David got someone to fill in as mother for his son. I certainly didn't want to do it. I feel sorry for her in a way because, true to type, David still chases me."

"Even though you've been happily married to Dougall for years?"

"Yep. It's an ongoing feud between David and Dougall. I'm the meat in the sandwich."

"So is this Chantel sheila then. I'd rather have your side of it than hers."

"Me too. How do you suggest I befriend her. She can't possibly like me."

"Could you use your rank and go to the address officially?"

"I suppose I could follow up on the idea of paying Tim's rent. But I don't want to run into David."

"You'd see if his car was there or not. He'd have to show up for army duty like any normal job."

"That's not a bad idea. I'll do it. Or try to."

The skating rink population drew an almost audible sigh of relief when the trio of Bridcombe girls vacated the premises. Driving home, Dulcy occupied the front passenger seat, Opal drove, and the sisters shared the back seat. The girls talked animatedly about the session.

"I hated that big fat kid who kept jostling everyone."

"I hated that show-off girl with the fancy pink tutu. She nearly knocked me down twirling around with her skinny leg stuck out. She was just begging to be spun faster."

"Yep what a sook just because she fell over. Little princess hey."

"Should have spun her harder."

"Yeah. I hate when I take pity."

"The family who skates together hates together." Opal said. "Now that you're all banned from the rink for another three months, you won't get to do that again for a while."

"They had it coming." Xanthe sulked.

"And going." Lirah laughed.

"It was worth it." Kinta added.

"Where do they get it from?" Opal asked her friend.

"Beats me Opal."

Encouraged by the girl's night out, and the feisty Bridcombes, Dulcy fronted David's beach house at the soonest opportunity. She chose a weekday when he would be on duty, further evidenced by his vacant car space.

Making friends with her ex's live-in woman had never been on Dulcy's agenda, but she did not go unarmed. Her weapon of choice; a delectable bakery chocolate cheese cake. Chantel answered the door.

"Oh. It's you."

"Chantel. May I call you that?"

"It's my name."

"I hope you'll call me Dulcy. That's my name." she hoped her forced smile looked friendly.

"I know. So?"

"Well, Chantel, it's like this: Seems our men have a ridiculous feud, and no one can sort that out except two strong minded women. You and me."

"Hmm. Maybe. What's in the box?"

"Chocolate cheese cake."

"Come in. Tea or coffee?"

"Dougall says you make a lovely cup of coffee." Dulcy spoke her first lie to Chantel.

They sat across from each other at the kitchen table. Chantel served the creamy cake with fresh strawberries she happened to have on hand. As intended, the bone china plates and little cake forks impressed Dulcy. Chantel rued having no linen serviettes, but made do with paper ones.

"This cake is a special treat. Thanks for bringing it, Dulcy."

"You have a flare for presentation, this is lovely how you've used the berries on the side, Chantel."

Never immune to being buttered up, Chantel smiled at last.

"So. Where do we begin?"

"Firstly Chantel, I want you to know I bear no ill feelings towards you. Never have. In fact, I didn't at any time wish David to be alone and unhappy. I am actually really glad he found you."

"Thanks."

"By the time you and David got together, it was well over between us. Long story most of which I'm sure you must know."

"Of course I know that story. Zelia's murder was hot gossip. I know David seemed guilty but it never made sense to me. He wouldn't want everyone knowing she had his baby. Plus it meant Davy was left motherless."

"He was a prime suspect. I wasn't allowed to be officially involved in his case because of our relationship. We were still married at the time you understand. But I worked behind the scenes to help exonerate him. I believed in his innocence."

Chantel identified genuine truth in Dulcy's comments. She had nothing to lose with her reply.

"I know he never really loved me, not truly deeply. But he needed a mother figure for Davy and I needed a father figure for Dominic. We managed to make a family of it for the boys."

"I admire you for that Chantel. I couldn't have done it."

Dulcy's admiration appealed to Chantel's need for justification. She wondered if they could sort their men out, between them.

"Guessing your husband told you all about how his last visit here went?"

"Yes," Dulcy told her second lie to Chantel, "what did you make of it?"

"They were both to blame. The rent on the flat started them off. "

"Dougall can be argumentative."

"I call David pig headed. But asking when he could rent out Tim's flat again? How insensitive is that?"

"Paying Tim's rent was Dougall's purpose to visit. If they both wanted the same thing, it beats me how they got arguing."

"They egged each other on."

"Dougall is adept at putting the boot in."

"David shouldn't have said the thing about your husband being too old."

"It's the stupid feud."

"I know. David almost went ballistic when your husband said how he'd use the flat for variety."

"Dougall knows how to needle."

"He does. When he said he'd try to keep the noise down but you get loud when you're loving it with him...I though it would come to blows."

I'll have a few words of my own for Dougall. The big mouth. Dulcy fumed in private.

"How horrible for you having to witness that." Dulcy sympathised.

"I didn't know where to look, to be honest. Anyway I told them both off."

"Good for you Chantel. What did you say to Dougall?"

"I said he behaved unprofessionally. He agreed and apologised which is more than David did."

"I don't mean to intrude on your personal life, Chantel, but do you find David is a bit controlling?"

"He likes to have control."

"Are you okay though?"

"I look after myself. But there is one thing I've never said about Tim that bothers me. David forbade me to say anything. Now I'm worried how it looks."

"I know he accused you of hitting on the tenant. David's jealous streak overrules his good sense at times. He used to accuse me of misbehaviour too."

"Dulcy, I hope you don't mind me saying, but he reckons you always had a thing for Dougall Grimslade. Even after so many years he can't get over you married him. It's like you hit him with the ultimate insult."

David's idea that Dulcy went for the older man as revenge, held weight in Chantel's private opinion. She wanted to hear Dulcy confirm it. How any woman would prefer someone like Grimslade over her gorgeous David, was beyond her understanding.

"To be fair, Chantel, I did have a hero-worship attraction to Dougall but I never hid it from David."

"So David was always jealous?"

"Yes. Always. I only acted on a desire to be with Dougall after I split up with David."

Chantel remained dubious about the attraction, but formed a suitable reply.

"I guess you two have that whodunit thing in common."

"And great sex. Dougall's cheeky grin makes me go weak at the knees. He is my soulmate."

"So whatever David imagines, doesn't apply?"

"No it does not. I'm sure you look after David well and he is lucky to have a beautiful woman like you Chantel. I'm trying to say his ongoing jealousy wouldn't stem from being sexually frustrated."

"I do my best to keep him happy." Chantel blushed modestly.

The intimate turn of conversation bonded Chantel to Dulcy, since great sex had always been a driving motivation for whatever she did. Speaking about David's controlling attitude, and being admired for being a strong woman, convinced Chantel to confess. It would be such a relief to get it off her chest, furthermore, David need never know.

"Dulcy. He did accuse me of chasing Tim."

"Did that give you pause to think he might be behind Tim's disappearance?"

"No. I know for sure David wasn't behind it. He just doesn't want to help you out. It's his stupid vendetta to make life difficult for you and Dougall."

"I agree David wouldn't have harmed Tim."

Dulcy spoke cautiously, waiting while Chantel visibly struggled with some inner angst.

"Dulcy, please don't ever let David know I spilled this, because he ordered me not to."

Dulcy realised Chantel's position to be vulnerable, different to how her own had been with David.

"I wouldn't put you in jeopardy, Chantel."

"Promise? I mean it's just that I am settled here and I don't want to lose that security."

"Does David have some water tight alibi we don't know about?"

"It's just that, Tim came with me to the cruise ship that Saturday. He helped me with my luggage and I gave him my keys because he was supposed to drive my car back here. But it was still in the parking lot two weeks later. So Tim didn't make it back to my car and David wasn't anywhere near there at the time."

Dulcy reeled with the new information. A dozen *what ifs* circled in her mind.

"Why would David order you to keep that quiet?" she gasped.

"He said I'd just bring trouble down on my own head. He said it wouldn't make any difference because Tim must already be dead. And I believed that too. I know David was being spiteful about not helping your detective team. I'm sorry."

Chantel began to cry and wring her hands.

"I have to go. Take care Chantel. Better not let David know I was here today."

"I won't. I hope he never finds out I told you that thing."

Back at headquarters Dougall raised an eyebrow towards Dulcy as she rushed in.

"Where have you been all morning?"

"Visiting Chantel Cheron."

"Um. Dulcy. You're supposed to clear investigations with your worthy superior." he said, smiling.

"It was personal. It wasn't supposed to be about the case, but I uncovered something important."

"Care to share?"

"Tim Fun drove Chantel to her cruise job that Saturday he went missing. He was supposed to bring her car back but it was still in the staff car park when she returned two weeks later."

"Bloody hell. So Tim's last known whereabouts is nowhere near any of the search areas. Why has it taken her so long to tell us? Did Dubois know as well?"

"David convinced her not to tell. He said why get involved when it wouldn't make any difference. Chantel agreed that Tim had been missing so long, he had to be dead. Of course, David wouldn't want to be helpful."

"That bastard! Seems he'd do anything to make me look incompetent."

"Not only you Dougall. All of us. The whole team. Including his old surfing buddy Angus. David has acted true to type. Loyalty has never been his strong suit."

"Now we've got to try and pick up a cold trail. Shit!"

Dulcy pardoned her husband's coarse language, she felt like ranting with a lot worse.

"Another thing Dougall, I've promised Chantel we won't say the information came from her."

"You can't promise that."

"Why not Dougall? It won't effect the case."

"Making a promise like that is highly unprofessional."

"Unprofessional? Oho. Like you being on actual police business and telling David we'd have sex in Tim's flat? And needling him by saying I make so much NOISE when I'm loving it with you? No wonder David doesn't want to assist our enquiry."

Dougall had the grace to blush.

"I know. Sorry. He got under my skin. So guessing Chantel told you all about that."

"I wrangled it out of her by letting her think I already knew about it."

"Clever." Dougall smiled.

"Don't think you can butter me up with compliments Dougall."

"Then I'll have to think of some other way."

For once, Dulcy cursed his come-hither grin that melted her resolve. She forced her lips not to twitch in a smile because she wanted to stay mad at him for longer.

"We've got work to do Dougall, now that we have a thread to follow."

"Right. Full contingent to the shipping dock. Someone might recall something, as late as this is."

Too much time had elapsed between when Tim went to the quay, and the present time, to take full advantage of Chantel's information. Grimslade could only rely on his habitual brainstorming method, helped by Dulcy's intuition. They checked the cruise liner car park records to confirm when and where Chantel's car had been parked.

"Chantel had to pay a hefty parking fee. No wonder she wanted her car brought home."

CCTV covered the parking lot. Records proved Chantel drove in with Tim as her passenger. It showed he helped with her luggage and accompanied her to the boarding ramp. They had a short conversation with a security guard, after which Chantel pecks Tim's cheek and pats his back. He seemed eager to depart.

"He's helped with her bags but apparently he doesn't return to her car."

"Judging by the meal he'd been thawing, and the clothes laid out for work the next day, he planned to go straight back to his flat."

"He might make a detour to the loos, and he'd be at risk in there."

"I agree. A smallish person on his own would be a target."

Investigations tracked two council workmen who were responsible for maintaining the public amenities. Nothing useful emerged from security footage, since the lenses had been vandalised. The cleaners said cameras were often disabled with black spray paint.

"Do you recall any sign of a fight in the men's block. Like blood?"

"There's often shit and piss on the floor and the walls. Our first attack is to blitz the place with a high-pressure hose. We don't look too closely at the stinking artwork but there could be blood."

"Yew. Boys will be boys." Dulcy said.

"Not only the men. Sometimes the ladies section gets disgusting too."

"Yew. Girls will be girls." Dougall countered.

The janitors shared an annoying smirk at Dulcy's expense, so Dougall surmised they would be more likely to contact him than a woman.

"Thanks for your help. If you remember anything at all later on, no matter how small, please take my card and give me a call."

"Can we ask what this is about?"

"We received a late tip-off about the police detective who went missing some weeks ago. He might have used this facility."

"Crikey. D'ya think he's been murdered?"

"The enquiry is ongoing. We hope to ascertain what happened."

The council workers made the most of that story down the pub at the end of their shifts.

13

On The Job

What was the Question?

Driving back after assessing the situation at the quay, Dulcy berated her husband. They were both on edge with pressure to solve Tim Fun's case.

"Thanks a lot for belittling me in front of those cleaners, Dougall."

"You started it. Sweetheart."

"My reaction was perfectly reasonable in the circumstances. The fact you had to embellish it with your smart arse comment was extremely unprofessional. Furthermore, this case is far from a joking matter. I can't imagine what has become of poor little Tim."

Dulcy choked off in a sob.

Immediately contrite and ashamed, Dougall pulled the car over into a lay-by and took her hand. Dulcy rarely cried. They habitually coped with stressful cases by using inappropriate humour. This time Dougall had overstepped some invisible mark, and he knew it.

"Dulcy my darling. I'm sorry. How about I give you a good back rub tonight to work out some of your kinks and anxieties."

Dulcy blew her nose.

"Alright. But I want a proper rub for at least thirty minutes with lavender massage oil. Not just a hasty prelude to you getting your leg over."

"I promise a proper half-hour massage."

"With lavender oil, don't forget."

"Then we'll negotiate the leg over. Okay? I've got a few kinks and anxieties myself."

"As long as you don't wake me up for it."

Later in bed Dulcy's moans of pleasure made Dougall regret promising a full half hour massage.

"Oh. That is wonderful. I love your big strong hands."

"Size matters hey?"

He pressed his thumbs into her shoulder blades while working circular motions with his fingertips.

"Mmm. Go harder on my shoulders and yes down my spine just like that. Ooh aah."

It occurred to Dougall to keep her talking so she didn't fall asleep, and this might be a good time to ask a question that had bugged him for years.

"We've been together for going on thirteen years now Dulcy, and there's something I've always wanted to ask. Not that it makes any difference now. I'm not obsessed or anything. But you know, just out of curiosity."

"Mmm. Go on." she replied sleepily.

"Is my...I mean...compared to your ex..."

"David?"

"Yes David. How many ex-s have you got?"

"Just the one so far."

Dougall stopped rubbing as that sunk in.

"Oh don't stop.. I was only joking. So what did you want to know?"

"Is anything of David's...um...bigger?"

"Bigger than what?" Dulcy hid her knowing smile in the pillow.

"Bigger than mine."

"Oh yes. Absolutely. Hugely. Enormously so."

Fortunately, Dougall didn't voice his inner reaction: *I feckin' knew it! He's not only younger, better looking and fitter, The bastard!*

"Not that it matters. Right? You're really happy with me aren't you Dulcy?"

"Well, I manage with your little ups and downs. But you know there are steps you could take to enhance personal growth."

Great! Could this get any worse?

"Really. I suppose you've looked into this."

"Sort of, I have come across similar shortfalls in the course of other research. The usual advice is to seek professional counselling to suss out options." she said.

Dougall shut up for a good five minutes. *Bloody hell. Why did I ask? Now it's going to come up like an elephant in the room every night. No, not an elephant. More like a puny little tiddler.*

"That was a beautiful massage my darling. You have such magic big strong hands. I feel so relaxed now. You're very quiet of a sudden. Are you sleepy?"

"I'm wide awake Dulcy. I might never rest easy again."

"Why?"

"My dear wife just told me she manages *to get by with my shortfall.* It's a bit of a shock to be honest."

Dulcy kindly let him off the hook.

"But Dougall my darling, I love that your ego is not as big as David's. Your vulnerable episodes are endearing, and far preferable to his braggadocio."

"My ego?"

Dougall breathed a sigh of relief. Dulcy smiled in the dark.

"Did you have another vulnerable moment Dougall?"

"Yes that's it. I was having a moment."

"Are you getting over your concerns now?"

"I am. So is my leg. While we're on the subject, I've often wondered about something else."

"To do with David?"

"Yes. It is to do with David. I know comparisons are odious. You might say I'm fishing for compliments again. Maybe I am. Be brutally honest Dulcy. I can take it. I just have to know."

"What was the question again?"

Her giggle gave her away. Dougall finally twigged she teased him for his off remark to the janitors.

"Shut up Dulcy."

"Okay. I will. Now you'll never know what I know."

Despite temporarily coping with anxieties by verbal sparring, the predicament of Tim Fun's disappearance weighed heavily. Back at headquarters early the following day, Dougall included Angus Bridcombe in discussions.

"Angus, the search area has shifted. A late tip-off pinpointed where Tim's plight probably began. It's at a quayside car park where the big ocean liners moor. We are behind the eight ball with this due to the time lapse. However, I'd like you to spearhead a full-on ground search of the surrounding area and the water under the wharves."

"I'm on it. I can deploy a good team of uniformed personnel immediately. Police divers have been on stand-by in case of any breakthrough with the river search. May I ask about your tip-off?"

"It came from Chantel Cheron. Your mate David Dubois prevented her from telling us sooner, but Dulcy winkled it out of her. And by the way, Chantel has been promised her disclosure will be private. She doesn't want Dubois finding she clued us in."

"Bloody David and his inflated ego." Angus got the gist immediately.

"It's enormous." Dulcy mimed a popular fishing boast holding her hands wide apart.

Dougall resorted to his practised deadpan expression. Angus left, keen to set his task in motion.

"If you're finished with your sly digs Dulcy, we need to brainstorm some scenarios. And by the way, no one is that big unless they're a freak of nature."

"Are we still talking about egos?"

"Just concentrate on the job Dulcy."

"I will if you will."

Sorely tempted to pull rank with a little reminder about respecting her superior officer, Dougall nevertheless let it go. After all, he had to live with the woman.

"Any ideas?" he asked.

"What if those council workers actually robbed Tim themselves?"

"And what? Got Tim out of there, stripped his clothes off and binned them miles away?"

"Seems someone did. Or stripped him first then moved him. Also, the deep water at the mooring is the obvious place to dump a body. The depths are murky and it's near the amenities building."

The worst case scenario appalled them, but the pair took refuge in their alter egos by switching to professional mode. Downhearted at the prospect, the Grimslades seriously considered Tim Fun could be in a watery grave underneath the wharves.

"I have to say, those council cleaners are not high on my list of suspects."

"Nor mine, but I'm clutching at straws. A single perpetrator is just as likely and harder to track. However, the degree of vandalism at the toilet blocks suggests hoodlums on the rampage."

"I agree. Hopefully Angus's search turns up any local gangs. We might weasel out a snitch to do a deal."

"So our list of possible suspects weakly consists of some random individual, some unknown gang of hoodlums, one or both of the council cleaners and I guess your charming ex isn't off the hook."

"David's camping alibi checked out." Dulcy reminded.

"What if he only bought the campsite but didn't stay there? He could have spied Chantel driving off with Tim and followed."

"Chantel didn't even know she had the job until the last minute. I verified that with the recruitment agency. Also CCTV doesn't show David at the quay at any time."

"He'd have known about the CCTV and avoided it." Dougall countered.

"I don't buy it. David wouldn't want to go through another grilling like he did with Zelia's murder. He'd be aware of being a main suspect in Tim's disappearance."

Dougall dismantled Dulcy's rationale.

"He could have parked somewhere else and waited in the public block."

"On the off-chance Tim would need to use the toilet? Also David wouldn't know if those security cameras were working or not."

"Dulcy, I realise you may still hold misguided loyalty for your ex."

"That's bull Dougall. Get over yourself. I am just working towards the truth. Don't make this personal. And don't shirk your share of the blame. If not for you and David circling each other with your hackles up like mad dogs, we'd be miles ahead on this case."

"How do you make that out?"

"Think about it Dougall."

"Okay. Perhaps Chantel might not have withheld information if Dubois didn't exert some hold over her. But that's on his head. Not mine."

Dulcy's exasperated sigh was not lost on her husband. His face reddened for his part in pushing Dubois' buttons. Dougall eyed his wife, for once he rued her accurate intuition.

"Dougall, I know from past experience, David isn't brave enough. He wouldn't have the guts to do it even if he wanted to. And where's the motive? Just suspecting Chantel had the hots for Tim doesn't cut it. I actually quite liked Chantel once I got to know her a bit, but between you and me, she's earned a reputation for going after any male with a pulse. So I don't see David singling out his rent paying tenant."

"Now that you mention it, I think the alluring Miss Cheron had a go at me. I got coffee and iced vovos." Dougall preened.

"Perhaps you should ask yourself why Chantel might come on to you Dougall."

"Perhaps she noticed my big strong hands?"

"That is entirely possible. After all, she did notice your big strong foot in your big strong mouth."

Dougall only smiled.

"How about putting the kettle on darling. I could use a brew."

"Do it yourself. I'm not a bloody kitchen maid."

Dougall plonked tea bags into two mugs with a smile and a flourish. He could stand making his wife jealous for once.

Angus Bridcombe and his team discovered a gang of hoodlums dealt a reign of terror in surrounding areas near the wharves. Well known to locals, the gang was said to be fearsome in actions and appearance. Signature dress consisted of baggy-bum jeans, hobnail boots and black t-shirts with holes cut out to show nipples pierced with safety pins.

The police crew had zero tolerance for terrorist cults and wasted no time in hunting them down.

Five teenagers matching the gang description idled on the edge of the wharf. Their boots dangled above the water since no ships were moored at the time.

One gave the alarm on seeing officers moving in. Flicking cigarettes into the briny, they took off in three different directions as if an evasive plan had been a preconceived strategy.

On rounding a corner, the biggest yobbo ran into a large immovable object, in the shape of Angus Bridcombe. When the runner bounced off the massive chest and fell over backwards, tripped by his own sagging pants, the sergeant casually slapped cuffs on him.

"Never heard of wearing a belt? That slack arse style looks like you've shit your daks son."

"I haven't done nothing."

"Yeah? Why did you run? And whats with the ironmongery?"

Angus yanked on a safety pin. One of the other officers laughed.

"You should've cuffed his wrists to the pins sergeant."

"Wish I'd thought of that." Angus replied mildly.

"Ow! That's police brutality and I haven't done nothing. You fuckin' pricks!"

"Take him in."

The lout made another attempt to run but two hefty officers frog marched him into a police wagon.

"Tell the chief to add resisting arrest to using abusive language."

Angus had the catch delivered to headquarters where the Grimslades grilled him relentlessly. He turned out to be an eighteen year old who still lived at home with his parents.

"Cut the histrionics, you know what this is about. And we don't care which of your gang goes down for the murder." Dougall lied.

"What murder? I haven't done nothing." the youth's face paled.

"He sounds like a broken record." Dulcy said.

"He'll have a record after this that's a promise." Dougall said.

"My dad will kill me. I'm supposed to be at TAFE doing my warehousing course."

"Aw. Maybe we can make this go away then." Dulcy said.

"It wasn't me." the subject gasped.

So he did know what it was about. The Grimslades hid the Eureka moment behind bland faces.

"Keep talking. We've got all day and all night. All year in fact." Dougall said, sitting back comfortably.

"I'm supposed to be home for dinner."

"That's tough. A big lad like you? Do you take the pins out of your tits before you go home?"

"I just put my shirt on backwards. Look, I can tell you this much if you don't land me in it."

"You're already in it. The longer you stuff us around the worse it will be for you."

"I never done it. It were Scuzza. He only kicked him a bit. See. Because he'd already been rolled and that made Scuzza see red."

"How do you know he'd been rolled?"

"His pockets were empty, not even any coin and he were on the floor."

"Where was this?"

"In the bog near the wharf."

"What was he wearing?"

"I dunno. Didn't take no notice did I."

"So, who stripped his clothes off?"

"None of us done that. We scarpered when the lookout said the witch doctor was coming. Probably that witch doctor done it."

The Grimslades filed the information away but didn't take it as gospel. They knew about prevarications and shifting blame.

"So what's this Scuzza's proper name?"

"Will you take me home if I tell?"

"We could. What do you think Inspector?" Dulcy asked her colleague.

"Maybe. If we get a proper name and where we can find the charming Scuzza."

"Orright. His name is Scanlon Gilshenan. He'll be at choir practise now. At the holy saints church."

"How fitting." Dulcy said.

"You gotta take me home now."

"We don't *gotta* do anything, son." Dougall replied.

"If your information is verified as accurate, I will contact your parents and see if they want to post bail." Dulcy smiled sweetly.

"You're a slut." snarled the bully.

Dougall gave his final instructions to two hard-faced police guards on duty.

"Throw it in the slammer. And remove the nappy pin decorations. I don't care how you do it."

"You can't do that. You're all a bunch of dirty friggin' arseholes." the snitch cried.

"No bail." Grimslade decreed.

While still at the quay, Sergeant Angus Bridcombe got the extra brief about Scuzza aka Scanlon Gilshenan via a quick phone call. He waited outside the church hall, picked the most likely offender and confirmed the presence of metal pins by a quick pat down.

The boy soprano, duly apprehended, lapsed into his usual belligerent persona. A hearty rendition of something far from a hymn serenaded the officers who drove the gang leader back to headquarters.

Eventually most of the gang had a turn at sitting in the hot seat. Their versions of events hardly differed. The detectives had to concede Tim was probably mugged before they got to him. Since the gang checked his pockets, he had been clothed at that point. According to the snitch, Tim then suffered a kicking from the pious Scuzza. All the gang agreed they'd scarpered and left the victim on the toilet floor.

"So you left him for dead."

"That Jew boy was alive last time we saw him." Scuzza exclaimed.

"You assumed him to be Jewish? Did you remove his pants?"

"Why would I? I'm not a poof."

"To see if circumcision bolstered your prejudice."

Scuzza looked blank. If he didn't know what circumcision meant he didn't admit it. Or, perhaps his own penis hood was foreshortened since about twenty percent of Australian newborn baby boys get circumcised. Back in the fifties, hygiene rather than religion meant about eighty percent were done.

"He just looked like one of them. And somebody else already got him for it. It's the trend hey. Not like his sort are flavour of the month."

"How do you know he was alive? You got a medical degree?" Dougall sneered.

"He groaned and vomited a bit."

Grimslade told the guards to house Scuzza with the snitch and listen to what they talked about.

"More than one mentioned a witch doctor." Dulcy said in the analysis.

"They've had time to collaborate on a fake story to shift blame."

"If there is someone called the witch doctor, he could be some sort of freelancer."

"Be good if we had a vigilante. We need all help we can get handling youth crime. I'll ask Angus to suss it out. He and his team will be canvassing the area for at least another week."

Over the coming days, Angus and his crew found no local knowledge pertaining to any witch doctor. Either the entity had gone to ground or never existed in the first place.

14

The BBQ

Respect

Warragul continued a duty of care for his *little brother* and took over most of the cooking and housework while his son Jarrah went out to work.

Thaddeus discovered Warragul's pension had never been stopped. Instalments kept being automatically paid into an account set up for him by social workers when he first went to prison. Since the old man hadn't drawn on it during his homelessness, a substantial sum accrued. It seemed a rich windfall.

Father and son decided to celebrate with a backyard barbecue.

"We'll get good steaks and a heap of prawns, hey?"

"How about we invite that Bridcombe mob."

"Yeah. Righto. I never thought I'd invite a copper to eat with us." Warragul laughed.

They went outside and viewed the blackened hotplate set on a frame of old bricks. A few plastic chairs stored in the laundry were brought out to be hosed off. Having no picnic table, plates had always simply balanced on laps.

"This looks crappy now that I think of having visitors here, and we need more chairs." Jarrah said.

"I been wanting to get you something. Now I know what it will be." his father replied.

Warragul insisted on paying for new barbecue furnishings as a gift to his son. Jarrah shopped for it, choosing a hooded cooker unit with a rotisserie and a solid outdoor timber table setting to seat eight.

"Now we gotta get a chook to go on that spit."

"Done. I got a beauty in the freezer. Remind me to thaw it overnight."

Jarrah phoned his old friend Angus and set a date for the get together.

"Just bring yourself and your family, Angus mate. We got heaps of food."

On a fine warm Saturday evening the five Bridcombes were welcomed to the backyard barbecue. The scent of freshly mown grass competed with delicious aromas of frying meats.

Told not to bring anything, nevertheless, the Bridcombes arrived with drinks, nibblies and sweets. Jarrah plugged his CD player into the laundry power point to provide background music.

Beset with persistent pain, Tim stayed in his room. He didn't complain, but what he could hear of the music, chatter and laughter tortured his senses.

He felt his stomach roil as the rich smell of cooking caused nausea.

Vaguely Tim knew his physical condition deteriorated. The idea that death would be a relief occupied his lucid moments more and more often.

Seven healthy appetites made good work of the steaks, chicken and prawns, yet hardly put a dent in the abundant feast.

"I'll take a plate in to my little brother. He might eat something." Warragul said.

"Give him more aspirin and put the kettle on old man. He'll want a cup of tea." Jarrah added.

"Yep. Never turned one down."

"Oh I didn't know you had a brother." Opal said, in mild surprise.

"Yes. Poor fella is a bit crook, has to rest in a dark room a lot of the time."

"He gets bad headaches." Jarrah explained.

"Migraines are hard to bear. My mother used to get them." Angus remarked.

Warragul went indoors with the plate of tasty morsels. Hoping to tempt his sick friend into eating something, he crept into Tim's room.

"Here's a nice cup of tea and two pills. I'll leave this tucker here beside you. There's a nice bit of steak, chicken and a few grilled prawns. Do you want anything else?"

"No. Thanks." Tim groaned.

"Alright. I'll shut the door and look in later."

While Warragul busied himself indoors, Jarrah explained that the little brother was mentally retarded.

"He doesn't know anything. Sad hey. He's so young too."

"How old is he?" Opal asked.

"Don't know exactly. I'd guess probably about nineteen."

"I suppose accurate birth records and education options aren't always available in the bush."

"Yeah. That'd be right." Jarrah shrugged.

He'd had a wake up call after learning his father couldn't read.

Warragul returned to the party.

"Is he okay?" Jarrah asked.

"He might eat it later."

The group partied on well after dark. Opal began stacking the plates, saying:

"I am so full. I couldn't eat another mouthful."

The girls rose from the table and told their mother to stay put.

"We'll do that Mum." Xanthe said. "Come on girls."

The three sisters gathered the used crockery and utensils and carried it all indoors to the kitchen sink. Kinta began washing up, Lirah dried while Xanthe had a quick loo break.

The twins chattered on as usual and did not hear Tim quietly exit his room on the way to the toilet.

The smell of fried food turned Tim's stomach. Fighting to control an urge to retch, he struggled against a dire need to throw up a thin gruel of porridge he'd eaten much earlier. Waiting his turn for the bathroom, Tim leant against the opposite wall, trying to remain steady on his feet.

Xanthe emerged from the bathroom in time to see the sick man's eyes roll back in his head, just before he slid down the wall to the floor. The ashen faced person appeared to be a skeletal replica of Tim Fun.

Her voice froze in her throat. *Timmy?* She knelt beside the prone form and took his thin limp hand in hers.

Lirah and Kinta entered the short hallway.

"Xanthe where are you. No skiving off getting out of the work. And we need the loo too."

"What are you doing? Who is that? Oh my god. He looks like Tim."

"I think it is him." Xanthe replied hoarsely.

"It looks like him only skinny and sick."

"It must be him. I'm sure it is him."

The twins ran outside screaming.

"TIM IS HERE. IT'S HIM. HE'S SICK." they garbled in unison.

The four adults gaped in disbelief. Angus recovered first from the shock announcement. He strode inside. Trained in first aid, Angus's professional mode kicked in.

"Opal, dial 000 ask for ambulance then hand the phone to me."

The rest of the party looked on in silence while the big man made an assessment. Angus used two fingers to clear a thin stream of vomit from Tim's mouth, after laying him over on his side.

Without further ado, Sergeant Angus Bridcombe calmly gave ambulance personnel the address and relevant statistics on the patients condition.

"Emergency situation. Adult male in his late twenties. Collapsed. Weak pulse. Yes I have cleared his mouth and put him in the recovery position. There seems no blockage to his airway but his breathing is shallow and intermittent."

It seemed an age waiting for the ambulance although it arrived within fifteen minutes. Medicos quickly did what they could to stabilise the patient and whisked Tim away to hospital with sirens blaring.

Angus called Dougall who had been romancing Dulcy on the patio in their Saturday night tradition.

"It's Angus."

"What awful timing again. What's gone wrong now?" Dulcy moaned.

"WHAT? I DON'T BELIEVE IT!" Dougall shouted. "TIM'S BEEN FOUND."

Dulcy had to sit down before she fell.

"Is he..?"

"He's alive so far. He's been taken to hospital."

"Where has he been? Did Angus find him?"

"Not sure. We'll have to wait to hear all about it. Angus says he has his hands full at the moment."

Back at Jarrah's house, everyone needed a stiff drink but settled for coffee. Opal had rarely witnessed her husband acting in his role as a trained responder. She hugged him closely.

"Angus you were magnificent."

"Daddy, you're a true hero." Xanthe agreed.

"I feel so proud of you Daddy." Kinta said tearfully.

"Respect." Lirah punched her father in the arm. Hard.

Angus soaked up the rare accolades from his family. Jarrah and Warragul agreed the policeman coped admirably. They'd been glad to have the competent off-duty officer take charge.

"So Little Brother has been a missing person, and you all know him?"

"He's our missing detective, Tim Fun." Angus replied. "The force has pulled out all stops to find him. It shifted to a recovery search after his dumped clothes were discovered."

Opal commented further.

"Everyone wanted to do something useful. That's why we all went to where his clothes were binned. We decided to walk across the bridge after our efforts fell flat."

"If you hadn't done that, I wouldn't have found my father." Jarrah said.

"So that means we did help find Tim by going to the park." Xanthe exclaimed.

"It does," Lirah agreed, "because you brought him here Jarrah."

"Wild Dog. How did you meet Tim in the first place?" Angus had to ask.

"Found him bashed up. I said, better come to my safe place before those bad boys come back." Wild Dog answered.

"He seemed like a disabled bloke. A retard. We been caring for him." Jarrah added.

Opal didn't want to sound harsh or judgemental so worded a question gently.

"Uncle. He must have needed a doctor when you found him."

Warragul appeared chastened and ashamed. Jarrah stepped up quickly to explain.

"I'll tell you the full story about my father so you can understand how it was."

Despite the policeman present, Jarrah spent an hour relating all that Warragul suffered. He told of the wrongful arrest and imprisonment that made his father want to disappear. He added information about the terrorist gang and why Warragul feared they would kill the lad.

"No one had come looking for a lost boy either." Jarrah added.

"A big search had been underway but focused in all the wrong areas." Opal said. "I understand how it was. You must see that too don't you Angus?"

"Yes I see how it happened."

Angus knew loopholes in law and dishonourable officers existed.

"We called him Little Brother. He seemed to be a lot better lately. Until yesterday when his headache got really bad again." Jarrah said.

"Tim isn't a retard. He is actually really clever." Xanthe said.

"He didn't look too clever puking on the floor here." Lirah reminded.

"He'll recover in hospital, won't he?" Kinta asked nervously.

"Let's hope so." Opal replied.

"We should go. I'll have the Grimslades chasing me first thing." Angus said. "We'll have to speak to doctors about Tim asap. Then there will be dealing with the press. All the usual hoo-ha."

"You might be on TV Daddy."

"Another hurdle." Angus mourned.

"Jarrah, stay in touch. Next time you both come to our place for dinner."

"Oh yes. Uncle, we want to hear more about the raven." Kinta begged.

"And the bone pointing thing. Can a girl become a witch doctor Uncle?" Lirah asked.

"You're halfway there." Opal smiled.

Warragul's heart lightened for being respected and called Uncle by Lirah and Kinta.

15

Prognoses

Out From Under

T im Fun underwent emergency surgery to relieve pressure on his brain. An aneurysm caused by his initial mugging, subsequent kicking, or both, had burst during the barbecue party.

Neurosurgeons drained fluid from Tim's brain by a keyhole incision using specialised instruments and an endoscope. Although considered a less invasive operation than removing a section of skull performed in craniotomy, his friends were warned, any brain surgery held risks.

The next two weeks spent in ICU would be critical to Tim's recovery. Sergeant Angus Bridcombe attended discussions at the hospital with detective couple Dulcy and Dougall Grimslade.

"Assuming the patient recovers, is he likely to suffer permanent impairment?" Dougall asked.

"It is too early to say. We will know more in three weeks. He can expect to be fatigued for about three months. Cognitive changes may be short or long term. It helps that the patient is young, not overweight, and we assume a non-smoker."

"He is a non-smoker, teetotaller and been quite a fitness fanatic in the past. He has always been a keen surfer and strong swimmer."

"Very good. He has given himself the best chance of surviving a trauma such as this. He may come out of it with few or no complications.

"What follow up treatment might he be given?"

"Another MRI scan to monitor blood vessels in his brain. It depends how well the treatment works."

"When may he receive visitors?"

"All being well, as early as tomorrow but he must be kept quiet and not over stimulated. No more than two at a time and next of kin have priority. I'm sure police are keen to question him, but I'd advise waiting until the patient gains some cognitive rehabilitation. If he is unable to remember what you ask, confusion will be stressful to him. Please keep questions to a minimum."

"We won't question Tim at all at this stage, but we would like to see him."

"I understand you are the three officers who led investigations."

"Yes, but we also have personal ties to Tim Fun. He is a friend and valued colleague."

Back at the station, the Grimslades deemed the prognosis given as cautious.

"Where there's life there's hope." Dougall said.

"The fact Tim is young and has always taken care of his health helps." Dulcy replied.

Neither Dougall nor Dulcy had seen Tim yet. Angus explained the surgeon's caution.

"I have to tell you, Tim appeared ghostly pale and emaciated when we found him. He looked only a shadow of himself. Xanthe found him first, but she barely recognised him."

"We're told the outcome had been touch and go but your quick response made all the difference, Angus. Good job mate."

"Yes well done Angus, you're a hero. Opal says you kept your cool and handled it magnificently."

"Yeah. Even Lirah punched my arm and said *respect*."

Perhaps Lirah's reaction meant more to Angus than any other as she'd always been the toughest nut. Angus covered his rising emotions by sticking to the facts.

"Jarrah and his father assured us Tim was well provided with food. But on reflection, perhaps he'd not been keeping it down."

"Severe headaches can make people bilious and interfere with sleep." Dulcy agreed.

"I could sleep for a week." Angus yawned.

"Take some time off Angus. You deserve it. Dulcy and I will visit Tim tomorrow if possible."

"I will. I know my daughters are champing on the bit to visit. They'll just have to wait. I think their presence might amount to over stimulation." Angus added.

"I think you are right." Dulcy replied.

Angus relayed the outcome to his family.

"Apart from police Tim can't have visitors at the moment."

"What else did the doctors say?"

"Just that it's too early to tell but he has a good chance of recovery because he doesn't smoke or drink alcohol."

Opal had already heard the bare facts from Dulcy, and knew Angus put a positive slant on it for the sake of their daughters.

The Grimslades waited another day and checked with medical staff before visiting the hospital.

Rubber soles squeaked on pristine clean floors as they trod the hushed halls following directions to the ICU ward.

Francis Funicular met them on her way out, dabbing at her tears with a white hanky. They greeted Tim's aunt and asked after her nephew.

"He didn't know me." she sobbed.

"We're told it takes time." Dougall replied kindly.

"Would you like to come to the canteen for a cup of tea?" Dulcy asked.

"No thanks anyway. I have to get back to my poodles. One of them is expecting."

"Are you okay to drive? We could give you a lift after we see Tim."

"Thanks again but I'm using taxis. Parking here is expensive anyway."

"Had you noticed any improvement in Tim since yesterday?"

"He looked a bit better without all the tubes, but I'm surprised they already had him up out of bed this morning and walking around. I'll come again tomorrow."

Police medical insurance enabled Tim Fun to received best care. Dougall and Dulcy crept into the private room and found Tim resting, surrounded by medical equipment. A light bandage around his head, the only evidence of his operation. He stirred awake and observed his new visitors.

"Hello Tim."

Tim waggled a finger towards the pair as if he could almost, but not quite, place who they were. It felt strange to the Grimslades having to identify themselves, but it had to be done.

"We're police detective friends from where you work Tim. I'm Dulcy and this is Dougall."

"Police." Tim murmured, frowning.

Tim still didn't seem to know them.

"We've been looking for you. You're our favourite young detective Tim. We are grateful you were rescued."

"Wild Dog." Tim whispered.

"Yes. Wild Dog took care of you after you got hurt."

Tim closed his eyes as a tear ran down his cheek.

"You're safe now Tim. You'll be back on your surfboard in no time." Dougall said.

"Surf." Tim's eyes sprang open as his brain made some connection.

"You love the surf. The ocean waves and the beach."

"Beach. Xanthe." Tim murmured.

Dulcy squeezed Dougall's hand. A nurse bustled in saying therapists were doing the rounds and would be seeing the patient in about five minutes.

"I think we should speak with his therapists and tell them what we've got from Tim just now."

The nurse said it would be highly irregular to have outside visitors present with the therapists.

"Police business." Dulcy flashed her badge.

The nurse stiffened and pursed her lips before exiting the room.

"You love doing that." Dougall said.

"It's a perk."

The therapists, two men of similar age to Tim, entered the room. Dougall introduced themselves and explained their presence, saying a few gentle reminders seemed to trigger Tim's memories.

"We hope that might be helpful to you. We know Tim Fun very well as our colleague and good friend." Dulcy added.

The therapists seemed aloof and didn't thank them for the input. One of them deigned a reply:

"Actually, we've known this patient well in the past ourselves. We went to the same school. However, we knew him as Timothy Funicular."

"Small world. Does Tim remember you at all?"

Reluctant to be questioned, Dougall only received a short answer.

"That is debatable."

Tim frowned at the therapists. The Grimslades caught it and supposed he'd had enough of visitors for one day.

"We will come again tomorrow Tim." Dougall saluted Tim in farewell.

On the way home Dougall remarked that Tim recalled Xanthe's name but not their own.

"Yet he hardly knows that girl, compared with working closely with us for several years. We come out being forgettable."

"Opal says the girls put a romantic twist to the trick they pulled on him. Xanthe believed herself to be in love, at least before this happened. The twins agreed. Apparently, they could *just tell* Tim loved Xanthe too."

"Are they psychics?"

"It's a girl thing Dougall. They start planning a wedding on the nuance of a glance from a boy."

"Did you ever?"

"Nope. You sprung your surprise proposal on me, conniving with your daughter and her sister-in-law. Sneaky lot your family."

"You got a bit more than a nuance of a glance from this boy."

"Quite a lot more actually. I'm not complaining."

"I guess you and Opal talk about me."

"Never." Dulcy lied.

"I thought you told her everything."

Dulcy glossed it over.

"Anyway, I can't wait to call Opal and tell her Tim put Xanthe in the mix of things he loved. It will be up to her if she tells her kids. I know they're all keen to visit him."

Opal absorbed the news and replied that she'd keep it secret for the time being.

"If Tim suffers a relapse it will only be worse on the girls, especially Xanthe."

Tim slowly recovered over the coming weeks and began to speak in complete sentences again.

Doctors ordered he be moved out of ICU into a ward with four others, saying extra socialisation would benefit him. Tim worked hard at his own rehabilitation and most enjoyed time spent in physio to regain his former strength and muscle tone.

Jarrah and Warragul were instantly remembered by Tim, as his most recent memories were unimpaired. He began to recognise his Aunt Francis and the Grimslades too, but no one could tell if it came from their frequent visits, or if his memory restored some of his past. Everyone dearly wanted to know but held off probing.

Having paid Tim's rent and acquired the flat keys, Dulcy brought in a few of his t-shirts, cotton shorts and track pants. She hoped wearing his own clothes would help.

Chantel had been home when Dulcy went to Tim's flat.

"I heard Tim has been found. I am so sorry for assuming he was dead."

"Chantel, I have to tell you that withholding his last know whereabouts could have resulted in his death. He had to have emergency surgery."

Chantel covered her mouth, shocked.

"I should have spoken up sooner. I'm consumed with guilt, and I deserve to be."

"Nevermind. Tim is safe now and hopefully improving."

"You won't let David know what I told?"

"I won't Chantel. But seriously, I don't know how a strong woman like yourself can live under a man's thumb."

Deep in thought, Chantel watched Dulcy drive away. That night when David returned, he met with Chantel's discontent.

"Your ex was here today to gather some of Tim's clothes. She said he had to have urgent surgery to save his life."

"So?"

"Tim could have been found sooner if we'd been helpful. He might have died."

David swigged on a can of beer and dismissed her concerns.

"Could have but didn't." he belched.

"We were wrong. Can't you see that David? I should never have let you sway me."

"You'll do as you're told under my roof. If you don't like it, you know what you can do."

"Yes. I do know, and I'm done with living under your thumb."

Upset by her own guilt and David's uncaring attitude, Chantel decided to get out from under. She strode into their bedroom and threw some extra items into a bag. It was added to the prepacked luggage kept in her car, ready for the next cruise job.

16

Tiffany & Ethan

Chantel Tells

With nowhere to go for the next four days, Chantel decided to phone her best girlfriend, Tiffany Birdwhistle, before going to a motel.

"Tiff. Hi. Any chance I could doss on your sofa for a few nights? Long story."

"Every chance. Come right on over Chantel. Do we need wine?"

"Wine would be good. I'll bring some."

"Just bring yourself and we'll have a good old get together."

"Will Ethan mind?"

"Of course not. He might not admit it, but he loves a bit of gossip."

"I can provide that at least. I look forward to your input." Chantel replied.

Tiffany and Chantel had been best friends since schooldays. Their futures began on a level playing field but separate journeys into womanhood dealt them different fortunes.

Despite being a single mother, Chantel achieved a high distinction diploma in hospitality and cookery yet only gained grunge work.

Tiffany went to university, studied journalism and landed plumb TV roles before marrying Ethan Birdwhistle.

"As you've probably guessed, I've left David."

"What's he done?"

"It's what we both did. I'm ashamed to admit we failed to give police a clue on Tim Fun's last known whereabouts. We thought it made no difference because Tim must already be dead, and we didn't want to get involved."

Chantel related her part in withholding vital information on Tim Fun's disappearance. Both Tiffany and Ethan deemed the couple to be definitely at fault. Nevertheless, as friends, they helped her come to terms with her guilt.

"You weren't the only ones who thought Tim Fun had to be deceased. News stories implied as much when the search shifted to a recovery operation."

"It seems cowardly now, not saying just to keep ourselves comfortable. David had been grilled by detectives and that put his back up."

"I guess Dougall Grimslade wouldn't be flavour of the month for David." Ethan said.

"You guess right. He absolutely hates Dougall. That's why he didn't want to help him solve the case. But I made friends with Dulcy. She promised not to tell David I blabbed, which doesn't matter now anyway. Then something she said about living under a man's thumb hit a nerve."

"Dulcy doesn't mince words."

"Well, she made me see I have always allowed myself to be influenced. In the past, it worked out for all of us to become a family. Dominic and Davy were already best mates."

"David also held some control over Dulcy. Her move up north is one example."

"Finding he bought that beach house to keep Zelia and his child had to be the worst. Dulcy pulled no punches having it out with him."

"I had it out with David too. I told him we were in the wrong and Tim might have died. He more or less said I had to obey him while I'm under his roof...so here I am. I'll be out of your hair soon though, my next cruise job starts in a few days. It's a three week stint so it gives me time to work out where I go from there."

They all sipped their wine, mulling over the situation. Ethan mentioned a practicality:

"Your de facto status means you can claim a share of the family home."

"Oh no. I wouldn't do that. Dominic and I lived in David's house for years. He never asked me for rent."

"Don't sell yourself short Chantel. You were a wife to him and a mother to his son all that time. From what you've said, he's made it intolerable for you to stay there. You deserve fair financial compensation." Tiffany replied.

After Chantel walked out, David Dubois found a tasty shepherd's pie in the oven she'd prepared for the evening meal they'd never share. He ate the whole lot straight out of the pie dish, washed down with another can of lager.

The empty dish clattered loudly when he tossed it in the sink. No way would he do any washing up, or bother to soak the pan. Certain Chantel would soon come crawling back, David smirked thinking she'd have no dinner.

Little did he suspect, he'd soon be missing her home cooking. Normally before a cruise job, Chantel shopped for groceries, precooked and froze a variety of nutritious meals for David in her absence. All he had to do was choose what he fancied and nuke it in the microwave.

Over the coming days, finding no ready-made dinners, it dawned on David that Chantel must have been more than a little miffed. *Bloody woman!* He phoned the recruitment service to confirm she had an upcoming cruise job.

David vowed to have words with her on return. Takeaways were no substitute for home cooking. He waited primed for a confrontation. Chantel returned after her stint on the holiday liner.

"So, you think you can just amble back in." he began.

"Just a quick visit to pick up some of my things." she snapped.

"You're not taking anything from my house."

"If you try to stop me, I'll call the police. I already have advice regarding my legal position David."

David imagined the Grimslades having a ball with that. They'd piss their pants laughing. He belatedly realised Chantel might claim something akin to alimony. That thought changed his tune.

"Don't be silly Chantel. We can work this out between us." he smarmed.

"How? What would be different David?"

"Come on, you know I'm all bluff Chantel. How about I take you out to dinner and then we sleep on it. I've missed you."

Chantel bit back on a retort saying he missed what she'd freely given for years. At the same time, she would dearly love a bout of 'make up' sex. She agreed to dinner and a tumble in bed.

David performed well up to her expectations. In the dawn of a new day, she listened to him singing happily in the shower preparing for his day of army work duty.

After David went to work, Chantel cleared her wardrobe, gathered what she wanted to take, and left. She'd already signed up for a back-to-back cruise duty and obtained a hotel room near the quay.

Her favourite cooking utensils, pots and pans fitted into three cardboard cartons. Those items were her own purchases made over the years and were all she really cared to keep.

Finding Chantel had gone and taken her belongings, David had reason to seek advice from his old surfing mate in the legal profession: Thaddeus Maekris.

"Good to see you again David. Come in. What can I do for you today?"

"I'm afraid I have another woman problem, Thad. My partner has left me over a clash of opinions. It was nothing much but I'm not sure where I stand, legally." David pulled a face.

"Is this likely to be a permanent move on her part?"

"Well, she's taken a lot of her cooking stuff and all her clothes. Her wardrobe is bare."

He outlined fears that Chantel could make financial claims.

"How long did Chantel live with you?"

"A dozen or more years."

"And you cohabited as husband and wife?"

"I suppose so, since we slept together."

"Did you father any children with this partner?"

"Not together. She already had a child by an unknown father. Her son is the same age as my Davy, so we brought them up as brothers. They've left home now."

"Did she work outside the home?"

"She did domestic study courses in cookery and that sort of thing. She didn't get a paid job until the boys were out of primary school. What's your prognosis Thad?"

"Chantel definitely qualifies as being in a de facto relationship with you. She has the same rights as if you were married to each other."

David went into a rant about it being his house and how he'd accepted her son as part of the deal. Thaddeus calmly reminded him he wasn't there to judge, only to give advice.

"Shit! Does that mean she could claim part of my property? Or make me pay her compensation?"

"It does. Though it could take a long time. I'd suggest you endeavour to settle amicably out of court."

Given his handsome face and enviable body, David couldn't believe his bad luck with women. First Zelia, then Dulcy and now even Chantel. He ran fingers through his thick dark auburn hair they'd all admired so much. Fat lot of good that did him.

Dubois was a good-looking man, so Thaddeus doubted if a long-term partner would leave him on a whim. The legal eagle wondered what might be unsaid and felt curious to know more. He made coffee for them both, playing for time.

Thaddeus knew Dulcy never made claims on her ex's assets, although she could have. Seemed David had enjoyed a dream run.

Back in the day, Thaddeus had wanted Dulcy Vestige for himself. He'd always considered the wholesome policewoman too good for Dubois. He had never met Chantel Cheron but made a suggestion in an attempt to find out more.

"If you like, I can act as mediator if your estranged partner will agree to a joint visit."

"She works as a kitchen hand on a cruise ship, but I'll try to get a message to her there. Thanks Thad."

"Don't thank me. Wait till you get my bill." Thaddeus smiled.

Aware he'd probably exhausted his quota of mates-rate visits, David forced a laugh.

David admitted to himself that he and Chantel were alike in many ways, and he didn't want to split up.

He supposed he did sort of love Chantel. It was not the desperate proprietary *in love* feeling he had for Dulcy. Nevertheless, it was a companionable love and their last session in bed had been as good as ever.

That last morning, while he sang in the shower, David made a self-resolution to be nicer to Chantel in future. He kicked himself for not doing so sooner, thinking perhaps she might have stayed.

17

Mothy Knickers

Checkmate

The Grimslades continued speaking to the therapists, Ty Billings and Frederick Benson, when visiting the hospital to see Tim.

Comparing notes to ascertain degrees of improvement, Billings and Benson bolstered their importance by extensive use of medical terminology. After one lengthy oration full of convoluted terms expounding the depths of their joint knowledge, Dulcy summed up:

"So, in a nutshell, Tim's improvement is on the higher end of expectations."

"Affirmative. Your conjecture coincides with our hypotheses." Billings said with a supercilious sniff.

"Good we're on the same page with that." Dougall replied with a wink to his wife.

Between themselves, the Grimslades dubbed the wordy therapists Bill and Ben.

"Dougall, does Tim seem discomforted to you whenever Bill and Ben come in?"

"Yes. I noticed that. The neurologist said questions Tim finds confusing would be stressful, and the lengthy technical jargon Bill and Ben use is ridiculously over the top."

"Trying to remember would be frustrating and feeling stupid would go against the grain. Tim so prided himself on accuracy. He took particular care after he wrongly identified the owners of David's beach house. You gave him your favourite *leaping to unverified assumptions* lecture, remember."

"Ah yes. He took that to heart. At least he noticed the suspect was a smoker since he smelt it on him."

"I still smile recalling when you asked if he knew the cigarette brand, and he said *'not by the smell'.*"

"Hmm. Clever little so and so."

"He aimed to be precise following your well worn and treasured lecture. I hope he gets all that smartness back again."

"So do I."

When an old memory surfaced through Tim's brain fog, he realised why the therapists' visits discomforted him.

Ty Billings and Frederick Benson had been ring leaders in nicknaming him Mothy Knickers back in high school. After identifying the reason for his mistrust, Tim pretended to be asleep when their visits were due, hoping they'd go away.

Feigning sleep, Tim heard what was said on their next visit. The Bill and Ben pair amused themselves by referring to the patient by his hated label:

"He's single and his next of kin is that old aunt who visits, so Mothy Knickers still applies."

"Indeed. Good old Mothy Knickers. He always preferred Shakespeare and Dickens to girls."

"That was just as well, since none of the girls ever wanted him."

"I know. Not even the ones who definitely had no moths in their knickers."

"Some of them didn't even have knickers."

Laughing at their own wit, Billings and Benson observed the 'sleeping' patient. Rather than wake Tim to assess his progress, they scribbled data on their clipboard notes to falsify their duty.

At the same time, a nurse tried to prevent four new visitors barging into the ward.

"You must wait until the therapy session is over."

The three girls went ahead regardless. Finally having their visit endorsed by Tim's doctors, the Bridcombes would not be put off by some pedantic rule.

Opal shrugged to the nurse and mouthed 'sorry'. Xanthe justified their headlong charge.

"Nope. Tim's doctors say he's ready to receive us and we've waited long enough. Thanks. Don't worry we will be very quiet and well behaved."

Opal stayed outside in the corridor trying to placate the nurse, hoping she didn't call security.

Taken aback when three gorgeous young girls barged in, the Bill and Ben pair gaped, smoothed their hair and straightened their ties.

But the beauties took no notice of the therapists. Instead, they surrounded Mothy Knicker's bed, where he appeared to be asleep. Tim's eyes flew open when Xanthe spoke.

"Oh Timmy. At last. Here we are. Did we wake you up?"

"No. I just had my eyes closed."

Xanthe took Tim's hands in hers and kissed his face.

"How I've missed you my wonderful man."

Lirah and Kinta sat on the end of the bed and claimed Tim's bare feet. Cradling a foot each to their heaving bosoms, they pecked little kisses onto his toes. The subject of their affections did not object although he couldn't recall ever knowing the twins. Kinta apologised for the trick they'd played on him.

"Darling Tim. We are so sorry for pouncing on you in bed that time. I hope it didn't feel like rape."

"He was up for it Kinta, I mean if doing it twice in one hour counts," Lirah added with a cheeky grin, "and he's even wearing his naughty t-shirt today, maybe it still gives him a thrill."

Tim wore one of his *Detectives Cop A Feel* t-shirts that Dulcy brought in.

"Not fair ganging up on my Timmy. Just keep your grubby mitts off my guy." Xanthe sulked.

"You just wanted to do him first. At least you got to do that thing underwater, Xanthe." Lirah reminded.

Opal's entrance abruptly cut short her three daughters' spicy reminisces. She addressed Tim:

"Hello there Tim. I'm told you are doing very well. I hope the girls aren't taxing you too much."

"I can handle them." Tim replied. He shammed confidence for the sake of the therapists.

"Apparently you can and very well. Even though you had to drag them by their hair like a caveman." Opal said with a stern eye to the twins.

"We forgave him for that." Kinta replied.

"Yep. It was the only way he could get us both through the door together." Lirah agreed.

Tim had no idea what he did with those twins and could not remember dragging anyone by their hair. The situation offered a superb opportunity to practice his deadpan expression, yet Tim raised one triumphant eyebrow towards the mockers from his school days.

Tim's checkmate dumbfounded Bill and Ben. Humbled, they took their leave without another word.

"You remember me don't you Timmy?" Xanthe begged.

"Bits of it are coming back to me. It's sort of like a movie rerun with white noise." he replied.

Xanthe calling him *her Timmy* and *my guy* buoyed his spirits. In a rush, the name Xanthe became imbued with feeling her grope his private parts underwater. The sound of surf as he went under explained the white noise.

Tim blushed when a part she had fondled seemed to remember it better than his brain did.

The visit gave him much to think about. He slept on it. Waking next morning the name of Bridcombe came to him. Xanthe Bridcombe. Yes!

He still could not recall anything that felt like being raped by the other two, which seemed very odd. *You'd think I'd remember that.*

Tim searched the cobwebby recesses of his memory to no avail.

18

Tea for Two

If Wishes Were Horses

Whiling away time in her hotel room, waiting for her cruise ship to moor, Chantel Chiron perused real estate ads. Hoping only to find a better rental, her attention riveted on a small business for sale: A tea shop on the esplanade not far from the surf club.

Chantel knew the place well. The old-fashioned tea parlour, sandwiched between an ice-creamery and a newsagent had become shabby over the years. A few outdoor picnic tables squatted sadly under faded beach umbrellas on a hot patio fronting the shop.

Through rose coloured glasses, Chantel imagined repainting the outdoor furniture and replacing the tattered umbrellas with a pergola and hanging baskets of bright flowers. A few potted palms would cool the area as well. She'd often day-dreamed of running something like it.

As a customer, Chantel was not surprised the run-down place enjoyed little patronage.

Scorning the meagre choices of dry muffins and scones, Chantel imagined the fresh cakes and buns she'd bake if she ran that business. She could do savoury finger foods too like smashed avocado on toast.

Perhaps eat-in or takeaway options could be offered. Her wishful grand menu included curries which would be easy to precook and freeze. The thwarted cook let her imagination run riot. She wouldn't waste much. Any leftover cakes could go into sherry trifles.

Chantel sighed over an old adage: *If wishes were horses, then beggars would ride.*

Yet it cost nothing to look. With another day to kill, an enquiry to the real estate agent earned Chantel an early inspection of the inner workings of the teahouse.

To her expert eye, the kitchen hardly passed the bare minimum of hygiene standards. Ample bench space appeared unnecessarily cluttered so everything would have to be shifted to properly clean and disinfect the surfaces.

Accustomed to a streamlined workspace, Chantel saw that just a couple of shelves would clear the benches. Having plenty of cupboards and a dishwasher somewhat saved the kitchens lack of appeal.

Beyond the kitchen, a staff toilet and wash basin hunkered in beside a storage room. A solid backdoor opened to a parking space.

The real estate agent knew the place to be a lemon. Strong competition from many more attractive food outlets on the esplanade left it for dead. The tea parlour hadn't shown a profit for months and the owners had lost all motivation. They kept the place open only in order to sell it.

The agent extolled the virtues of location and pushed for a commitment.

"You could secure this place on ten percent deposit today. That would hold it temporarily pending finance."

Chantel did not have that much in savings. Her mind whirled with the notion of claiming against David's assets. Tiffany and Ethan thought she'd have a strong case.

"What if I can't raise finance?"

"You'd lose the deposit."

He said it cheerily as if that would never happen.

"I could do five percent deposit." she gulped.

The agent did not display the happy dance his inner being performed, instead he put on his best doubtful face.

"You might be lucky. I'll have a conversation with the vendors and get back to you."

Chantel returned to her hotel room, suddenly aghast that she'd been prepared to risk her entire savings. She'd be skint with no place to live. Then again, the vendors probably wouldn't accept five percent anyway. Yet, she could not stem her wishful dreams. If somehow she could swing it, perhaps she could bunk in the tea shop storage room and use the public showers on the beach.

In the agent's assessment, the applicant might have trouble raising finance and would lose her deposit. He couldn't see how she'd run the tea shop without giving up her cruise job, and that would be glaringly obvious to any money lender as well. But that was not his problem. He was just doing his job. He hurried to seal a deal before Chantel got cold feet and backed out.

"Miss Cheron. The vendors will accept five percent today. But only because they need it to secure another place that expires by 5pm."

Chantel heard herself say she'd arrange a bank transfer.

"Very well. Come into my office and I'll draw up a contract, pending finance."

The contract allowed six weeks grace unless she could validate a reason for an extension.

After biting the bullet and signing away her life savings, Chantel broke into a sweat. About to embark on her cruise duty, David messaged to ask if she would agree to a joint visit with his solicitor. This opening had been welcomed as a precursor to obtaining means to finance the tea shop.

"Okay. Make the appointment for three weeks time."

Surprised how easily Chantel complied, David hoped it meant she'd be reasonable. At the same time he knew it could mean exactly the opposite.

Chantel treated herself to a hairdo at the cruise liner salon and made a special effort to look business-like for the appointment at Thaddeus Maekris's legal office. A feminine blouse teamed with a tailored suit flattered her good figure. High heels and a minimum of tasteful gold jewellery completed the ensemble.

David Dubois and Chantel Cheron arrived separately, but at the same time. Thaddeus Maekris invited the couple into his office, noting Miss Cheron's attractive appearance. Although happily married to his wife Poppy, Thaddeus envied David Dubois' success with women.

"Good morning Mr. Maekris." Chantel shook his hand.

"Call me Thaddeus please."

"Thank you Thaddeus, and please call me Chantel." she smiled.

Chantel sat in the proffered chair and crossed shapely legs clad in sheerest nylon. David felt a stab of jealousy, aware Thaddeus admired her.

"I imagine an amicable agreement would be preferred by both of you." Thaddeus began.

"Yes. If possible." David replied.

Chantel merely nodded. Thaddeus underlined the length of their union.

"I have taken the liberty of obtaining the current real estate value of the home you have shared for the past twelve or more years."

"The house is in my name." David reminded.

"Miss Cheron has the same rights as a spouse."

Chantel interrupted.

"I do have an amount in mind."

To the puzzlement of the two men in the room, she named the exact amount needed to acquire the tea shop, without rounding it out. The figure fell quite obviously short of fifty percent of the beach house value.

"That is a very specific sum." Thaddeus remarked.

"You'd be happy with that much?" David had to ask.

"Yes, but only if I get it within the next three weeks."

"Do you have a deadline to meet?" Thaddeus understood she must have.

"Yes. I have a holding deposit on another property. It expires in three weeks."

David knew he could raise the amount Chantel wanted, but regretted it meant ending their relationship. He preferred she came back to him and resumed where they left off. Although it went against his grain to plead in front of Thaddeus, he did so anyway.

"Chantel, I rather hoped we might get back together."

"I'm not asking for much David."

"It's not the money." he said.

"It is for me. Sorry David. But I have a chance to get something I really want now."

"Something or someone?"

David said it jealously without thinking and immediately wished he hadn't. Thaddeus got the drift. He'd always thought Dubois a fool. He wanted to advise Chantel to hold out for more money so he worked towards that end.

"Perhaps if you care to elaborate on your plans, Chantel, I may offer helpful advice?"

"Alright. Laugh if you like but I want to buy that old tea shop on the esplanade."

"Why would you want that dive? You've got a dream job on the holiday liners." David exclaimed.

"It has never been a dream job, David. I've been stuck in a rut."

Thaddeus intervened.

"Chantel, I understand the specific amount you ask for probably is what you require to secure the tea shop."

"It is. I haven't intended to fleece David."

"Have you considered overheads like renovations and starting up costs?" Thaddeus asked.

"If she's happy with the amount she asked for..." David cut in.

"My role is to help you both arrive at an equitable settlement. Without bias." Thaddeus reminded.

"What do you suggest as a fair thing, Thaddeus." Chantel asked.

He scribbled down some numbers and arrived at a sum nearer to what Chantel could legally claim.

Initially David felt like punching Thaddeus, but they'd been good friends since their surfing days. He slumped in his chair because he really did want Chantel back.

"Would you like another day or so to think it over?" Thaddeus asked.

"No. Thanks Thaddeus. I know what I want out of this. I'll accept the minimum amount I asked for and make do." Chantel replied.

David knew what he most wanted as well. It was for Chantel to come home to him.

"Chantel, I will buy that damn tea shop for you and help set it up. Whatever it takes. But I just want you back with me."

Thaddeus jumped on it.

"I can draw up a contract making the tea shop in Chantel's own name as part of her settlement, free and clear. David, I note your commitment towards setting it up and will extrapolate a sum of money pursuant to expectations. You keep the beach house in your name. Do you both agree?"

"I do." David replied.

"Huh. Never thought you'd utter those two words in my favour." Chantel laughed.

"I'll marry you if you want."

It wasn't a dream proposal and Chantel never at any time of her life wanted marriage.

"Thanks but no thanks David." she replied coolly.

Having his ace offer rejected smote a hard blow to David. He imagined Chantel always yearned to marry him. Her offhanded dismissal witnessed by Thaddeus cut David's ego down to size. Thaddeus admired Miss Chantel Cheron ever more for her dignified stance.

"But you'll come home if I buy the tea shop for you and pay to fix it up?"

"It is convenient for me to do so at this point. As a trial run." Chantel replied.

A tough glint in the woman's eye put David to the test. Thaddeus saw it clearly and David strongly suspected it.

19

Forget I Asked

What Do You Think

Dulcy Grimslade drove Tim Fun home on his discharge from hospital. She and Chantel Chiron had changed his bed linen, caught up with laundry and had the place smelling fresh and sparkling clean, just as he liked it.

Tim refused transitional care providers. Foremost, he had no desire to continue therapy with the Bill and Ben pair.

"How good to be home." Tim sighed as he entered his flat.

"You remember this place then."

"I do now that I am here...oh goodness...I left something thawing in the fridge."

"Tim, that was weeks ago when you first went missing. I had to throw it out." Dulcy said.

"Nevermind Tim, I will provide your meals. I'll be home every night now that I've given up the cruise job." Chantel promised.

Happy to assuage lingering guilt, Chantel intended Tim would be well fed at her own expense. At least until, or if, his health and memory were completely restored.

"Where is my car?" Tim asked.

"It's stored in the police pound. But Tim, we have to ensure you're safe to drive before you get behind the wheel."

"How will I get to work?"

"Tim dear, you won't have to worry about work for months yet. You are entitled to paid leave to fully recuperate. Enjoy it and perhaps spend some time at the beach."

"Okay. I suppose that makes sense. Do you know what happened to my surfboard?"

"Ethan says it's still at the surf club where you left it."

Relieved Tim's memory filled in some answers, Dulcy went back to work.

Xanthe and the twins were forbidden to visit Tim Fun at his flat. Their parents discussed the likelihood of Xanthe taking her puppy love for Tim too far.

"She's too immature, and I think Tim is way too vulnerable to handle our darling girls right now." Opal said.

"It would be better if they didn't see Tim at all." Angus replied.

"We can't stop them seeing him on the beach, if he's there. And school holidays are coming up. Xanthe has applied for part time work at Chantel's tea shop. That might at least keep her out of mischief."

A sandwich board sign outside the refurbished tea parlour announced *Under New Management.*

Before opening day David added a light shade cloth over the sturdy new pergola. He sanded and resealed all the outdoor furniture with timber paint. The whole effect with bright hanging baskets and potted palms transformed the once drab exterior.

Chantel appreciated David's efforts and their relationship took on a whole new vibe.

The old fashioned tea parlour, renamed *"Chantel's"* attracted an upsurge of custom. Delicious aromas of baked goods and curries wafted across the beach, drawing people in by their noses.

Quick to note her hired help, Xanthe Bridcombe, attracted a younger patronage, Chantel took on her twin sisters as well during school holidays. As the tea shop became the new buzz on the esplanade, the extra help became necessary.

Every night after closing the shop, Chantel packed meals to take home for Tim and themselves. Tim didn't mind eating alone. He enjoyed the solitude of his flat after so long in hospital. Even the good company of Warragul and Jarrah did not compare to his own private space. At last he was able to sleep naked again, the only way he ever felt really comfortable in bed.

Tim awoke after his first night at home feeling wonderfully rested. He pulled on board shorts, and wandered down the road to the surf club before sun up. The place hadn't opened yet, so he sat by the shore savouring the fresh salty breeze off the ocean. He caught the smell of delicious cooking coming from further up the esplanade, though he did not connect it with Chantel's early departure.

Before opening the clubhouse for the day, Ethan Birdwhistle joined Tim on the beach.

"How are you Tim? Alright?"

"Getting there." Tim replied.

Tim knew the face and the voice but the name escaped him. Another lifesaver arrived and called a greeting.

"Morning Ethan. Give us a hand with the tower will you."

Ethan! That's it! Tim just needed a jog to his memory. *Phew. How could I forget the legendary Ethan?* He recalled being in awe of Ethan's reputation with bikini clad beach belles before he married Tiffany.

The tall lifeguard stand secured inside the clubhouse, needed two to drag it down in position on the sand.

"Ethan, I'll help set out the flags." Tim said.

"Thanks mate."

Ethan had no idea of the mental struggle Tim had just overcome. Tim greeted his surfboard like another old friend, and soon paddled out beyond the breakers. Catching his first wave after so long filled his heart with joy.

Aware Tim Fun had been through an horrific ordeal, Ethan kept a close eye on his friend. Tim paddled back out, and seemed to take a very long time just sitting astride his board, ignoring good swells that other surfers hastened to ride.

Memories of Xanthe held Tim in limbo. He forgot about riding waves back to shore, wishing that young girl would surface beside him again and say *boo*. He wouldn't even care if she tipped him off into the sea and did that thing underwater. He recalled how she'd invited him to touch her, then remembered why he could not. Nothing had changed except his growing obsession.

Ethan asked another surfer to check if Tim was okay.

"He's just been sitting out there for nearly an hour. See if you can bring him back in."

"He's that police detective who went missing isn't he?"

"Yep. That's what bothers me. If he won't make a move, I'll take the surf ski out and fetch him."

Tim woke from his daydream when nudged to come in. He dragged his board up to the surf club. On the way, he spoke to Ethan, who manned the lifeguard tower.

"I'll have to keep storing my board here for a while, Ethan. I don't have my car back and I'm not cleared to drive yet."

"Are you ok to get home?"

"Sure. Thanks. It's just a stroll up the road."

Tim had left his door key in the peg basket again. Perhaps subconsciously he wanted Xanthe to invade his privacy again.

As Isla's brother in-in-law, Ethan chose to phone her father to report on Tim's behaviour that morning.

"Dougall, Tim just seemed to be in a trance. He might have stayed out in the ocean all day if we didn't make him come in. I'm not sure if that's his new normal but I'd rather say something than leave it hanging."

"Thanks Ethan. He has vague moments. We're not sure what he remembers. But I'll drop by his flat this evening to check on him."

Dougall found Tim out in the back yard pegging his board shorts and towel on the clothesline.

"How's your first day home been?"

"Pretty good thanks. I went for a surf and caught up with Ethan."

"That's good. Did you stay out for long?"

"Um. I just rode two waves. I left my board at the surf club."

"Good. You don't want to overdo it too soon, Tim."

"No."

Chantel arrived home at that moment and brought Tim's dinner in, before bustling upstairs. Dougall said hello, goodbye and prepared to leave. Tim waylaid him for a few moments.

"Dougall, I hope this isn't overstepping any mark, but I've been meaning to ask you something."

"Ask away Tim."

"I know you and Dulcy are very happily married." Tim paused getting his act together.

"Yes we are. Go on."

"Well, it hasn't escaped my notice that there is...um...quite an age difference. Between you and Dulcy I mean."

"Oh that. Well Tim, Dulcy looks young for her age. I am painfully aware that I do not, and the opposite is true of myself. Actually, only eight years separates us in age."

Dougall had never been slow on the uptake, but in this instance, he couldn't imagine why Tim raised the subject. After what Tim had suffered, Dougall put the strange question down to oddities whirring about in the younger man's head.

"Has that been of some concern to you?" Dougall asked gently.

"No. No. Just you know... wondering if that difference ever caused ...anything. I don't know. Forget I asked."

That night, in bed, Dougall related the conversation to Dulcy, who got the gist immediately. To her, Tim's question seemed glaringly obvious. He entertained being with young Xanthe, and wanted to hear a big age difference might be okay. Dougall somehow missed the simple answer.

"What do you think he meant?"

"I've racked my brains. I hesitate to mention what came to mind. But his mental state might have temporarily quashed his former inhibitions. He became embarrassed and was quick to say *forget I asked*."

"Spit it out Dougall."

"Alright. Could Tim harbour affections for you Dulcy?"

"In what way?" she smiled to herself. *Really?*

"You know, the usual way, like if he could fill any needs where I might be lacking due to my age."

"What sort of needs?" Dulcy couldn't help digging for her own amusement.

"Physical sort of needs. You must know what I mean."

Dulcy almost stifled a giggle. Dougall got it.

"I reckon you're pulling my leg again."

"You're so easy." she burst out laughing aloud.

"What then? Clever clogs. I suppose you have all the answers."

"Dougall, you do know Tim and Xanthe are supposed to be in love, except she is only sixteen and he is twenty-nine."

"That's ridiculous. The Bridcombe girls used that argument to excuse invading Tim's flat. Those girls were just romanticising the joke like the silly teenagers they proved themselves to be."

"I know for a fact, Opal was only seventeen when she fell for Angus. I'll let you in on a girls' secret: Right from the start, Opal planned to seduce Angus into wanting marriage and let him think it was his own idea. I'd say that worked out well for my wily friend."

"Opal might think she orchestrated the result. But Angus is about five years older so I'm sure he knew. He's probably been the wilier one allowing her to believe in her power."

"Nope I don't think so. Anyway Xanthe is a product of them both but more like her mother. Opal said Angus pointed that out himself."

"So you're saying Xanthe has seduced Tim into wanting a close relationship with her?"

"Yes. You must see the theory is neither impossible nor implausible."

Dougall experienced a light-bulb moment.

"Aha. So Tim was sounding me out on our age difference because he is much older than Xanthe."

"Hey Dougall. You should be a detective."

"Very droll Dulcy. You've used that old one before."

"Haven't we just established you're not that old?"

"I'm in the mood to establish it again."

"Will you be gentle?"

"As gentle as you like."

"You should know what I like by now."

Dulcy squealed in delight as Dougall growled and pounced on her.

20

Connecting the Dots

Oliver Twist

An upside to Tim's memory blanks meant he could re-read his favourite old books as if they were new to him. Many well-worn parts jumped out, but finer plot twists entertained him again. The more he read, the better his memory refreshed to connect the dots.

Tim's mornings were spent surfing early and helping out at the surf club before walking home. Knowing school holiday season had begun, he continually looked for Xanthe or her sisters on the beach. When they didn't appear, he imagined the Bridcombes must have gone away for the holidays.

Afternoons, Tim rested and read books until Chantel brought his meal. He ate alone, showered and went to bed. He missed going back to work more than having his car. Yet the car had to come first in order to go back to work. He put his case to Dulcy the next time she looked in on him.

"Dulcy, I have a routine follow up appointment with Neurology coming up soon. It'd be good if I could drive myself in for it."

"Well Tim, that will depend on passing your driving test. I can arrange that for you though."

That night Dulcy conveyed her fears that Tim might be in for a disappointment.

"He's kept up surfing every morning. Ethan says his balance and timing appear as skilled as ever. Plus, he's been the usual good help at the clubhouse. I think surfing and driving are like riding a bike. The ability might rely on muscle memory more than conscious thought."

"I hope you're right Dougall. There's only one way to find out."

The Grimslades organised for Angus Bridcombe to assess Tim's driving capacity in a test drive. Optimistically, Dougall put Tim's car battery on a charger and checked the tyres. He ensured the oil and other fluids were topped up ready to go.

Angus sat in the back seat of a local driving school vehicle. A stern driving instructor sat in front with Tim behind the wheel. The instructor tasked Tim with driving in busy traffic, hill starts, reverse parking and road rules, but couldn't fault his knowledge, physical reactions or driving skills.

"You did well Tim," Angus said, "You'll have your car back by this evening."

"Thanks Angus. I'm glad you were available to oversee my test. I thought you might have taken the family away for the school holidays."

"No rest for the wicked Tim. The girls all have holiday jobs, so they've been kept gainfully employed. For once."

After the debacle with Bridcombe's daughters, Tim avoided asking too much. Yet he wondered where those girls might be working, sure it wouldn't be too far from home.

Tim drove himself into his medical appointment where he underwent cognitive examinations.

The Bill and Ben therapists formed part of the testing team, much to Tim's distaste. Neither met Tim's eye but took refuge behind their clipboards. Tim forced a greeting:

"Good morning Mr. Benson and Mr. Billings."

"Good morning, Mr. Funicular." Benson pretended indifference to their last encounter.

Tim knew the therapists were not entitled to be called Dr. Benson and Dr. Billings. He could not resist rubbing it in that he had earned a prefix.

"DC Timothy Funicular." Tim corrected. "But you should have my preferred name of Tim Fun on your file."

"Oh yes, that's right. You've adopted a *fun* name." Billings sniffed derisively.

At that point, the senior neurology specialist, who had performed Tim's keyhole surgery, entered.

"How are you doing young Tim? You're looking spry."

"I am quite well again. Thank you doctor. I believe my memory has fully restored to what could be considered a normal level. I even remember my childhood and high school days. In fact, I recall attending the same schools and being in the same classes with Mr. Billings and Mr. Benson here."

Tim said it with an acid glance towards Bill and Ben.

"Excellent. Now we must get on. If our worthy therapists ply their cognitive checks, I shall oversee proceedings."

Benson and Billings shared a sly smile. They wound up their session with oral exams tinged with sarcasm, intended to needle Tim.

"Mr. Funicular. Sorry! I mean DC Funicular. Do you recall your nickname during high school?"

Tim did not back down from the plain attempt to cause embarrassment.

"Yes. It was Mothy Knickers."

Detecting the barely concealed animosity between his patient and the therapists, the good doctor connected the dots and threw the ball into the other court. He raised his eyebrows and pursed his lips as he said:

"Good grief. Tell me Mr. Billings and Mr. Benson, how did that nickname come about."

"Timothy always had his nose in a book when everyone else had begun dating." Billings smirked.

The doctor interpreted Tim's self-conscious facial expression, and borrowed a line from Charles Dickens:

"We never tire of the friendships we form with books."

Tim caught the quote as a buffer to his humiliation. He reciprocated in kind with a Charles Dickens quote from *David Copperfield:*

"New thoughts and hopes were whirling through my mind, and all the colours of my life were changing."

Billings and Benson had no idea what Mothy Knickers and the neurology specialist waffled on about. They exchanged slight shrugs although both felt to be on the back foot. The head of their department fixed the pair with a steely gaze.

"Mothy Knickers. How very inventive." he said.

"It is still just friendly kidding as old school friends." Benson added in defence of their teasing.

The doctor had his doubts. He wasn't born yesterday. He provided another Dickens quote for Tim's benefit:

"Some people are nobody's enemies but their own".

"Oliver Twist. One of my all-time favourites." Tim smiled, as he'd recently re-read it.

"Well done young man. Your memory serves you well."

The doctor shook Tim's hand and patted his back before his patient exited the treatment room.

Billings and Benson presented their clipboard notes for the surgeon's endorsement and prepared to depart.

"Not so fast you two. I'd like a word before you scarper." the head surgeon scowled.

Red faced, the therapists endured a half hour lecture on ethical behaviour towards patients, in regard to continuing their careers at the hospital.

21

Here's The Thing

Plenty More Fish in the Sea

If Xanthe and the twins thought waitress duties would be a walk in the park, their tea shop jobs proved otherwise. They were run off their feet all day during the school holiday period.

Lirah paused in the kitchen, wiped her brow and re-twisted a scrunchy around her long pony tail.

"What a way to spend the holidays. At least we get to meet a lot of male talent." she winked.

"The pay is better than our pocket money, but be good if we got both." Kinta said.

"I can't believe Mum and Dad stopped our allowances just because we're working."

"It's supposed to prepare us for real life." Xanthe replied dully.

Xanthe had been feeling blue. She had hoped to resume chasing Tim Fun, but Chantel required help before opening time at the tea parlour.

Already hard at work when Tim went surfing, and strictly forbidden to go to his flat, limited Xanthe's chances.

Tim emerged from the surf feeling wonderful after an extra long session riding the waves. He rinsed salt water off under the cold outdoor shower in front of the clubhouse, then helped Ethan with the lifeguard tower.

"You'll be back at work soon."

"Hoping I will now that I've got my car back."

"So no more problems with...you know...the thing."

"A few minor glitches but the doctor gave me the all clear. I've got my appetite back. I could eat a horse at the moment." Tim rubbed his flat belly.

"They say the tea house is great for cooked breakfasts now, and the waitresses are pretty hot too."

"Sounds like a plan. I might check it out."

Tim fronted *Chantel's* and been delighted to see the hot waitresses were none other than the Bridcombe sisters. Chantel waved to him from behind the counter. Finally it dawned on Tim that Chantel ran the tea house. *Duh. Call myself a detective.*

"Timmy!" Xanthe rushed to take his hand and guide him to a table.

Tim's day just kept getting better.

"What's good?"

"Me." Xanthe replied.

"I meant on the menu." Tim blushed.

"I'm on the menu for you Timmy."

Tim shied off making a public show of her attraction.

"I need to eat." he put on a serious face.

"Wow. You're grumpy when you're hungry."

"I'm famished."

"Okay. I'll bring you a big brekkie for starters." Xanthe winked.

"I only keep a few gold coins zipped in my board shorts pocket, so maybe just beans on toast."

"Call it my treat Timmy."

Xanthe bustled to put together a plate of bacon, eggs, sausage and baked beans. Lirah and Kinta doted special attention on Tim's table too, bringing the freshest bread rolls hot from the oven as a starter.

More customers walked in, lured by aromas of bacon and baking bread. Soon the place became jam packed with no spare seats. People had to be content with breakfast in takeaway containers. Tim saw he shouldn't linger at his table once he'd finished eating. Xanthe rushed to his side as he got up to leave.

"Timmy. I've been dying to see you. Will you meet me on the beach later? I'm not allowed to go to your flat."

"Won't your parents be picking you up?"

"Yes. But you could take me home Timmy. I'll say I worked overtime to help Chantel clean up. Lirah and Kinta will back me. Then I'll say you offered to take me home when..."

It came as no surprise that Angus and Opal did not want him seeing Xanthe. As much as Tim yearned for time alone with the girl, he would not go behind her parent's backs. He cut her off:

"No. Sorry Xanthe. I can't do that."

Tim exited *Chantel's* without a backward glance. The abrupt rejection did not sit well with Xanthe. She took temporary refuge by taking a loo break. Fighting to control her tears, Xanthe's emotions see-sawed between anger and frustration. Chantel called her out after she'd been missing for ten minutes.

"Xanthe. Are you alright?"

"Yes. I won't be long." her voice broke on a sob.

Chantel asked her sisters if they knew what was wrong with Xanthe.

"It's Tim Fun. He just left. And he said he didn't want to meet her later."

"She's completely in love with him." Kinta explained.

"Tim? Oh no. Well nevermind. I'll have a little chat with Xanthe later if we get a moment to ourselves."

"Why did she say *oh no*?" Kinta whispered.

"Tim's too old for Xanthe. I bet that's why." Lirah replied.

After closing up for the day, Chantel and the girls sat together over cups of tea and leftover cakes.

"So Xanthe. Your sisters tell me you have a crush on Tim Fun."

"It's not just a crush. I love him. He's the one for me. I just know it." Xanthe's tears welled up.

"Xanthe, I don't know how to break this to you. But here's the thing. Tim is gay. I think you all know it means females don't do it for him. Of course, gay guys often make great platonic friends. Just like another girlfriend."

The three Bridcombes stared back, for once rendered speechless.

"How do you know?" Xanthe asked.

"Everyone knows. It's so obvious. Not that there's anything wrong with that."

"NO. No way." Xanthe cried.

"But we…" Lirah began but stalled on those two words.

"No Lirah…that doesn't mean…" Kinta added her own partial comment.

"Xanthe. That explains why…" Lirah did not need to finish her sentence.

"You gave it your best shot Xanthe." Kinta began to cry in sympathy.

Chantel felt bad for bursting the bubble. But better Xanthe found out before making more of a fool of herself. Chantel still cringed over her own little episode.

"I think your Dad is here to pick you up. Nevermind Xanthe. Plenty of fish in the sea. I'll see you all tomorrow."

With Xanthe and Kinta still in tears, the sisters bundled into Angus's car.

"What's wrong? Don't tell me you've all been sacked?"

"No Dad. As if. Chantel just told us that Tim Fun is gay so that's broken Xanthe's heart. And Kinta is just being a sook as usual." Lirah said.

"Plenty more fish in the sea." Angus repeated the old adage.

"That's what Chantel said too."

Angus did not believe Tim Fun to be homosexual, yet it served his purpose. That night, after the girls had retired to bed, he told Opal.

"So I said, plenty more fish in the sea."

"That's a rather off handed thing to say to her Angus. Can't you understand Xanthe's heartbreak? Tim is her first serious infatuation with the opposite sex."

"That's it Opal. Infatuation is not proper in love."

"So you're happy to let her go on believing Tim is gay?"

"Do you have a better suggestion? Otherwise she will chase him until she gets him. Just like you did with me." Angus reminded.

"Oho. That was not the same thing."

"It could easily become the same thing. How long do you imagine Tim will resist her? You said yourself, Xanthe is too immature."

At first light the following morning, Xanthe appeared at the breakfast table with her eyes red and puffy from crying all night. Opal felt her own heart break to see her daughter so upset.

"Xanthe looks like the puffer fish from hell." Lirah remarked.

"Shut up Lirah." her twin replied in mild rebuke. "But you do Xanthe. Sorry."

Tactless as ever, Lirah waffled on.

"Chantel reckons everyone knows Tim is gay. She said it's as obvious as dogs balls."

"She did not say dogs balls Lirah. Stick to the facts."

Lirah sailed on unperturbed:

"Anyway, since Dad works with him he had to know. So, how come he flipped out over us being in Tim's flat? It's not as if he'd want to do the terrible deed worse than death with us female people."

"Worse than death hey?" Opal remarked. "Have you been reading too many old romance books?"

"You can't read too many old romance books Mum."

Kinta applauded her twin's reasoning.

"Hey you've got a point there. I hadn't thought of that. Good thinking Lirah. And by the way I am not a sook." Kinta managed to agree and disagree in the same breath.

"Gay or not, your father accused Tim of wrongful behaviour because it could have been." Opal said.

The girls busied themselves with cereal and milk while their probing minds churned up questions.

"Mum, if you knew all along that Tim is gay, why didn't you tell Xanthe?" Kinta asked.

"Yes Mum, why? You did know about Tim being gay. Right?" Lirah gripped the idea like a terrier.

Opal strove to be honest with her daughters and could not outright lie.

"I really couldn't say it ever crossed my mind. It's not a subject I feel comfortable talking about."

The girls had never known their outspoken mother to beat about the bush. They narrow-eyed each other over their cornflakes. Taking Opal's dodge as a glimmer of hope, Xanthe decided there and then to find out for sure. If Tim proved to be gay, she couldn't feel worse than she did already.

Xanthe stood under a cold shower until she turned blue, and the puffiness left her eyes. The girls arrived on time for work not long after sunrise though tropical rain kept the morning gloomy.

Torrential rain did not deter most board riders, including Tim. He drove down to the surf club for an hours surfing. His dry towel and change of clothes were in his car.

Despite knowing Angus and Opal disapproved of any close relationship with Xanthe, Tim couldn't wait to see her again.

After a bracing morning in water that felt warmer than the air, Tim towelled off, changed, and went to the tea shop again for breakfast. He told himself: *Nothing wrong with seeing her in a crowded public place.*

Wet weather that morning meant *Chantel's* was far from crowded. Under the dripping pergola, the outdoor tables and chairs remained vacant.

Tim parked out front, ran inside, took a seat and ordered scrambled eggs. Xanthe served his breakfast with hardly a word. Her heart throb realised his hasty departure the day before probably hurt her feelings.

"Xanthe, thanks for yesterday." he referred to the big breakfast.

"I understand why you left in a hurry and I'm sorry if I embarrassed you. " she replied.

"Not at all. I just didn't want to take up a table when you got so busy."

Heavy rain made business so slow, Chantel idly viewed the weather from behind the gleaming counter that she'd wiped down for the tenth time.

"This rain has set in. Oh well, we all need a break I guess."

She gave her waitresses the option of cleaning duties, scrubbing walls and floors, or taking the day off.

"Yay!" Lirah air punched in glee.

"You love to clean that much?" Chantel laughed.

"I vote we go to see a movie." Kinta said.

"It's pouring. I suppose we could get a cab."

"Tim is here. He could drive us."

Roped into taxi duty, the rest of Tim's day was decided for him by the Bridcombe sisters.

22

Epic Adventure

Creepy Old Men

The twins were keen to see a musical comedy starring a popular boy band, but Xanthe wasn't in the mood for it.

"I'd rather see the epic outback adventure; it's supposed to have great scenery and wildlife. Plus, it's a double feature."

"You can't go alone Xanthe. What if some creepy old man is in there? You know what Mum has warned us about."

Xanthe's favourite goddess of love, Aphrodite, answered her prayers when Lirah came up with a brilliant idea.

"I know! Tim can go with you."

Tim had only just dropped them off, planning to go home and read. About to pull out of his parking space, he stomped on the brakes when the twins pounded on his car roof.

Remembering Angus doing something similar, Tim reflected that the Bridcombe family seemed to enjoy assaulting his innocent Fiat.

"Tim! You have to go with Xanthe or some old creepy old men will get her."

"What? Where? What creepy old men?"

"The ones in the movie theatre."

Tim could hardly get out of accompanying Xanthe, leaving her un-protected. When Tim paid for both their tickets, it felt like a real date. Serendipity at being thrown together for a couple of hours in a dark cinema, held extra spice for its forbidden aspect.

"Where do you want to sit?" he asked.

"Back row please. I can't stand being too close to the screen. It gives me a headache."

Thankfully Tim no longer suffered terrible headaches, but he knew all about them. He ushered her in during the movie previews and ads. Xanthe chose the darkest corner at the end of the row.

"Did you want popcorn and a drink? I'll go out and get some if you like."

"Ask me again at half time Timmy. Right now, I don't want to waste a minute of being alone with you."

"Xanthe...I..."

On the spot, he couldn't frame a suitable reply without encouraging her ardent advances.

"Timmy, you like me don't you?"

"I do. Very much. As a friend. You must realise our differences remain a hurdle to anything more."

He referred to the thirteen year age gap. She pursued the homosexuality rumour.

"Timmy, people say you are very well read and informed."

"Do they?"

Tim preened a little. Xanthe would never tell him that the nasty girls at the surf club said he talked like a toff and was way up himself for having some sort of higher education.

"I have always been a book nerd I guess. It has served me well at times."

Tim replied modestly, thinking of his recent coup over Bill and Ben. Despite being so well informed, her next question seemed disconnected.

"Right. So, please tell me what makes someone know if they're gay?"

For a fleeting moment, he wondered if Xanthe swung both ways. Caution shortened his reply.

"I guess it's about who they feel attracted to."

"Aren't you attracted to me though?"

Aha. He twigged.

"Did Chantel say something about me?"

"Yes. She told us about your um...tastes. Not that there's anything wrong with that."

Oh no. His white lie to his amorous landlady came back to bite him.

"Xanthe. I'm not gay."

Xanthe's heart lifted. *I knew it!*

"Why does Chantel think you are then?"

Tim avoided dobbing Chantel in for making a lustful move on him.

"I might have given her that impression." he hedged.

The theatre lights dimmed and opening music heralded the start of the movie.

"So Timmy..."

They had the back row to themselves, but someone sitting two rows in front shushed them.

Xanthe took Tim's hand in hers. Her touch rocketed straight to his core. He couldn't resist allowing it with a blatant lie to himself: *Just friends. Enjoying a movie together.*

She wore a short black waitress frock, less the white apron she'd left at the tea shop. The dress rode up when she hunkered into the seat. Her skin appeared to glow hot and cold in the flickering lights from the big screen. The sight drew Tim's gaze to linger on the top of her legs, as she intended.

"Timmy I love you." she whispered.

Xanthe kissed his hand and placed it on her bare thigh. He felt the silky soft skin and struggled to take his hand back. Instead, she placed her own hand on his rising erection.

"No." he groaned.

"Yes." she soothed.

Shush. The irritated viewer in front hissed.

"Timmy. We could go back to your flat. No one would know."

"Oh dear god. No Xanthe."

"Why not? Do you want me to find someone else to be my first?"

"NO. Don't think that Xanthe."

"What choice do I have?"

Tim knew Xanthe could have any number of willing partners. Maybe she'd even choose someone older than himself. He'd be a prize mug if that came about.

The patron in front stood up, turned around and stared at them. *Will you two shut up? Some of us want to listen to the movie.* Tim scrunched down into his seat.

"Sorry." he muttered.

Xanthe lowered her voice to be barely audible over the movie dialogue. She breathed an ultimatum close to Tim's ear, giving him goosebumps.

"Kiss me now or never Timmy. Last chance."

She place her roving hand on his cheek and leaned her face in towards him. Tim thought if just one kiss stopped her talking, it was no sacrifice. He pressed his lips to her cheek, going for a quick brotherly type of peck. Xanthe had other ideas. She turned her head and met his lips with her own.

Tim's dreams of kissing Xanthe's lips did not prepare him for the delicious reality. Egged on by her murmurs of pleasure, within a few minutes, he boldly dared to touch her breasts. Aware of two reasons to make nipples harden, he ruled out feeling too cold.

Fascinated by the response he generated, Tim dropped his hand to caress Xanthe's thigh.   Instinctively driven, Tim moved his hand up under her skirt, to stroke the front of her fine lace panties. He became lost in another world when her legs parted in invitation.

A loud volley of gunshots from the movie startled Tim out of his trance. He managed to stop short of exploring further inside Xanthe's pantie elastic.

"Don't stop." she begged.

"I must. We mustn't." he groaned.

When the half-time curtain came down, they were still kissing. The irate theatre goer gave advice as he marched up the aisle past the back row lovers: *Get a room.*

Tim blushed scarlet. Xanthe poked her tongue out.

"What an old fogey. He's probably one of the creepy men in cinemas that Mum told us about. But we really should take his advice."

"We really shouldn't." Tim replied.

"We've got over an hour before we meet the twins and it's only five minutes to your flat."

Xanthe coaxed. Tim needed no more incentive to agree. He couldn't bear to think she'd go elsewhere for her first time. Or any time, if he were perfectly honest.

They vacated their seats and hurriedly followed others out to the canteen area. Sadly all plans were thwarted when the twins appeared in the foyer with Opal.

"We rang Mum to get us because our movie ended and we want lunch." Kinta said.

"So we waited to let you know because you've still got the second half of your double feature."

Xanthe's mother did not seem happy. Opal's demeanour, not lost on Tim, had him redden with guilt for what he had been about to do. Chickening out again had not been in the plan, yet he had no choice.

"This movie is actually pretty boring to me. I almost fell asleep. So I'd rather go home and take a nap. Opal you're welcome to my ticket if you want to take my place beside Xanthe."

Xanthe glared at her sisters. Opal silently thanked Tim's good sense. She decided to take his ticket to separate the couple.

"What about us then?" Kinta said.

"I can drop you home." Tim offered.

"That is very good of you Tim. Thanks. They can get their own lunch at home then."

Opal pecked Tim's cheek and smelt Xanthe's perfume on him. Back inside for the second half of the movie, they took seats in a middle row. It was where they usually sat. Opal asked for an update.

"What happened in the first part of the plot Xanthe?"

"Mum. I have absolutely no idea." Xanthe replied honestly.

"Have you been a very naughty girl?"

"Don't stress Mum. I'm going to marry him."

"Will Tim have any say in the matter?"

"Of course he will. I'll even let him think it's his own idea."

Opal experienced a frisson of deja vu that transported her back to when she first met Angus. She saw the writing on the wall and decided Xanthe could do a lot worse than Tim Fun.

That night after the movies the twins raved over the boy band's performance during tea time.

"You would have loved it, Xanthe. Better than that old documentary thing or whatever it was."

Lirah blathered on while Xanthe kept quiet, concentrating on her meal. Kinta kicked Lirah under the table.

"Ow. That hurt. What did I do?"

"Sorry my foot slipped." Kinta replied as her eyes darted between her parents.

"I only saw the second part but it was actually quite spectacular." Opal said.

Angus's radar kicked in.

"Don't tell me you sat alone for the first half Xanthe."

"No Daddy. Tim drove us there so he sat with me until Mum got there."

"I see. That was convenient. Weren't you all supposed to be at work?"

"There was nothing to do. Only a few customers came in because of the rain."

"Chantel said we could go home unless we wanted to scrub walls and floors."

"And you didn't want to get your hands dirty?"

"We're supposed to be on holidays Daddy. We've already spent most of it working."

"Welcome to real life." Angus replied.

Opal intervened before it got out of hand.

"Have you given any thought to what you want to do when you leave high school? Xanthe you only have one more year. It will go by quickly. The two years will fly by for the twins too."

Xanthe did not say she just wanted to marry Tim and have his babies. Instead, she gave her second choice.

"Chantel has taught me a lot and I kind of like cooking and stuff like that."

"So you might go on and study to be a baker or even a chef? That would be nice." Opal smiled.

"Maybe I will."

"And Kinta?"

"I want to be a famous film star or a famous fashion model, but I wouldn't mind becoming a pro roller derby player either."

"Pro roller derby? Is that even a thing?" Lirah asked. "I'd do that."

"Suggest you both think of proper careers." Angus advised.

"Well I'm never going to just get married and churn out babies like sausages." Lirah declared.

Xanthe and Opal exchanged a look that spoke volumes. Angus winced since that was the life he'd given his young wife. Opal produced three babies before her twentieth birthday.

"It's not for everyone but I'm happy with my lot." she smiled at Angus.

Angus smiled back gratefully. Opal patted his big hand with her small one, across the table.

"Now look what you've done Lirah. They've gone all mushy." Kinta giggled.

Xanthe wanted nothing more than a loving relationship like her parents had. It occurred she could have it all, as Tim's wife, mother to his children and also follow in Chantel's footsteps with a food career.

Tim could not escape a self-truth: He was definitely, wrongly, desperately and ignobly head over heels in love with a sixteen year old girl, thirteen years his junior. That she claimed to love him too, seemed nothing short of a miracle.

He relived over and over how splendidly his hands-on seduction techniques worked like magic. Ignoring a voice in his head arguing that Xanthe controlled proceedings, all his prior failures with girls were negated in the cinema.

If not for Opal and the twins appearing in the theatre foyer, he would have consummated his love for Xanthe that day. He explored mixed sentiments of disappointment, frustration and relief that it hadn't happened. *Yet.* The tantalising *yet* shone like a beacon just beyond his reach.

Tim continued to leave his back door key in the peg basket, and the chain off the latch, adding guilt to complicate his emotions. Angus and Opal would have his guts for garters if they cottoned on to a loose affair happening with young Xanthe.

Nothing could change the age difference but Tim spent time making calculations. When Xanthe reached eighteen, he'd be thirty-one. When she reached twenty, he'd be thirty-three. Somehow the gap seemed less glaring as time went by.

For the first time in his life, Tim contemplated marriage. If her parents agreed and Xanthe accepted a legal union, another worry niggled: A teenager might regret throwing her youthful freedom away. Perhaps resentment would grow and fester.

Even so, IF Xanthe crept into his flat again like before, Tim would forget his self advice.

As Tim's recovery strengthened, he had thanked Chantel for her kindness in bringing his meals but determined to provide for himself.

"You've been so kind Chantel and if I can ever be of help to you, just say."

He sincerely hoped she didn't take that the wrong way.

Rain still pelted down. Tim nuked a freezer meal. He didn't approve of eating in bed, but this time he relaxed his rule. *Why not?* It had been a day full of relaxing rules. That got him going again over the exhilarating episode with Xanthe in the movies.

Yearning for her overwhelmed him. He put his face into the pillow and cried out in anguish.

Upstairs, Chantel thought she heard something over the rain drumming on the roof.

"No. Just frogs in the drain pipes." David yawned.

Tim puzzled over the twins asking if it felt like rape when they apparently jumped him in bed. *Did that happen?* A shame he couldn't recall an alleged double whammy. Finally, exhausted, he fell into a deep sleep.

In the witching hour, lingering wisps of cobwebs were swept away. Portals to haunted halls in Tim's mind creaked ajar and he crept inside to see what was within.

He awoke with the certain knowledge of why he had dragged the twins out by their ponytails.

Tim suddenly remembered all the Bridcombe teens had fondled him intimately.

Red-faced he recalled his inevitable eruptions. Hadn't volcanoes been mentioned? Did someone say Vesuvius?

Belatedly embarrassed, Tim couldn't face any wanton Bridcombe sister for breakfast at *Chantel's*.

He went straight home after his morning surf and decided it was high time he went back to work.

23

All Work

& No Play

The following morning, Tim ate some cereal, drank some milk, donned good blue jeans and a shirt and tie. He fronted early at work to find the Grimslades and Angus partaking of pungent coffee from the office machine.

"Tim! Good to see you. But you know you're owed more time off." Dougall exclaimed.

"Can it be rolled over? I am so bored. I've re-read everything on my bookshelf."

"I believe you've also been to the movies." Angus said it like an accusation.

Dulcy detected a challenge and noted Tim's blush. She shot a knowing glance to Dougall. Tim cleared his throat and replied:

"Yes Angus. Spur of the moment. The girls feared creepy old men in the theatre, and Xanthe wanted to see a different show. Anyway, I gave my ticket to Opal for the second half."

"Got to watch out for creepy old men hitting on young girls." Angus growled.

Tim nodded and dropped his gaze. *Cripes, how much does he know? Carry on, carry on.*

Dougall got him past the uncomfortable moment.

"Well Tim, there is a backlog of research you could get going on. It'd be great to catch up. But if you feel under the weather later, just leave it and go on home."

Tim gratefully took refuge behind the big screen of a desk computer.

Seasonal weather played a part in what happened next.

The wet season in South East Queensland, when it happened at all, was driven by monsoons and South East winds. In a good year, adequate quenching rain fell on the parched land between the months of December and March. In bad years, nature delivered floods or drought, instead.

Australians in every state and territory inevitably had to cope with The Big Wet, The Big Dry, the Big Floods and the Big Flaming Bushfires as a part of life, death and misfortunes.

Even before Tim returned to his detective work, The Big Wet set in with a vengeance.

Torrential rain meant *Chantel's* tea house barely had enough work for one waitress let alone three. The twins were glad to get out of it. They'd had enough of the job and looked forward to a relaxing Christmas before going back to school in the new year.

Chantel loved that the Bridcombe girls had sassy personalities, and delivered backchat to cheeky customers in good humour. She hoped to get the twins back even after the holidays, and gave them first options to work weekends when business picked up.

Glad Xanthe chose to stay on, Chantel particularly liked the eldest Bridcombe sister for sharing her keen interest in culinary pursuits. Xanthe kept coming in every day, mainly in hopes of seeing Tim. To her great disappointment, he no longer came in for breakfast, or any other time.

Angus casually mentioned Tim Fun had returned to duty at the police station, but that didn't excuse Tim's absence to Xanthe. Despite feeling rejected, ignored and let down, she yearned to see him.

There came a day when Opal dropped Xanthe to *Chantel's* an hour earlier than usual. She and the twins were off to the city for Christmas shopping. They all knew Chantel would already be at the tea shop baking and prepping. Xanthe could have gone in to make an early start. However, the short distance to Tim's flat enticed her with the possibility he'd not have left for work yet.

Xanthe ran splashing along the road through puddles. Her clothes remained dry, protected by a hooded rain cape but her shoes were soaked. Elated to see Tim's car parked outside the flat, Xanthe drew up panting and tapped on the door.

What now? Tim cursed as he'd just stepped out of the shower. Without towelling off, he quickly pulled on a pair of shorts.

"Xanthe!"

"I had to see you Timmy. Are you going to invite me in or leave me standing in the rain?"

Tim ushered her inside. The front door opened straight into his bed-sitting room.

"Sorry it's a mess, I haven't made the bed yet."

"I'm sorry to be dripping on your floor. Can I hang my cape somewhere?"

Tim helped her out of the raincoat, and hung it on his hatstand where it still dripped on the floor. He didn't care about that. Xanthe kicked her wet shoes off by the door. Without another word she slipped out of her dress and stood before him in her lacy underwear.

Despite Xanthe offering herself, the dream come true had flawed timing for Tim. He had envisaged a slow romantic build up to their first time, not a quickie before work.

"Xanthe. This isn't right." he moaned.

"You were pretty up for it at the movies." she said.

"I was out of my mind. I'm glad your mother turned up."

Xanthe didn't believe him. She shed her bra and dangled it on one finger.

"Do you like my titties?"

Tim almost fainted with desire. He choked a weak and waning protest in a husky voice.

"I can't take advantage like this. You are only sixteen. I'm twenty-nine."

"I don't want some fumbling youth Timmy. I want you to be my first."

"Xanthe. I would be just as fumbling except a lot older, I've n-never had the p-pleasure."

"I think you have Timmy."

"I mean in the established conventional understanding of sexual intercourse." Tim blushed crimson.

Xanthe stared. So all the rumours about him at the surf club must be right. He had really never ever scored with any of the dates he took out. It made her want him all the more. He could be all hers.

"Timmy I think we could muddle our way through it together." she crooned. "Anyway, practice makes perfect."

She slipped her panties down, kicked them towards the bunk and circled slowly to show him every side of her taut body. Tim lost his struggle with right and wrong.

"Xanthe, your body is absolutely breathtaking." he gasped.

"I want to see all of you too. Yes?"

Confident his rigid display would never be more impressive, he agreed with one strangled word.

"Yes."

Tim's shorts clung damply from his shower. Xanthe knelt while working them down his muscular thighs. His throbbing penis begged to be kissed so she planted one right on the pink tip.

He groaned in ecstasy and pulled her pony tail loose, slipping the brown glittery scrunchy over his wrist. Xanthe's long dark hair fell in soft waves about her shoulders.

"Timmy my darling. You are beautiful. Every part of you is perfect."

Afraid he'd lose complete control before the main event, he pulled her upright. Tim smelt the stimulating scent of his own manhood on her lips when she stood and kissed him. Without breaking the kiss, he gently guided her towards his bed.

Alas, the imminent culmination of their desire died a sudden death. A loud rapping on the door and a deep shout shrivelled more than the couple's intentions.

"TIM FUN! OPEN UP."

"OH NO. THAT'S DADDY." Xanthe gasped in a horrified stage whisper.

Panic gripped the naked couple. Tim recovered first:

"Quick. Grab you stuff and get dressed in the bathroom."

Xanthe gathered her dress, bra and raincoat then spent precious seconds looking for her panties she'd kicked under the bed earlier. Tim hopped about on one leg trying to get into his jeans, with one pants leg still turned inside out.

"Hurry Xanthe." he gasped.

"TIM! We've got a situation." Angus yelled while pounding on the door harder than before.

That represented the understatement of the century to the guilt ridden wannabe lovers.

"J-just out of the shower Angus. C-can you give me a minute?"

Xanthe quietly slipped out the back door, her shoes in her hands. Tim found a shirt and opened the door to the unwelcomed sight of big scowling Sergeant Angus Bridcombe, Xanthe's father.

Angus strode into the room and noted the rumpled single bunk. His mind illustrated how it must have been when his three naughty daughters invaded this flat. Tim didn't need to be psychic to read the giant's mind. The disgruntled father snapped a demand to Tim that brooked no argument.

"Forget the bloody tie. Grab your boots. You can put them on in the car. You're coming with me."

Tim obeyed, pocketed his wallet and keys and slid into the passenger seat of the 4x4 police vehicle. He scarcely had time to buckle up before Angus floored the accelerator.

Meanwhile, Xanthe arrived at *Chantel's* at her normal starting time. Yet so much had happened in the past hour, it seemed like another lifetime.

"Good morning Xanthe. Your hair is lovely but you'll have to tie it back. Kitchen rules. Sorry."

"Oh. Yes. Good morning. I must have lost my scrunchy. Do you have a rubber band or something?"

Mystified when the 4x4, blue lights flashing, sped towards a rural area, Tim had no idea why Angus singled him out for this mission. The police sergeant offered no explanation nor any conversation. Rain lessened the further west they travelled. Without the swish of windscreen wipers, silence loomed ominously, only starkly punctuated by the siren when used to navigate traffic hazards.

A pang of conscience prickled Tim for his very recent misbehaviour with the driver's virginal young daughter. Surely Xanthe's father didn't know of it, yet the older man's surly attitude denied that. Aware Angus's reticence determined towards some dire purpose, suspense twanged Tim's taut nerves.

"Where are we going Angus?"

"Rural property."

"Why?" Tim gulped.

He could not think why Angus wanted his company for an apparent urgent quest. Tim's vivid and guilt ridden imagination conjured up an industrial wood chipper and a large compost pit.

Tight lipped, Angus worried over his decision to attend an armed hostage event without proper back-up. Instead, he chose to take a young detective who was possibly not fully fit for active duty. Yet Tim Fun seemed the logical choice for the particular problem.

Eventually, Xanthe's stern father deigned a reply.

"My mate Jarrah took his father along to help on some big land-scaping job. They sheltered from a heavy downpour under a patio awning. The home owner saw them through a window and went ape shit."

"Have they been hurt?"

"Not yet. Owner came out with a rifle. Jarrah tried to apologise for using the patio, but they got locked in a shed at gunpoint. Just lucky Jarrah had his phone. He called me because his father fears police. You know about that."

"I do know, but Wild Dog trusts me and he knows you. What about the mad landowner, won't he call police?"

"Don't think so. Jarrah says the bloke is out of his tree, high on something. He can hear him marching around the shed raving about doing away with them. Says he wouldn't have employed Jarrah's firm if he knew they were blacks."

"So just a dyed in the wool racist raving mad junkie with a gun?"

"Yep, with an ambition to exact some sort of *make my day* revenge."

"Thanks for inviting me along Angus."

"We'll talk about that later."

Tim wasn't sure if he'd just been threatened.

Angus pulled the 4x4 into a double gateway and drove between bordering trees up a long track into the property. They came across Jarrah's work ute parked near a locked shed. But the landowner had gone indoors out of the rain. Angus called out and Jarrah replied.

"We're in here. Careful mate, he's a real nutter."

"Are you both alright?" Tim asked.

"Pretty pissed off."

Wild Dog spoke up: "Is that you little brother?"

"Yes my old friend. You saved me once and I've come to save you this time."

The nutter instantly appeared in the open doorway of the house and aimed a rant at Tim.

"I heard that! So *little brother* is it? Another bloody abo. You all in cahoots? Think you can take my land?"

"Settle down mister. Do you live alone here?" Angus asked in a reasonable tone of voice, trying to engage the irate man into making normal conversation.

"Aha. Casing the joint are you? Bad luck because I am never alone. I've got my trusty point-two-two all loaded and ready to go. It's my handy little helper for eliminating pests."

Tim spoke in a low aside to Angus.

"Got your taser?"

"Yes but I have to get close enough."

"What are you hissing about? Think I can't hear you?"

Angus began strolling slowly towards the house, speaking calmly.

"No one wants to take your land, mate. Let's sit down out of this rain and we'll talk about it in a neighbourly fashion. Any chance of a cup of tea?"

"Think you can sneak your way into my house? Cadge a feed off me? You one of them white blackfellas? Yeah that'd be right. I know the police force is full of you buggers now. That uniform doesn't fool me."

Angus extended a hand towards the unhinged man in a gesture of peace. The man sprung fully out of the doorway and pointed his rifle at the giant officer's chest. He would have to be a very bad shot to miss such a broad target. Angus put his hands in the air.

"Hey. Take it easy."

"Shut up and lay down in the dirt where you belong."

Angus fell to his knees in the muddied yard.

"Right down! Put your face in the mud."

Angus did as told but reached a hand to his taser hoping to roll over and zap the maniac if he came close enough.

"Keep your hands over your head or I'll blast your balls off."

Angus valued his balls and had no option but to obey. He hoped Tim might cause some distraction for a chance to use the stun gun. That hope faded when the steel barrel pressed to the back of his head. The gunman saved the smaller less threatening figure standing nearby for later.

Sensing the safety catch release, the agile younger detective rushed in. The split second as the trigger engaged, Tim body-slammed the shooter and knocked him off balance. The gun skidded away out of reach but Tim's swift action did not prevent the shot being fired.

The nutcase scurried, slipping in the mud, to secure the firearm. Tim deftly kicked it away and strode three paces to pick it up. Blood oozed from Bridcombe's head. It appeared, alas, he'd been too late to save Xanthe's father.

A cold purpose possessed DC Timothy Funicular. He ejected the spent cartridge, deliberately worked the bolt to reload and levelled the rifle for an avenging kill shot. The killer fell to his knees and begged for his life.

Jarrah and his father heard what was said before the first unmistakable crack of the gunshot reverberated against the walls of the metal shed. Warragul stood in front of his son, sure the nutter would come for them. He'd be first in line but hoped for time to crash into the killer and save Jarrah.

A millisecond before Tim Fun's trigger finger tightened, Sergeant Bridcombe groaned, rolled over, and got to his knees. He'd been stunned by the loud report so close to his head. Quick to recover, Angus registered Tim's executioner stance in the nick of time to prevent him making a dreadful mistake.

"STOP! Don't do it Tim. He isn't worth it."

Angus Bridcombe understood Tim Fun had been about to serve unlawful justice on his behalf.

Despite blood spraying from a wound to his ear, the hefty officer stood and ably cuffed the disarmed landowner. The man spat, yelled abuse and struggled against his captives to no avail.

"You fuckin' black bastards."

"Shut up you stupid prick. I just saved your life." Bridcombe growled.

A hairs breadth from taking a man's life in cold blood, Tim overcame his deadly objective calmly. Angus noted the young detective's steady hand and unruffled demeanour. Xanthe's father gained new respect for her choice.

Tim lightened the mood for his terrified friends in the shed, as he unbolted the door.

"Relax. All over red rover."

When Jarrah and Wild Dog emerged visibly shaken, Angus safely discharged the ammunition and stowed the rifle in the 4x4.

"Guess we won't get paid for this job then." Jarrah remarked sagely.

Angus knew Wild Dog's mistrust of authorities and saw no reason to call more police in.

"If you feel okay to drive, Jarrah, take your father home. We'll sort out the legalities later."

"Crikey son," Warragul said, "I thought gardening would be a safe job."

Until this day, Jarrah had never been happy to leave a job unfinished. Wild Dog helped gather their tools. They drove away grateful to be alive, albeit to the tune of the crazed prisoner's ribald discontent.

Angus put a stop to the loud invective with one well aimed beefy fist.

"You didn't see that Tim." he advised.

"See what? Anyway thanks for letting old Warragul go home. You need to get that bullet wound looked at."

"Let's offload this garbage first. Then I'll see about finding a band aid."

Angus felt his damaged ear that smarted like blazes. His hand came away bloodied from the sizeable chunk taken off.

"Shit. That mongrel has ruined my good looks."

"Could have been worse."

"Tim. I owe you."

"You'd have done the same for me."

"Always." Angus vowed.

Deep in thought, Angus drove them back to HQ and dispensed of their prisoner. Next came the arduous task of paperwork, the most unloved part of the sergeant's existence. This time he had to explain why he'd taken it upon himself to go without proper back-up. Tim endeared himself again:

"I'll prepare the paperwork while you go see the doc."

Happy to be going home to his family almost in one piece, instead of to the morgue, Angus had to ask something. The question had bugged him all day from when he first arrived at Tim's flat.

"Tim. Tell me why you're wearing Xanthe's hair doodad on your wrist? It's one I gave her and I watched her putting her pony tail up with it this morning."

For the first time, Tim realised he still wore Xanthe's glittery brown scrunchy.

He'd almost taken her virginity that morning, but he hadn't. He'd almost shot a man dead that day, but he hadn't. Meeting Angus's hard face proved no less disturbing.

"I pulled the thing out of Xanthe's hair when I saw her this morning."

Sergeant Bridcombe's wide square jaw clench as speculation brewed. The grinding of molars might have been Tim's vivid imagination, though that's how he remembered it.

The Grimslades' sudden entry interrupted any ongoing inquisition. Blood still dripped onto Angus's collar, since he'd rubbed his damaged ear a few times. The bloodied and muddied state of their sergeant raised more than an eyebrow. By contrast, Tim Fun appeared as cool and neat as a pin.

"Oh my god! What have you done?" Dulcy cried.

"Angus got shot." Tim said matter-of-factly. It now seemed the lesser of concerns.

"Had a tricky incident this morning." Angus added.

"Why wasn't I called? Am I the chief honcho around here or am I redundant?" Dougall riled.

"Long story." Tim offered.

"I've got all day. Apparently, I've nothing else to do." Dougall shot back.

"I'm off to the hospital." Angus escaped leaving Tim to sort it out.

24

Pigs Might Fly

Scathingly Brilliant

Safely home that night, Angus retold the shocking saga to his dismayed family. He edited a few parts not legally done in the line of duty. Opal summed it up.

"Tim Fun saved your life Angus."

"That's true. He did."

"Tim is a hero." Kinta cried.

"He must be tougher than he looks." Lirah marvelled.

"That's why I love him." Xanthe clasped her hands to her heart.

Angus eyed his eldest daughter sternly.

"Xanthe. Tell me why Tim was wearing your hair doodad on his wrist."

Angus's daughter also knew how to edit a tale.

"He took it out of my hair when I saw him this morning."

"Where did you see him?"

"Did you ask him?" she parried.

"I want your version Xanthe."

Xanthe wondered to what extent Tim might have modified the facts. She looked between her unsmiling parents who waited to hear her answer.

"I dropped you off earlier than usual at *Chantel's*." Opal gave her a starting point.

"Oh yes. How did your Christmas shopping go?"

Xanthe used the distraction hoping in vain to change the subject.

"We got loads of good stuff." Kinta jumped in to save her sister.

"Maybe we should have picked up a big pack of pantie liners for Dad's ear." Lirah laughed.

"And a red hat." Opal joined in the joke hoping to lighten Angus's dark mood.

"Nice try girls. Xanthe I'm waiting."

"Alright. I went to his flat before work this morning, because I was early. I still got to work on time, by the way. You can ask Chantel."

"Xanthe. You have been expressly forbidden to go to Tim's flat."

"I wasn't going inside but it was raining, so I had to."

"Is that when Tim took the thing out of your hair?"

"Yes."

"Why would he be letting your hair down Xanthe?"

"I needed to tidy it. So…"

"No lies Xanthe. Were you there when I knocked on the door?"

Xanthe replied to her father without telling a lie.

"Yes Daddy. But I knew you'd take it out on poor Timmy so I ran out the back way."

"So I'm some sort of ogre? The wicked overbearing father? When all I've done is try to save you from yourself Xanthe?"

"Daddy. I don't want to be saved from Timmy. I love him. I'm going to marry him."

"WHAT! Has he proposed to you without even a by your leave to me. Your father?"

"No. He doesn't know I'm going to marry him yet. But I'm working on it." Xanthe admitted.

Opal could relate to her daughter as she'd exercised similar tactics herself in beguiling Angus.

"None of us need more upset now. We'll discuss it properly tomorrow. We've all had a terrible shock and we're lucky to have our family all together tonight, alive. We should be counting our blessings instead of arguing." Opal said.

"And don't forget that's thanks to my Timmy." Xanthe reminded.

"Exactly when did he become *your* Timmy?" Angus growled.

"I haven't done the horizontal tango with him *yet* Daddy, if that's what you think."

"Only because he wouldn't." the ever tactless Lirah offered.

"Even though he loves her to bits." Kinta added.

"Yet? What do you mean by *yet*."

"Exactly what you think it means Daddy."

Xanthe provoked her father defying him to object. Opal took charge before a family war erupted.

"I said that's enough! Go to bed. All of you."

Opal's frown to her husband clearly indicated they'd discuss it in private between themselves. Later in bed, the concerned parents struggled to come up with a viable solution.

"Why couldn't we have three sons instead of three daughters." Angus moaned.

"Oh sure. Instead of three possible grandchildren a year we could potentially get dozens."

"Yeah. I guess my sons would be chips off the old block." Angus smiled smugly.

"What do you mean by that?"

"Nothing dearest. Just joking."

Hmmm.

"Jokes aside Angus, I believe we can't keep Xanthe and Tim apart, and the inevitable will happen. Wouldn't it be better if we condone their friendship so they don't go behind our backs? Remember what we were like."

"At least you were a year older and finished school, Opal."

"Only just."

"But they are not us. Giving them free rein could end in heart-break for Xanthe. Or Tim."

"We all owe a deep debt of gratitude to Tim. Remember he saved your life today."

"But we don't owe him the hand of our first born. Do we? Couldn't we just nominate him for a bravery medal? Have you even considered that Tim won't want to be tied down to marriage Opal?"

"Nope that is not a consideration at all. Xanthe will make sure of that."

"We could put her in boarding school for a year." Angus dared to suggest.

"Wash your mouth out Angus."

"Right. Bad idea."

"Also, Xanthe is being mentored by Chantel at the tea parlour which will help her enormously in reaching her career ambitions."

"Right. Yes. True. Okay I suggest a compromise."

"Go on."

"What if we tell Xanthe if she waits until she has left school before entertaining any serious relationship, we will give it our blessing."

"Get real Angus. Where's the incentive in that for her?"

"We need an added incentive for sure. But the thing is, it gives her time to change her mind. You know what a scatterbrain she can be, and she might go off Tim by then."

"Pigs might fly. By the way darling, how is your ear? Is it very painful?"

"It's hurting. I might need more pain killers to get to sleep. How do you feel about having a permanently maimed husband?"

"It's a real turn off."

"Is it?"

"Of course not. You're stuck with me because nothing would turn me off my big fella. But what happened today reminded me we should make the most of every happiness while we can."

"I guess that applies to Xanthe and Tim too." Angus said quietly.

Meanwhile in the girls' bedroom the sisters shared scandalous secrets.

"He let your hair down? That is just so romantic. Did you do the tango with him Xanthe?"

"No. Dad turned up at the absolutely worst time. Anyway I got to see Tim stark naked."

"So what. We've both done that."

"But I felt his willy."

"Big deal. We've done that too."

"I kissed it."

"Yew! That's gross. You win. I'm never doing that to a boy." Kinta pulled a disgusted face.

On the other hand, Lirah wanted a clinical analysis.

"That's interesting. Did he like having his willy kissed? How did he react?"

"He groaned a lot and pulled me up off my knees for a proper kiss."

"Okay. Righto. That sounds like he didn't like it. I must remember that. I don't know why we aren't taught this sort of detail in sex education at school."

"What did you do then?"

"We kept kissing and he sort of walked me backwards towards the bed. That's when Dad banged on the door and shouted."

"Holey heck. I'd have fainted or had a heart attack."

"We panicked to get dressed. I'd lost my knickers somewhere and Tim couldn't get his jeans on because one pants leg was turned inside out."

"That sounds really funny. You might laugh about it someday."

"I'm sure I won't. Missing out on having Tim at that moment had to be the most disappointing let down of my whole life."

"You'll get him someday Xanthe." Kinta sympathised.

"Bet Mum and Dad are talking about you right now." Lirah added.

"Yeah. Can't wait to hear what horrors they come up with tomorrow."

The following evening, Opal and Angus took Xanthe aside for a serious talk.

"Why can't we be in on the discussion? We're part of this family too." Lirah complained.

"It's not as if you all won't whisper about it half the night." Opal replied mildly.

"It's not the same. And we might learn something from your many years of wisdom." Kinta said.

Angus shrugged to his wife.

"Okay but no butting in."

"Cool."

"Alright. Xanthe. We know you think you're in love with Tim Fun."

"I know I AM. You want a serious talk and I am serious. Mum I know you were only seventeen when you nailed Dad."

"But you are only sixteen, still at school and Tim is almost thirty. Also *nailed* is not a nice way of describing the loving and proper relationship between your mother and me." Angus retorted.

"Xanthe darling, at least wait until you finish school to make any big life changing decisions. No use rushing in and regretting it later." Opal tried.

"I suppose you've grilled Timmy even though he's the hero who saved your life."

"I am perfectly entitled to ask Tim Fun what his intentions may be."

"Intentions? Oh no Daddy you didn't! I don't want Tim to be forced! It sounds like a hillbilly shotgun sort of thing. You'll just ruin all my careful and subtle efforts."

Opal hid a smile. Xanthe was indeed very like herself. Angus hadn't let on how little he gleaned from the young detective. Tim only admitted to taking Xanthe's scrunchie out of her hair.

"Alright I will leave the shotgun at home. But you must promise to limit your friendship with Tim. Make no mistake about my meaning Xanthe. Keep it strictly platonic."

"I think that means you can square dance but not tango." Kinta said.

"So, not even strictly ballroom?" Lirah asked.

"I said NO butting in! I mean NO dancing at all. We will see how you *both* feel after you've left high school." Angus decreed.

Opal added the only incentive she thought might work.

"If you and Tim *both* still want a closer relationship by the time you leave school, you will have our blessings."

Xanthe stormed off and slammed the bedroom door. The twins crept in after her. Pounding her fists into a pillow Xanthe cried out her angst to her twin sisters.

"Mum and Dad are so unfair. They even said if *both* of you still want it, as if Tim won't want me by then. They must think he'll go off me in that time. What if he does? He might get interested in some other girl."

Lirah began painting her nails with a new polish bought during their Christmas shopping spree.

"That's true. Kinta and I will be sixteen by then. The age of consent. Do you think Tim would like this colour?"

"Oh that is a cruel dig Lirah. Don't worry Xanthe. She's just teasing. We made a twin's pact never to meddle with Tim Fun again."

"Someone else might." Xanthe wailed.

Kinta shed tears in sympathy. Lirah casually mentioned a loophole:

"Mum and Dad said *after you leave high school.* So, all you have to do is NOT go back to school next year. Technically that means you have already left school NOW Xanthe."

Newfound hope sprang into the thwarted lover's heart. Xanthe sat up.

"Lirah that is scathingly brilliant. You're an absolute genius."

"I know." Lirah blew on her painted fingernails to harden the varnish.

Kinta wished she was as scathingly brilliant as her twin.

25

Less Clever

She's a He

Coastal rain eased to a drizzle by the next day. Except for a handful of stalwart surfers, the beach remained deserted.

Tim went out early as usual to catch a wave or three. He'd avoided having Angus grill him about Xanthe so far. Yet it loomed uppermost in his mind.

He showered and changed ready for work, planning to go to *Chantel's* for breakfast to see Xanthe and return her hair band.

Tim momentarily faltered finding Opal and the twins were also inside the tea house. Xanthe bustled around from behind the counter, hugged him and kissed his cheek.

Opal noted Tim's adoring gaze settle on her eldest. She could not condemn Tim for falling in love with her daughter. The task ahead to keep them apart seemed pointless.

"Tim, will you join us? I'd like to buy your breakfast, whatever you'd like but I can recommend the pancakes." Opal smiled.

"Thank you. That is so kind." he replied politely, bowing slightly in respect of Xanthe's mother.

"It's the very least I can do. We owe you a huge debt for saving the man of our house."

"You're our hero. Forever. We all love you to bits." Kinta exclaimed.

"Dad says you fought off a mad junkie who tried to murder him. I'm impressed." Lirah added.

"And it takes a lot to impress Lirah." Kinta added.

The incident replayed in Tim's mind. He attempted a modest reply.

"It all happened so fast. Thankfully, Angus recovered before I...um...anyway it might have ended differently."

Opal stored Tim's near slip of the tongue in the back of her mind to question Angus later.

Tim appreciated the invitation for breakfast but rued not getting a chance to talk to Xanthe alone. When he finally arrived at work, he still had the brown glittery scrunchie in his pocket.

Angus happened to poke his head around the office door and caught Tim with his eyes closed, dreamily holding Xanthe's hair accessory to his lips.

Xanthe's father ducked back outside without being seen. He could not upbraid Tim for being so besotted with his eldest, since he owed his life to him.

Acknowledging Xanthe could do a hell of a lot worse than Tim Fun softened Angus's attitude. He began to find himself more worried that she'd change her fickle mind.

Advantages in having one daughter settled with a worthy partner tipped the scales. He imagined angst ahead if the twins went for deadbeats in heavy metal bands, cowboys or *aargh* religious fanatics.

After knocking off work, Tim could not settle down. His small flat felt lonely and claustrophobic. Instead of reaching for a book to read as usual, for once he opted for a long walk outside, enjoying the sea breeze in the cool of evening.

After suffering one mugging, Tim avoided darker areas. He strolled where dog walkers and night joggers populated the well lit esplanade. His footsteps gravitated towards *Chantel's Tea Parlour*, which was closed. He noted the light of an active security alarm blinked inside.

Hands in pockets, Tim drew out Xanthe's headband savouring a faint trace of her scent, as he held it to his nose. Perhaps he would see her in the morning, return it, and ask for another souvenir. Or would she think that was creepy and weird? He had so little experience of courting, he had no idea.

Within an hour, Tim smelt a hint of more rain on a sudden icy breeze gusting off the ocean. Made aware he had walked quite a long way to the cul-de-sac end of the esplanade, he turned for home.

Distracted by a billboard posted on a building site, Tim stopped in his tracks.

The sign announced a low rise block of eight units under construction. The units were designed to have storage and car parking on the ground floor underneath each residence. By the time Tim stood contemplating possibilities, rain pelted down and he became soaked to the skin.

Tim jogged back to his flat to keep warm. He peeled off his sodden clothes while looking up the relevant real estate website selling the new apartments.

Tim found units could be bought off the plan. Artistic depictions of spacious interiors fired his imagination. Judicious investments had grown his savings to a point where he could acquire one of the desirable homes. He knew the value of equity in ownership rather than paying dead rent, but until Xanthe, had never known a reason to give up his cheap and convenient flat.

Now he imagined having a decent home to offer. If Xanthe accepted him at all, for any length of time, he'd have known more happiness than he ever expected in his lifetime.

Tim immediately emailed the agents to book an appointment. He checked his available funds and researched home loans for how much he could borrow on his wage. The agents responded promptly.

"You are wise to secure early. We expect the remaining units to go like hot cakes."

"I can well understand that. Have many sold?"

"Yes. Five are spoken for. There are two in the back row still available and one in front on the north east corner. Of course, the front one commands a premium price for having a wrap around patio enabling the better views."

By the following evening, Tim Fun had dibs on a swanky three bedroom home unit opening onto north and east facing patios with sea views. Holding cards close to his chest, his purchase would remain his secret for the time being.

Tim went to *Chantel's* the next morning. Rain had eased, so customers chose to sit outdoors in the sunshine. Relieved to find Xanthe alone behind the counter, he reluctantly returned the cherished scrunchie.

"I meant to return this yesterday but I forgot."

Xanthe swapped it for the rainbow striped she wore that day.

"You can keep this one if you like Timmy, to remind you of me."

He slipped the rainbow one over his wrist. Knowledge of his latest scrunchie fetish made Xanthe seem very insightful. He liked that his love was so clever.

"I'm sorry your dad caught me wearing the shiny brown one. I had to admit I'd taken it when I saw you that morning. I didn't say where we met."

"He knows I went to your flat. I said I ran out the back way so he didn't take it out on you."

"Xanthe. I went too far that morning and I'm sorry."

"I'm sorry I kissed you on the willy. I know you didn't like it." she whispered.

That comment made Xanthe seem less clever.

Chantel hurried out from the kitchen with a tray of fresh cakes and interrupted the conversation.

"Hello here's our favourite tenant. Good morning Tim."

"Hello and goodbye Chantel. I'm late for work. Sunshine is good for a change hey?"

Chantel and Xanthe watched Tim stride from the shop.

"Looks like Tim is coming out." Chantel said.

"More like going out isn't he?"

"No. Coming out of the closet."

"Huh?"

"Didn't you notice the rainbow band on his wrist? That's a gay symbol you know. He's going public about being gay as if it wasn't bleeding obvious."

"Wow. You know so much Chantel."

"Stick around Xanthe. I can teach you a thing or two about men and cooking." Chantel winked.

Xanthe like Chantel. It might be tricky if or when Tim's real status emerged. Xanthe changed the subject:

"Chantel, what if I didn't go back to school next year. Could I work here permanently?"

"I'd love that. Have you spoken about it to your parents?"

"Not yet. I was just thinking. I want to have a proper food career, but the school subjects are so general. I'd rather focus on what I really want to do."

"Well, I got my accreditation through TAFE courses in cookery and hospitality. I actually only did two years of high school, myself."

"Maybe I could juggle work and the study courses."

"I'd help you achieve that Xanthe. I'm already about to trial a new casual for when you are unavailable. So we could work around your schedule."

"Is she anyone I know?"

"She's a he. A nice young man named Sebastian Ornery."

"Oh. Well I don't know anyone by that name. Suppose he won't be wearing a little black dress."

"I've asked him to wear black if possible and I'll supply the white apron."

"Cool."

26

The Loophole

We've Been Had

Opal and Angus Bridcombe discussed Xanthe and Tim in the privacy of their bedroom, away from the pricked ears of curious offspring.

"Angus, I've been thinking. Xanthe could do a lot worse than Tim Fun. He's a decent sort."

"No coward either. He kept a level head under pressure dealing with that psycho."

"What really happened? I get the impression you haven't told the whole story."

Angus never could hide anything from Opal for long.

"I was stunned by the blast so close to my head. Tim thought I'd been murdered so he got the rifle and aimed to execute my killer. I came to my senses just in time to prevent him shooting the idiot."

"So Tim wanted to avenge you. That's loyalty."

"That's right. He held his nerve too, rock steady. No after shock dramas. Cool as a cucumber."

"He's got my respect." Opal said.

"Mine too. I agree Xanthe could do a lot worse. Now I'm hoping she doesn't go off him."

"Yes. I hope he waits for her too."

Xanthe's parents back-flipped with the idea they should encourage the romance. A quiet tapping on their bedroom door intruded on their inner musings.

"It's me Xanthe. Can I come in or do you need a minute?"

"Speak of the devil." Angus muttered.

"Come in Xanthe. What's up?"

"I want to tell you I've made a decision. I'd rather go to a tech college next year and focus on my foodie career."

The Bridcombe parents stared at their eldest. Opal wondered if Chantel put that idea into her head. Angus thought of the savings in not equipping her for school. The girls grew out of uniforms so fast, and they cost the earth. Opal sussed out any interference.

"Did Chantel talk you into this idea so she'd be able to keep you working in the tea shop?"

"It's completely my own idea, but I did ask Chantel for information."

"What sort of information were you given?"

"I asked how to become accredited. Chantel said she got her certificates or whatever through TAFE. It got me thinking that if I do the same, I could concentrate on what I want to study instead of wasting a year on stuff I won't use."

"Do you plan to keep on at *Chantel's* when you're not at college?"

"Yes. Chantel says I can continue part time and she'd work around my hours to help me achieve what I want. By the way, there are other people who want to work there and there's already a new casual on trial. So, I'm lucky to have a guarantee of steady employment."

Angus saw he would have one less allowance to provide on top of saving on school uniforms. It didn't seem wise to point out economic reasons to Opal. He only raised an enquiring eyebrow to his wife.

"I guess that bundle of papers under your arm supports your idea." Opal surmised.

"Yes Mum. I've done extensive research and earmarked the courses and schedules."

Xanthe laid out a sheaf of print-outs and brochures. Her parents took some time looking over it all. Angus identified one problem:

"How will you get to there? The nearest institute is half an hour away."

"I thought of that too. If Mum enrolled for the same courses, we could go together."

Opal felt a frisson of excitement for a new interest in her life. She could do it!

"I wouldn't mind having a go at further education. Knowledge is no burden." she said.

"Oh yes Mum. We could help each other, and sometimes I could cook for the family to give you a break."

"Now there's an incentive." Opal took to the idea ever more keenly.

Angus knew it would be no use arguing the point. Opal's excitement warmed his heart. He supposed her never ending mundane routine must be boring.

"Alright. Seems you've both got it all worked out." Angus agreed.

"So I can do it? Promise? Cross your hearts?"

"It's a good idea and you've worked hard on presenting it. So it's a yes Xanthe."

Xanthe gleefully kissed them both and ran to tell her sisters. They heard the twins squeal with delight. Opal remarked on the result.

"They sound very happy. Apparently, they were all in on this."

"As long as you're happy I am." Angus said.
Opal showed him how happy she felt.

The witching hour of the night worked its eerie magic. Opal suddenly sat bolt upright in bed. Angus rolled over sleepily.

"Is something the matter?"

"Angus. We've been had."

"What? How?"

"Xanthe won't be going back to high school. She got us to promise. So she's already finished there."

"So?"

"Think about it Angus."

"Those little buggers! They've pulled a swifty. I'm betting Lirah's bush lawyering is behind this."

"Lirah has a gift. If only she used it for good instead of evil." Opal sighed.

"Maybe she'll choose a law career when she leaves school."

"Kinta is always easily led by Lirah but obviously they're all in on it. Where do they get it from?"

"Think about it Opal." Angus countered with her own words.

"Hmm. We can't expect offshoots of the *poked club* to give up without a fight."

"And there's your answer. I rest my case."

"Now you sound like Lirah yourself."

"She is a smart cookie."

"Okay. It only means they've plotted a way for Xanthe to see Tim Fun romantically. And didn't we agree she could do worse?"

"Yes...but they're getting away with it. I suppose we can't renege?"

"No Angus. We can't expect them to keep promises if we break ours. Plus, I really want to do those study courses."

"You could go it alone."

"I don't want to go alone. I want to go with Xanthe so we can share the experience." Opal sulked.

Angus realised their conniving daughters had worked the clincher into the deal by involving their mother.

"Keep your knickers on Opal."

"That's not what you said earlier."

"I'm wide awake now. I think you should make us a nice cup of tea."

"Why me?"

"Because I'm the man and you're the woman."

Angus dared to jest in haste and got to repent at leisure.

27

Karma

Very Naughty

Sebastian Ornery arrived for his first day of work at *Chantel's* on his racer bicycle which he stowed in the backdoor porch. Dressed in skintight black biker shorts and a black t-shirt, he cut a trim figure.

The athletic young man tied a pristine white apron around his narrow waist, making a big bow at the back. He spun around and aped a fashion model pose. Xanthe liked his flamboyant behaviour, thinking he'd be a cheerful workmate.

"How do I look?"

"Spiffing." Xanthe smiled.

"You'll do." Chantel said.

Tim arrived for breakfast early. Before entering the tea shop, he drew Xanthe's rainbow band from his pocket and slipped it over his wrist. He wanted his darling girl to see he wore it.

Sebastian minced out from behind the counter to serve Tim as his test customer. The fabric wrist adornment drew his immediate interest.

"Ooh. What can I do you for?" Sebastian cooed.

"Pardon?"

"My little joke Sweetie. Seriously, I can recommend everything on the menu."

"Have you tried everything yourself?"

"I have actually." Sebastian waggled his eyebrows suggestively.

Surreptitiously monitoring the new boy's first dealings with a customer, Chantel and Xanthe shook their heads. His outlandish behaviour went a few steps too far. Fortunately, Tim copped the impertinence, and not someone else.

"I'll have a word with Sebastian." Chantel said.

"Okay. I'll try to placate Tim. He looks a bit miffed." Xanthe replied helpfully.

Xanthe jumped at the chance to take Tim outside to the front footpath, for a private conversation.

"Oh Timmy. You've won another heart." she laughed.

"Did Chantel say something about me being gay to the new boy?"

"I doubt it. But you're wearing my scrunchie like it's a bracelet and apparently rainbow colours signal being gay."

Tim ripped the band off his wrist and gave it back to Xanthe.

"Even so. That fellow is decidedly forward if you ask me." Tim huffed.

"Nevermind Timmy. Chantel is ticking Sebastian off right now."

"Good. Xanthe I need to talk to you. I know your parents don't approve of our close friendship."

"Mum and Dad think we'll go off each other in a year. They made me promise to cool it until I leave high school."

"That's twelve months away." Tim groaned.

"The good news is I have already left high school." Xanthe grinned.

"No! You mustn't abandon your education, Xanthe. I won't ever go off you. I promise to wait."

Xanthe explained the loophole Lirah noticed and about going to TAFE instead of school.

"Lirah came up with a diabolical scheme to bypass your parents' wishes?"

"Yes. Isn't she clever? She's the most wicked of us all. As you know, that is quite an achievement."

Tim struggled with approving the result.

"I want to be with you like mad Xanthe, but I don't like tricking your parents. Our ongoing relationship is too important to me. I don't want to lose their respect."

"But Timmy, Mum and Dad will get over it. They've always liked you a lot. Now they like you even more for saving Dad's life."

"Xanthe, it wouldn't be ethical to exploit the situation by twisting your parents' instruction. I want to keep their approval. Please see it from my position."

Xanthe would have argued the point except more customers turned up.

"Great. Now we have an audience. I guess we'll talk about this later in private."

Tim cringed as four young women arrived at *Chantel's*. He'd taken each of them out for dinner at different times. The nasty bunch had relayed Tim's inept overtures widely, providing a great source of amusement to some at the surf club. A sad-sack reputation for his lack of success with girls dogged Tim for years.

One of his past dud-dates smirked:

"If it isn't our funny boy. Trying out your famous chat lines again Tim?"

One mimicked a Tim Fun phrase they'd often laughed about... *if I may be so bold.*

"That's spot on to the fancy way he talks. He's such a scream." they squealed.

They fell about giggling. Tim's discomfort escalated when Sebastian walked outside to the footpath looking for Xanthe. He delivered a message from their boss:

"Chantel, bless her, says are you going to stand out here yakking all day? There's work to be done."

"I should go." Tim said. He didn't feel like eating breakfast anymore.

"Bye Sweetie. Don't be a stranger. Do come back soon." Sebastian blew a cheeky kiss before mincing back into the tea house. Chantel's talk hadn't touched the surface with the new boy.

The four unpleasant girls gaped with delight at this rich new gossip material. Their victim knew, unless he knocked it on the head immediately, he'd be linked with Sebastian in a gay relationship before the day was done.

To that end, Tim moved in close to Xanthe. He encircled her slim waist with loving arms and planted a passionate kiss on her lips. His beautiful girlfriend melted against him and eagerly prolonged the embrace.

"Oh, darling Timmy I've been longing to do that again. I love you so."

"Just a friendly reminder Xanthe. I'll wait for you."

"Me too. For you. I won't have to fight Lirah and Kinta off anymore either. They've promised not to jump you in bed ever again."

Agog, the catty girls eavesdropped unashamedly. Tim used their own taunt on purpose.

"If I may be so bold, they were both very naughty girls."

"I guarantee they didn't learn *that* in sex education at school. Anyway, they accept you're mine now Timmy. And I'll murder anyone who tries to steal you."

Xanthe's dark eyes blazed a warning to the nosy onlookers. Tim afforded the four speechless females a wink before swaggering away, hands in his pockets.

Buoyed with success, Tim detoured down the esplanade to see industrious work underway on the home unit block.

His upmarket new address would be eminently prestigious as *Number One at One The Esplanade*.

Life was good.

28

The Merry Season

She Could Do a Lot Worse

Christmas revellers were particularly well behaved that season. Only a handful failed breathalyser tests and only a few became abusive. Worst offenders spent a night in the odoriferous clink. Overall, however, Angus had a fairly easy time attending to yule tide duties, for once.

In two minds whether to say more to Tim about Xanthe, Angus pondered the situation during down times at work. On the one hand, he wanted to take responsibility. On the other hand, he didn't want to interfere with his daughter's so called *careful and subtle efforts.*

Tim could usually be found tapping away on one of the office computers, otherwise in the kitchenette making tea. One such tea break coincided with Tim and Angus bumping into each other there.

"What is that stuff you drink Tim?"

"Herbal teas. This one is ginger and lemon. Very healthful. You're welcome to try any of them."

"Yeah. Nah. But good for you taking care of your health. It shows. You could almost still pass for twenty-three."

The thinly veiled reference to his age made Tim decide he should clear the air about Xanthe.

"I guess you want to hear my intentions regarding your daughter. I'd be lying if I didn't admit to a strong attraction."

Angus thought Tim must be a mind reader. Perhaps those herbal teas did something other than smell like carpet cleaner.

"Tim. Xanthe imagines she is in love, but she is only sixteen. Young girls are inclined to be fickle and behave rashly."

"I am aware of it. Xanthe said you and Opal hope she grows out of her attachment to me."

"You obviously both feel strongly at the moment and we do understand that. We asked her to put romantic notions on hold and we ask the same of you. In your favour Tim, we also agreed she could do a lot worse."

A lot worse? Tim wondered what they compared him to. A geriatric? A political extremist? A serial killer? He stated his case with trepidation yet honestly:

"I only pray Xanthe would want me forever as I do her."

"Forever? That is ambitious given the risk that it's only a passing phase for Xanthe.   I predict difficulty in keeping the friendship platonic, but please never forget you're the liable adult in this, Tim."

"My intentions are honourable Angus."

"I trust they are Tim."

Angus knew even the best of intentions can fail where love and sex were concerned. Yet he'd said his piece and left it at that for the time being. He discussed the conversation word for word with Opal before bedtime.

"Oh Angus, tell me you didn't say she could do a lot worse. That would sound like a backhander to a sensitive person like Tim."

"Why? It's what we've said more than once ourselves."

Opal sighed because Angus didn't get it.

"Nevermind. But he said his intentions are honourable for a permanent relationship. It sounds like he might propose marriage."

"I'm sure he'll propose something anyway." Angus's reply smacked of sarcasm.

"Well, Xanthe could do a lot worse."

"There you go Opal."

29

Tim's Eventful Year

Rumour Has It

The eventful year Tim Fun turned twenty-nine shaped up as his best but also his hardest: A sea nymph named Xanthe rose from the ocean to captivate him: He survived a mugging and brain surgery and eventually recovered his memory: Fate granted an opportunity to save three good men who, in one way or another, put themselves out for him. He felt truly blessed to repay Wild Dog, Jarrah and Angus.

Within the same year, karma exacted small revenge on the Bill and Ben bullies from high school and the unkind back-stabbing females who used Tim as a meal ticket: On top of it all, he invested in a luxury new apartment with a sea view:

The hard part proved to be waiting and hoping to make Xanthe his own.

Tim wanted to buy Xanthe a Christmas gift. He would have liked to give her a friendship ring but a precursor to a possible engagement defied her parents' directive to keep it platonic. Instead, he chose a fine gold chain with a mermaid pendant, since the marine motif signified their first meeting in the sea.

The jeweller followed his instructions and bedded the delicate necklace securely in blue velvet, in a flat container that clearly did not look like a ring box. He knew the entire Bridcombe family would rattle it and read the gift tag, which simply said *To Xanthe from your friend Timmy.*

Tim pocketed the gift, and during breakfast at *Chantel's* he asked Xanthe if there were somewhere they could talk in private. Eager to steal some kisses, she took his hand and rushed him through the kitchen area behind Chantel's back, to the storage room.

"I'm already missing you Xanthe. But I'm leaving this morning to stay at my Aunt Fran's place for a week. I'll still be on call for work if they need me, and it's only an hour away."

Tim loved his Aunt Fran and owed her for his upbringing. Francis Funicular lived alone apart from her family of pedigree poodles and looked forward to her nephew's presence at Christmas time.

"Oh no! I won't see you for the whole week?"

"I can't let my aunt down, she'll have gone to a lot of trouble for my visit. "

Tim relished spending the week being spoiled rotten and reminiscing over his aunt's adventures. As a wedding celebrant, Miss Funicular officiated at some unusual events. Not the least being when DI Dougall Grimslade's daughter married. Back then, Francis narrowly avoided being murdered along with the rest of the double wedding party. *{cite The Peckish by Jo Milanne}.*

Angus's advice about young girls being fickle influenced Tim's next idea:

"Xanthe, please don't take this the wrong way, but I think you should use this week apart to explore your true feelings about us. I mean, ongoing with me."

Tim said it gently, hoping she wouldn't take it as a rejection and be hurt. Yet, angry tears stung Xanthe's eyes. Head high, she dropped Tim's hand and spun away, folding her arms.

"Okay. That's a good idea. Will you be investigating your own true feelings DC Funicular?"

Uh oh. Xanthe used a formal address instead of her fond nickname for him.

"Xanthe. I already know my true feelings."

"But apparently I don't know mine? Perhaps I'll kiss Sebastian for a comparison to judge you by."

Mutiny coloured both their faces. Tim hated thinking of Xanthe kissing Sebastian or anyone else. He challenged her exasperating threat.

"Good luck with that. I rather imagine he supports an opposing predilection."

"Nope. Sebastian only bungs on the gay act because Chantel came onto him on his first interview."

Tim knew that could be true since he'd resorted to the same strategy in a similar situation. Several objections sprang to mind.

"Why complicate your feelings with someone else Xanthe?"

"I can handle more than one thing at a time." she shot back.

"I'm not saying you can't, but I just want you to be sure about me being your one thing."

"And I'm just saying I need a comparison."

Provoked into staking his claim, Tim took a step towards her. She retreated a step. He took another step forward and her next backward step nudged her up against a solid table. Pinned, she had nowhere else to go.

The ghost of a smile flickered about Xanthe's mouth. Tim realised she toyed with his emotions to lure him into chasing her. Yet, he hungrily took the hook.

Maddened beyond his honourable intentions, Tim lifted her slim body, sat her on the table and moved between her legs in one deft manoeuvre. Xanthe eagerly met his lips with her own in shared greed. Her taunt to goad Tim worked like the charm she intended.

Lost in possessive passion, Tim hitched her dress up and began bumping a rhythm against the thin silk of her underwear as they kissed. Xanthe revelled in his heated reaction and frantic desire. She clung with her legs wrapped about him, urging him on.

A slight noise from the adjoining bathroom jolted Tim to his senses. They hadn't even closed the storeroom door. Relieved no one caught them indulging in the forbidden pleasure, Tim broke away suddenly. He fought to quell his desire, annoyed with himself for manhandling Xanthe.

"Oh no Timmy don't stop. I love when you take charge." she cooed.

Tim lifted her down from the table and straightened her skirt. He attempted to justify his actions:

"That's just a sample for your study comparison to judge me by." he panted.

"Timmy I don't want anyone else. How could you even think it?"

He might have said because he is a responsible adult, except his fierce loss of control denied that.

"My week away is a chance for a cooling off period." he persisted.

"I don't want to cool it Timmy. I would elope with you this very minute if we could."

Elope?

Tim presented Xanthe's Christmas gift shyly, his natural reserve at odds with his lustful behaviour.

"I got you this small token. I'll be thinking of you opening it on Christmas morning."

"Oh Timmy. You darling man. Mum and Dad said I mustn't give you anything personal. But there's a present for you from all of us under our tree. We'll give it to you when you get back."

"That will be New Years Eve."

"We'll all be together at the surf club party so we will bring our family gift for you then."

Reminded he was trusted to behave properly, Tim resisted a farewell kiss. Nevertheless, regaining some composure seemed too little too late.

"See you next week Xanthe. Give my best wishes to your family for a happy Christmas."

Before heading to Aunt Francis's place, Tim swung a detour to the end of the esplanade to check on his new apartment build. He stood outside the chainwire fencing admiring the work done so far. About to get back into his car, a couple of cheerful voices hailed him.

"Tim! Good morning. Ah look out. Sorry the dogs are over excited today."

A boisterous whippet hurled himself at Tim for a pat and a feisty toy poodle sunk his teeth into Tim's shoe. Both dogs had come from Francis Funicular's kennels. She bred the poodle and re-homed the whippet whose owner passed away.

"Speak of the devils. I'm just off to my Aunt Francis's place for Christmas." Tim laughed.

His friends, Ethan and Tiffany Birdwhistle hurried to leash the dogs.

"We bring them up here for a free run on the beach, but the little buggers took off when they saw you."

"No harm done. Nice to be admired."

Tiffany eyed Tim speculatively.

"Rumour has it you're fighting off a bunch of admirers lately."

The gossip mongers had wasted no time in spreading tittle-tattle. Ethan joined in the ribbing:

"All three of the Bridcombe sisters. Wow Tim. Who'd have thought?"

"The rumours may be greatly exaggerated. Furthermore, talk is cheap. " Tim blushed scarlet.

"Hey mate. I fully understand. Tiff was still at school when we first got together."

Tim made no reply other than an evasive hand gesture. He estimated Ethan to be only about five or six years older than Tiffany. His own age gap with Xanthe was more than twice that.

Ethan bustled their dogs into the car while Tiffany tidied her wind-blown hair and reapplied strawberry lip balm.

"So what brings you to this neck of the woods Tim? Thinking of buying into these new apartments?"

"It seems a good investment." he hedged.

"For sure." Ethan agreed. "Anyway, back to work for us. Have a merry Christmas and say hello to Francis from us. Tell her we're still married, ha ha, and that Frou Frou Pebbles and Noodle are doing well."

Mischievous antics frequently earned Birdwhistles' poodle a less complimentary F prefix. Tim ruefully regarded the teeth marks in his good leather shoe, but he felt too happy to bother about it.

Taking a final look at the building site, Tim left on a high note, ever more hopeful he'd not reside there alone, because Xanthe had said she'd elope with him if she could.

30

Aunt Francis

I Suppose She's Dead Ugly

Francis Funicular and her family of poodles greeted Tim with unleashed enthusiasm. He'd brought a bagful of doggy treats and gifts to go under the Christmas tree.

The experienced dog owner protected the tree with poodle-proof portable metal panels, otherwise the tree and gifts would all be shredded in no time.

"You're looking very well Timothy after suffering such a hard year. I feared we might never enjoy another Christmas together."

"All in the past Aunty Fran. I wish you were spared that worry but I am feeling on top of the world now. You are looking wonderful yourself."

Tim and Francis easily settled into their familiar relationship. Before long, the wedding celebrant had her nephew in stitches chortling over amusing wedding events.

"By the way, the two Birdwhistle couples remain happily married and their dogs are thriving on the extended love as well."

"Most marriages I've validated do last. I received Christmas cards from the Birdwhistles and many others I've joined in matrimony."

"Not holy matrimony?"

"Some pairings are decidedly unholy my dear." Francis laughed. "But it is not for me to judge."

Tim used her comment to lead into a topic he wished to discuss.

"Do you get many couples who have wide differences in their ages?"

"Oh yes. Many do. Particularly mail order brides to elderly men."

"Goodness. Does that still go on?"

"Always has and probably always will."

"How about within our own cultural norms?"

"Oh yes very often there are wide age differences."

"Really? What are some broad differences you've encountered?"

"Ten, fifteen even twenty years is quite common."

Francis knew her nephew well, and savvied to a reason for his curiosity.

"So Timothy my dear, any news you want to share with me?"

"Like what?" his blush gave him away.

"Have you met someone interesting?"

"I have actually." he admitted.

Tim rose from his armchair. Hands in his pockets, he paced the room. Francis sensed his anxiety.

"Is there an age gap that concerns you?"

Tim thought his aunt must have second sight.

"There is."

"Okay. That needn't be a problem though. How many years?"

"Sixteen."

Francis imagined an older woman easily seducing her shy nephew. He'd never been popular at school and apparently lived a secluded bachelor existence. She attempted to mitigate:

"Well. If you're happy knowing a forty-five year old partner rules out having children with her..."

"No Aunty, she isn't sixteen years older. The girl is only sixteen years old herself."

Francis breathed a sigh of relief. She imagined Tim had come out of his shell at long last, and been sufficiently enamoured to woo the teenager.

"Oh! How lovely for you my dear. What's her name?"

"Xanthe Bridcombe. I know all her immediate family. Her father is a police sergeant. We work out of the same station."

"Do her parents approve?"

"Conditionally. Of course they demand we limit our...um...liaison for the time being."

"I see. I guess you find that difficult?"

"Very."

Tim went on to tell how he'd saved Angus's life and the obligation to honour his trust.

"Here I am believing you have a nice safe desk job while you're off gun fighting."

"It just happened. Probably a one-off. I do spend the majority of my time on computer research."

Francis realised her nephew had really come of age.

"What are your hopes with Xanthe?"

"I want to marry her."

"Is she of the same mind?"

"Well, she says she'd elope with me right now if she could."

Francis wondered if Tim hoped she'd legalise an elopement.

"Aah... I should tell you a person must be eighteen to marry without parental consent."

"I hope Xanthe's parents will consent."

"Timothy my dear, she has to be seventeen to marry even with their consent."

"I'll turn thirty in the year she turns seventeen. Even if they agree."

"Goodness me Timothy. Thirty isn't old. It's an ideal age for a man to marry. Are you seriously thinking of eloping?"

"No. That is simply not a viable option. Also, going ahead, I hope to maintain a healthy relationship with her family."

Tim felt downcast. The wait of another year already seemed a lifetime away and could drag on.

"You're allowed to see her I gather?"

"Yes, but only as just friends. She is not allowed to come to my flat anymore."

Anymore? Francis fairly accurately pictured a reason for that.

"Enjoy this innocent time together to get to know each other's minds." Francis smiled.

"I tried to be sensible by suggesting my week down here could be a cooling off period."

"Did Xanthe think that made sense?"

"Nope. Got me into all sorts of trouble."

Francis smiled her understanding.

"Your day will come. Have you made plans towards the future?"

"I'm buying a beach side apartment. It's in a block of eight still under construction. Completion is scheduled within weeks. I haven't told anyone else about it yet."

"Perfect. An autumn wedding perhaps. It's my favourite season of the year."

"I live in hope her parents give consent. In any case if it doesn't happen, I will be moving into the place by myself."

"Xanthe is a very lucky young woman to have you Timothy. I can't wait to meet her."

"Thanks for your support Aunty Fran. It means a great deal to me."

"I suppose she's dead ugly." Francis joked.

"Hideous." he grinned.

31

The Heat Is On

Supreme Irony

Francis had New Year celebrations planned with her dog club and Tim looked forward to a special end of year bonfire party at his surf club. He returned home from his aunt's place on New Years Eve. His first stop was to see if Xanthe was at work in the tea parlour.

Chantel's was open but not busy. He'd missed out on meeting Xanthe who'd taken the afternoon off. Sebastian seemed particularly glad to see him.

"Tim Fun! How providential. Will you be attending the bonfire party? I have something you might like to see." he smarmed his last sentence suggestively.

Sebastian's waggling eyebrows made Tim's skin crawl. He snapped a brief and barely polite reply.

"What is it then?"

"Big surprise. All will be revealed. See you later."

Sebastian's annoying attempt at mystery was dismissed. If Tim's private comment bubble could be read, it said: *What a jerk. Thanks for the warning. I'll make a special effort to avoid the creep.*

Meeting up with Xanthe at the beach party filled Tim's mind. He rushed home to shower and get ready. Anticipating New Years kisses, he lavishly spritzed his face with fresh lemon scented aftershave.

Xanthe threw herself into Tim's arms when he arrived at the beach, only just before Lirah and Kinta did the same. The three sisters kissed his cheeks and the twins punched his arms amiably.

The gossip mongers at the surf club read a lot more into Tim Fun's triple Bridcombe greeting. They nudged each other and sniggered amongst themselves. *Told you so. He's got all three on the hook.*

"Wow. You smell as good as you look." Kinta said.

"Lemon or lime." Lirah stuck her nose against his cheek again to identify the scent.

Xanthe whispered in his ear while pretending to sniff the aftershave.

"I could eat you alive." she said.

"You must like lemons." he replied.

"I like yours."

She fingered her mermaid pendant with a cheeky grin. Somehow, that reminded Tim of being groped underwater.

Opal and Angus exchanged helpless shrugs witnessing their daughters' wild hellos. They welcomed Tim more sedately.

"He's already fitting in with the family." Opal said in an aside to Angus.

"I'll be more impressed if he sticks to his undertaking to keep it platonic." Angus replied dourly.

Opal stuck up for Tim.

"Xanthe said he wanted her to use his week away as a cooling off period. That's sounds well principled to me."

"Maybe he's going off her."

"I doubt it. But I sincerely hope not."

Tim had never felt more accepted than sitting with the five members of the Bridcombe family at the bonfire party. They presented him with their Christmas gift, a beautiful tapestry bound book of classic quotes by famous people.

"I love it!" Tim almost teared up.

"Mum and Xanthe picked it." Kinta smiled.

"I reckoned it'd be good for a nerd like you too." Lirah added.

"We're all happy you like it Tim. Aren't we Angus." Opal prompted.

"I'm beside myself." Angus replied.

Tim sat between the twins instead of next to Xanthe. It wouldn't do to be tempted into touching each other. When the countdown rang in the New Year, skyrockets exploded plumes of stars which rivalled lightning flashes far out to sea.

Opal and Angus embraced in the traditional kiss. The twins snaffled surprised boys they knew from school who couldn't believe their luck. Aware of being watched, Tim and Xanthe reined in their fervour and kissed chastely. Distant thunderclaps echoed to their quickening heartbeats.

The Bridcombes left for home soon after the final notes of Auld Lang Syne were sung. People hurried to pack up when heavy raindrops splattered the beach and the bonfire hissed and steamed.

Sebastian Ornery had kept an eye on Tim Fun throughout the party celebrations. The impending storm fitted in with his plans very well. He waved and made a beeline towards his mark. Tim cursed it was too late to pretend he hadn't seen the nuisance. He'd ably avoided Sebastian all night by sitting within the cocoon of Xanthe's family.

"Looks like a storm coming. Don't suppose you could give me a lift home Tim? I've only got my push bike and I left it at the tea house."

Tim couldn't get out of it in the circumstances. Following directions, he drove Sebastian to his family's home ten minutes inland from *Chantel's* tea parlour.

"I've got my own bedsit over the garage. Come up for a minute so I can show you that thing I talked about earlier."

"Can it wait for another time?"

"Depends on how serious you are about Xanthe."

A darker tone of voice and Sebastian's mention of Xanthe sounded ominous. Suspecting some wrong, Tim surreptitiously pressed record on his phone as he stepped from his car. The practised move had been honed during detective surveillance training.

Once inside a small sitting room, Sebastian clicked his TV on and started a video playing.

"By the way, I've made copies."

Tim blanched at the display of himself humping Xanthe in the storeroom of the tea house. The close contact made it appear full copulation took place.

"You fucking pervert!" Tim yelled.

For the second time in his life, Tim physically attacked another person. He smashed a fist into Sebastian's leering face. Surprised at the painful response that bloodied his nose, Sebastian fell back onto his sofa. He had imagined Tim would be more of a wimp.

Angered by the instant reprisal, Sebastian increased his taunting:

"Ooh Timmy don't stop." he mimicked Xanthe's voice. "She's like a bitch on heat hey."

If Tim could execute Sebastian Ornery on the spot, he would do so without a qualm. Yet the icy intent stilled him into disguising his wrath.

"There are stiff penalties for filming people without their knowledge." Tim said coldly.

"Oh sure. And you want everyone to see this. How will it go down with Xanthe's charming family?"

"What do you expect to gain out of this."

"Hmmm. I was going to let you off lightly until you hit me. Let's start with me having a go with Xanthe. If you arrange that to my satisfaction, I'll decide how much money I want afterwards."

"You're exacerbating your perversion with blackmail."

"Congratulations. You figured it out. So how much is it worth to keep this cute little film clip off social media?"

"You won't do that without damning yourself."

"You think not? I have any number of fake accounts." Sebastian sneered. "It won't be traced to me."

Having no option but to believe him, Tim shrugged as if he didn't care. He pretending to capitulate:

"Very clever. Alright Sebastian. Leave it with me." he faked nonchalance while inwardly seething.

Sebastian congratulated himself for pulling off the extortion. He had a copy of the video for Tim so he could be reminded why he must obey.

"Hang on, before you go, here's your own copy so you can watch it again and get your rocks off properly. Little cracker isn't she?"

Sebastian selected a USB drive in a plastic packet and handed it over. Tim couldn't wait to get out of there to check the success of his own covert recording.

Grateful to find he'd caught the blackmailer's incriminating speech, Tim revelled to the sound of his fist connecting with Sebastian's smarmy face as well.

Tim knew he must share this embarrassing problem with Dougall Grimslade as soon as possible. Since New Years Day morning would be downtime for most people, Tim waited until late afternoon before phoning.

"Dougall. Sorry to bother you today of all days, but I find myself beset with a pressing problem."

Dulcy heard her husband's heaved sigh and saw his grimace. She shamelessly listened in to his side of the conversation. Dougall waggled a finger at her in pretended reprimand.

"Does it involve Angus Bridcombe?" he asked.

Dougall could not forget the last debacle when he'd deflected a punch meant for Tim.

"Indirectly, only I am totally at fault this time. I'm afraid the issue is extremely personal."

"Better tell me about it."

"I'm threatened with blackmail by a staff member at *Chantel's*. He's filmed me with Xanthe Bridcombe in a compromising situation. Threatens to put it online if I don't comply with his demands."

"Where did this happen?"

"In the store room of the tea house. It was a spur of moment lapse for me after a slight argument with Xanthe. I went after her possessively if you understand my meaning. We even left the door open."

"In a state of undress?"

Dulcy's ears pricked up.

"No but that isn't clear in the footage. Though I had pushed her dress up...and um...lost control."

"Tim Tim Tim. Nevermind. I've been there and done similar things in my misbegotten youth."

Dulcy raised an eyebrow. He'd explain later.

"Angus wouldn't be best pleased if he sees it."

Tim confessed he hoped for a permanent relationship with Xanthe when she reached a suitable age, and how he'd striven to gain her parents' approval. He choked on telling the blackmail demands made by Sebastian.

"Have you proof?"

"Yes. I've recorded the conversation on my phone."

"Then we've got him Tim."

"But he claims to have fake online accounts where he can post the video anonymously. If he does it, the damage will be done. Of course I'll prosecute regardless."

"The penalty is up to two years in prison for illegal filming, even without the other demands. Did you tell him that?"

"I told him there were penalties but it doesn't bother him. He is sure I won't want it made public. He is absolutely right about that."

"Hmmm. Tricky. Let me think about it. Do you want to come over for tea? Dulcy is warming a tasty casserole as we speak."

Dulcy took the cue. She rushed to take the beef casserole from the fridge, put it in the oven and set the table for three.

Tim drove over to the Grimslade's place after cautiously copying the phone recording to his lap top. He took Sebastian's flash drive supposing Dougall might need to see it, but hated having to provide his lustful performance as evidence.

Dulcy welcomed Tim with a kiss to his cheek.

"You've got Dougall intrigued. He's been doodling crime scene diagrams ever since your phone call. He hasn't said what it's all about by the way."

"It's about me being an idiot. Blackmail. Potential drubbings from Angus and Opal Bridcombe. I know Opal is your best friend Dulcy, but can you please keep this confidential?"

"Of course. Goodness. Now you have me intrigued as well."

Dulcy thought it couldn't be all that bad. Dougall emerged from his study and sat at the dining table.

"I apologise for bothering you today. Anyway I have this audio recording."

Tim set his phone on the table and played the conversation.

"What a sleaze!" Dulcy cried. "We definitely have to crucify this scum bag."

"Is that sound effect what I think it is?"

"Yes. I lost control. Again."

Tim flexed his sore knuckles. Dougall got the gist.

"Hmmm. I guess the film must be pretty graphic. Is it?"

The dreaded time had come to show the video. Tim sheepishly relinquished the storage device.

"I'll help with the dishes while you inspect the damage."

"No Tim. You should be present." Dougall insisted.

"No hurry. It will all go in the dishwasher later." Dulcy added.

NO! Tim realised his hosts would both view his disgrace. He'd have to grin and bear it, or grimace and bear it in this case.

Sebastian supplied a longer version for Tim's copy. It began when he first entered the store room with Xanthe, and ended with him rutting against her in abandoned gusto. Tim shrunk in humiliation, hiding his face behind his hands.

The Grimslades had witnessed far worse in the course of policing duties and approached the blackmail material in a profession-al manner. Nevertheless, their reactions were watered down for Tim's sake.

"Well that's not so bad Tim. But I can see how he could use it against you and Xanthe."

Dulcy analysed the scene.

"Obviously neither of you noticed him standing in the doorway."

In his angst, the action figure film star had overlooked the direc-tional aspect.

"Wait. He wasn't in the doorway. The shooting angle comes from the side wall that separates the bathroom."

"Aha. He had a handy little peephole in place. Now that changes everything." Dougall smiled like a crocodile.

"Why would he want to film inside the store room?"

"Tim Tim Tim. I excuse your inability to draw the obvious con-clusion due to the circumstance."

Dulcy got it but waited for the younger detective to catch up. Tim finally tumbled:

"That stinking pervert! He's been spying on the girls in the bath-room."

"But this time, he's used the reverse option." Dulcy confirmed.

"Initially, I say we nab him on a Peeping Tom charge. It will justify entering his premises and seizing his records." Dougall said.

"Guessing he keeps copies of everything to titillate himself later." Dulcy agreed.

"I am particularly sickened that he's used Xanthe like that. I hope he doesn't get to publish my shame on social media." Tim added.

Keen to take Sebastian down, the Grimslades needed no further persuasion.

"We have to move quickly and catch him by surprise."

"Okay. Here's what we do. I put Chantel in the picture and get her to file an immediate complaint about the peep hole. She should realise the culprit is the only male member of staff." Dougall said.

"You won't tell her about me and Xanthe will you?" Tim asked.

"No need Tim. I'll say you asked to use the bathroom and discovered the spy hole."

"Won't she wonder how I noticed it but none of the girls did?"

"Guessing you stand up to take a pee Tim. You'd be looking straight at it."

"Ah. Right. I just hope Chantel co-operates." Tim said.

"She will. Chantel has rather a thing for my man. Doesn't she Dougall darling?"

"Who could blame her." Dougall preened.

Not for the first time, Tim detected teasing ripostes between his senior colleagues.

Informed of Sebastian's offence, Chantel readily agreed to file a complaint. She'd been disgusted by discovery of the peep hole.

Disguised between cleaning products on a raised shelf over the toilet bowl, the aperture faced a large mirror above the washbasin opposite. The reflection allowed a full view of anyone using the toilet or changing clothes in the bathroom.

The storeroom side of the spy hole hid behind a picture card list of suppliers. Loosely attached by a string, it could be quietly pushed aside.

Accustomed to looking after herself, Chantel Chiron hid her newly formed revulsion of her male employee well. Dougall asked her to leave all as is until it could be photographed, and she delayed changing anything on the shelf in case the culprit be forewarned.

Armed with Chantel's official complaint, the Grimslades climbed a staircase to Sebastian's flat, and tapped on his door. The occupant answered their polite knock wearing only a pair of boxer shorts. It seemed he'd been sleeping.

Blearily preoccupied with scratching a sweaty armpit, Sebastian did not recognise the pair as police detectives. By their mode of dress, he took them to be bible bashers.

"Piss off. I'm not interested."

Dougall and Dulcy instantly flashed their IDs before he tried banging the door in their faces.

"Sebastian Ornery. We have a warrant to search your premises."

"Bullshit. Why?"

"Use your imagination. If you resist you will be arrested and removed."

"Resist this." he snarled.

Realising Tim Fun double crossed him, Sebastian played for time to exacted a spiteful revenge.

Bracing his hands against the sides of the doorway he kicked out with both feet. Dougall fell against Dulcy who stood slightly behind him. They stumbled down the stairs together breaking their falls somewhat by grabbing the handrails.

Delaying the search by attacking the Grimslades gave Sebastian an opportunity to publish Tim's embarrassing episode to social media. It only took a couple of clicks.

Dougall's first concern was for his wife.

"Are you hurt Dulcy?"

"Not much. You?"

"I'll survive."

Dougall whipped out his phone and called for back-up. Help soon arrived in the shape of three burly uniformed officers including Xanthe's father, Sergeant Angus Bridcombe.

The two vehicles, a black Mariah and a squad car scattered gravel as the drivers braked hard in the driveway. The support team barged up the stairs with an intention to break into the flat.

Sebastian opened the door in the nick of time. He tried shamming an innocent face.

"What's this? Don't tell me that doddering comedy act are actually real police? They couldn't even stay on their feet. What a laugh. I thought they were incompetent scammers out to rob me."

His act didn't fool any of the crew. Forced into the paddy wagon with his hands cuffed behind his back, Sebastian managed a smirk.

"I see you're amused. You find this funny?" Angus Bridcombe growled.

"My amusement will only be topped by yours." Sebastian sniggered.

Xanthe's father's reaction when he viewed her wanton performance would be priceless. Sebastian regretted he could only imagine it. Dougall Grimslade knew what amused their prisoner. He slammed the van doors to shut him up.

"He's just out to needle everyone. Let's not entertain him Angus."

"Right you are. Well, I should get back. Do you want one of the lads to stay and help carry stuff?"

"Despite being a doddering comedy act, I think we can manage thanks mate."

Dulcy had been most offended by Sebastian's remark.

"As you know, I'm only Opal's age."

"Nevermind Dulcy, anyone over thirty has one foot in the grave according to some younger generations. Ageism is rife these days."

"True. There's a lack of respect we didn't used to see." Dougall added

"Well, entitled youths will find out what it feels like if they live long enough. The only options are to grow old or die young." Angus replied.

Driving back to HQ Angus thought about Tim Fun's twenty-nine years compared to Xanthe's sweet sixteen. She'd be twenty-six when Tim was thirty-nine. That seemed okay but he couldn't see them waiting more than one year, let alone ten.

Sebastian Ornery was taken to the city correctional centre where he'd be held pending a hearing.

While the Grimslades took possession of computers, laptops, mobile phones and every storage device they could find, an elderly woman emerged from the main house. She gave her name as Mrs. Ornery.

"What's my worthless son done?" she demanded.

"Attacked police personnel while resisting an official order."

"Good. He can be your problem now." she went back inside and slammed her door shut.

Sebastian's confiscated devices turned up a variety of exploitation material and pornography. Technology experts unravelled his several false online media accounts and reported findings to the Grimslades. Possible charges amounted to far more than two years of prison.

Dougall informed Tim that his personal act with Xanthe had featured in Sebastian's latest public post.

"It wasn't up there for long. The tech team took all his offensive reels off social platforms. However, any of it may still be presented as evidence in a court case."

"And Angus was there with you today?"

"He headed the back-up team. The accused was arrested and taken away. It was over within minutes."

"If Angus testifies his part in court, as he so often does, won't he be able to view the video?"

"Faces are blurred to protect the victims."

"Always?"

"I believe so. I can request to have the video suppressed or at least muted. But your audio recording is a main exhibit since it's pivotal to the blackmail intentions, and he mentions Xanthe by name in that."

Ruing that the vital evidence to damn Sebastian Ornery could also damn themselves, Tim uttered a favourite quote by Robert A. Heinlein - *The supreme irony of life is that hardly anyone gets out of it alive.*

"You can't make omelettes without breaking eggs, Tim."

"How long before the case goes before a magistrate?"

"Due to the serious nature of offences, I'd say within five weeks."

32

The Virgins

Did You Have to Tell Everyone?

Considering his options, Tim could sweat it out for five weeks risking Angus seeing and hearing the evidence in court or simply preempt it by confessing.

Tim chose the latter.

Xanthe had to be told everything and agree with his decision. He met her at *Chantel's* before opening time.

"Hi Timmy. Guess what. Sebastian has been sacked! Chantel says he's been spying on us using the bathroom."

"Yes. I know, but I'm afraid there is more Xanthe."

Before Xanthe could reply, Chantel emerged from the kitchen, wiping her hands on a tea towel.

"Good morning Tim. I believe Sebastian is having the book thrown at him."

"He is in custody awaiting trial. Investigations found his perversions cover a wide range of illegal activities."

"I'm glad I could help. His sneaky peep hole is covered up now of course. He seemed such a nice young man too."

"You can never tell."

Chantel went back to kneading dough in the kitchen while Tim took Xanthe aside to tell her the worst.

"Xanthe I'm sorry to tell you, Sebastian secretly filmed us *almost* having sex in the storeroom, only it looks convincing. He showed me the video after the New Years bash. Our private moment looks so real he used it as a blackmail attempt. I refused to be coerced. So now it's going to be evidence."

Aghast, Xanthe paled. She remembered wrapping her legs around Tim and begging him to go on.

"NO! I even urged you on. Oh Timmy. What a disaster. Apart from Sebastian, how many others have seen us like that?"

"My senior colleagues had to be shown. I'm assured it was taken off the internet within a day or so."

"The internet! That means thousands will have ogled us." Xanthe cried.

"The techs say distribution was probably limited to a handful of voyeurs who subscribe to Sebastian's porn posts. An upside is, his readership links have interested special task forces. Hopefully they'll catch a few more offenders."

"Yuck. All those sickos getting off watching us."

"Don't fret too much. Apparently, our performance would be considered mild and boring compared to the usual level of content posted by Sebastian."

"Aren't we entitled to own that video ourselves because we are in it? We could destroy it."

"I doubt we'd be allowed since it constitutes evidence. Even if the footage is suppressed, there's vital audio that mentions your name."

"Dad testifies his arrests in court. He will see it all and go absolutely ballistic. What can we do?"

"The honourable path is for me to confess and throw myself on your father's mercy. I'm letting you know that is what I intend to do."

"Timmy, he won't show much mercy. But I will be by your side. I won't let you face him alone."

"No Xanthe. Best you stay out of it. It's all my fault and I blame myself."

"You must know I deliberately teased you by bluffing about kissing Sebastian."

"I'm the adult Xanthe."

Even after the tea parlour opened for breakfast, they bickered back and forth at every spare moment. Xanthe argued her father would be less inclined to violence if she were present.

"Timmy, if it came to blows that will be the end of any happy relationship between you and Dad."

Tim was adamant. He knew repercussions could last for years and ruin the family harmony, whichever path he chose.

"I've made up my mind." he said.

Tim went into work early and sat at his desktop computer. The Grimslades and Angus arrived soon after. Angus had the task of compiling his account of the Sebastian Ornery arrest. His big hands struck so many typos on a keyboard, he often narrated his input to Tim or Dulcy to type up. This time, Dulcy stepped in to do it.

"Keep it simple Angus. You only have to say you responded to our call for support and duly apprehended the perpetrator. The magistrate will ask if he or she wants to know more."

"Alright. For my own information can you fill me in on more details?"

"We were following up on a complaint that led to a blackmail attempt."

Tim knew the Grimslades were now on the spot for his sake. His chair scraped the floor as he hurriedly stood up and faced Xanthe's father.

"Please allow me to intervene at this point. Angus, the case involves me personally. The blackmail came out of an incident at the tea parlour."

"Chantel's place? That's where Xanthe is working."

"Yes. The man you arrested began working there recently. I'm afraid the incident also involved Xanthe."

"How exactly?" Angus's face grew stern.

Dougall butted in.

"The accused fashioned a peep hole between a store room and the bathroom. He apparently used it to spy on others, and also to video private acts."

Tim continued:

"I'm sorry to say Angus, I supplied reason to incite his blackmail attempt."

"Assuming with my daughter. What did you do?" Angus growled.

"I engaged in a close encounter with Xanthe. It appears worse on film than it actually was."

Angus glared at the Grimslades and Tim.

"You've all seen this bit of film that amounts to blackmail material. I want to see it."

"I'd rather you didn't." Tim said.

"I'd rather I did." Angus roared.

Dulcy stepped in.

"We hope to limit displaying visuals since Sebastian Ornery incriminates himself on audio footage Tim managed to achieve."

"Seems Tim managed to achieve more than that." Angus snarled.

"Angus. I only briefly lost control and succumbed to my great affection for Xanthe."

"Great affection. Is that what it's called nowadays."

Dougall explained further:

"The video is only graphic enough to scare the victim. Tim came to us to catch the blackmailer, and we have sorted it out."

"Yes and that's that. Now Angus let's get on with your statement." Dulcy tried to end the drama.

Angus would not be placated. He shouted:

"This is MY daughter you are talking about here!"

Tim changed his stance:

"Please don't withhold the evidence on my behalf. Despite my mortification, I concede Xanthe's father has every right to view the footage."

He hoped Dougall muted the soundtrack, so Xanthe's father did not hear her seductive teasing. Before showing the evidence, Dougall sent Dulcy and Tim to investigate another outside case, so he could speak to Angus alone.

"Angus mate. I was forced through my job to view my own daughter in comprising situations. It still haunts me. So I strongly advise you to avoid watching that blackmail footage."

"It's that bad is it?"

"No. Dulcy agreed it wasn't too bad. But then we are not Xanthe's parents."

"I need to discuss this with Opal."

"That's a good idea. Go home and talk it over."

Angus gritted his teeth, jammed his hat back on and drove home.

He found Opal standing on a chair, dusting the ceiling fans.

"Back so soon? Did you forget something?"

"No. Better put the kettle on Opal. There's a serious matter we need to discuss."

"What about?"

"Xanthe and Tim. You'd better get down off that chair."

"Uh oh. What have they done?"

"What we feared they would do. Not only that, but they were covertly filmed by a blackmailer."

"NO!"

"It was done by that prick I arrested who pushed the Grimslades down the stairs."

"Have you seen the video yourself?"

"No that's what we need to talk about. Dougall advises us not to watch it. Of course his experience of Isla's abduction was horrible."

"Has Dulcy seen it?"

"Yes. She thinks it isn't too bad. Can you phone her about it Opal? I reckon she'll give you a straight answer."

Dulcy picked up on the first ring. She'd been expecting this.

"Hi Opal. Guessing you want to know about that blackmail video."

"How bad is it?"

"Remember schoolies week when we were seventeen? It's like when you got Angus alone in our holiday house."

"Um. You might need to be more specific."

"The kitchen table thing you described?"

"Dammit! That's how we made Xanthe."

Angus heard his wife's side of the conversation.

"Well that's crystal clear. How about we bring the culprits in for a stern talk before the twins get home."

The twins were still on school holidays but were on a sleepover at a girlfriend's pillow fight party.

Tim and Xanthe were interrogated, embarrassed and separated that very evening. Angus allowed Opal to begin chastising the pair:

"Did you even consider pregnancy as a consequence?"

"Be wonderful if I got put up the duff by what we only did. There'd have to be some perks in the second immaculate conception." Xanthe retorted scornfully.

"Up the duff? Where do you learn such crude terms?"

"Catholic school Mummy."

"Keep a civil tongue in your head Xanthe." her father warned.

Nevertheless, her parents wanted to believe in their daughter's innocence. Tim spoke up.

"Ahem. The footage is misleading. What happened was…um…a dry run. We were not unclothed. It was all my fault. I got carried away."

"Oh Timmy. You can't take all the blame. I taunted you."

Angus and Opal could well imagine their forward daughter doing just that. Angus couldn't let it go.

"Tim you were trusted to behave properly. Xanthe is only sixteen!"

"Well Daddy, I am still a virgin at sixteen, and Timmy is still a virgin too."

A crimson blush flooded Tim's face. His humiliation intensified a hundred fold.

"Oh my god Xanthe! Did you have to tell everyone?"

"Why not? Do you think it's shameful for guys to be virgins but it's a virtue for girls?"

"No I...but it's also a matter of..." he didn't want to mention his age.

The Bridcombe parents perceived Tim Fun to be the more vulnerable partner in the equation. Thus, he emerged an even better prospect as a son-in-law. Opal addressed her daughter:

"So Xanthe. What are your intentions towards Tim?"

Before Xanthe replied, Tim cut in:

"Excuse me Opal. If I may be so bold. As the man, I should declare my intentions first."

Whoa! Angus gave Tim credit for crossing Opal. He eyed his feisty wife waiting for her indignation to erupt and shoot Tim down in flames. But Xanthe riled up first.

"Timmy! You must not override my mother's question."

"Xanthe. I am merely stating how it should be. I happen to prefer the chivalrous way."

"How it should be? You mean as the man you get to decide."

"No Xanthe. My way, a woman is given first option to reject an offer. If it were the other way around, the woman risks a loss of pride by having her bid turned down. It is a long standing tradition for a gentleman to declare his intentions first."

"Bull. Where is this written? You're just making up a sermon like a stuffy old book nerd." she cried.

Stuffy old book nerd! Xanthe's put down on top of having his virginal status announced galled Tim.

He became very hot under the collar.

"And you are spouting off like an immature sixteen year old."

"It didn't stop you coming after me for my body. Now you accuse me of being immature."

"Your behaviour is. I'm surprised you don't stamp your little feet. Furthermore Xanthe, if you aspire to my continued respect, please never contradict me in front of others."

A grudging admiration grew in Angus's estimation of Tim Fun. Xanthe stormed out and slammed the door to the girls' bedroom.

"Well done Tim. That sorts her out. Sometimes a man has to put his foot down." Angus grinned.

"I apologise for airing grievances. My emotions got the better of me. No offence was intended."

Tim bowed slightly to Opal who set her jaw and sided with her daughter.

"I thought you were different Tim Fun. Now I see you're just another big dick."

Tim bit his tongue on an inadvisable reply. Opal stormed out and slammed her bedroom door.

Angus shrugged his wife's outburst off, and took two ales from the fridge.

"Can I buy you a beer Tim?"

Tim abstained from alcohol, but in this case he accepted readily, and even drank it straight from the stubby bottle. Angus burped and asked the question:

"So what are your intentions towards Xanthe?"

"I'm not sure that is still relevant."

"She'll get over it. So will Opal."

"If they do get over it. I'd ask for Xanthe's hand in marriage when she is of age of course."

"You got my blessing Tim. I reckon she could do a helluva lot worse."

"Thank you. I think."

The next morning at police headquarters, the Grimslades were astounded to see Angus and Tim getting along like best mates.

The irony was not lost on Tim that he'd gained Angus's approval but lost Xanthe's and Opal's,

Angus congratulated himself on separating Tim and Xanthe at least for the time being, so he could relax for a while. He advised Tim not to crawl to her.

"Xanthe is just like Opal. Let her see your empty chair and give her time to regret it."

Tim already missed Xanthe, but he respected Angus's experience so took his advice.

Angus hadn't mentioned Sebastian's video again and Dulcy and Dougall could not contain their curiosity.

"Seems you and Angus came to an amicable agreement Tim."

"At great expense. We're both in the doghouse now with Xanthe and Opal."

Dulcy didn't pry further only because she'd get the full story from Opal, who happened to phone at that very moment.

"Speak of the devil. I was just thinking of you Opal."

"Bloody men Dulcy! They're all big dicks."

"You've never complained about that before." Dulcy laughed.

"I'm past seeing the funny side Dulcy, and you know what I mean."

"Okay. I have an idea this is about Angus and Tim since they are acting like good buddies."

"They all bloody stick together. Angus sided with Tim against me and Xanthe. I could hear them chatting and laughing about it while they guzzled beer. And Xanthe is heartbroken. If only I could have warned her but teenaged girls never listen."

Opal bent Dulcy's ear for a good half hour.

33

Moving On

Woman to Woman

Tim continued surfing in the mornings, but on Angus's advice, stayed away from *Chantel's*.

Xanthe maintained her aloof stance. She rehearsed serving Tim's breakfast without a word. In her imagination, she'd sashay away wriggling her hips. She might even flirt outrageously with other male customers. Alas, she didn't get to perform her fantasy pantomime because Tim didn't show up.

Just as Angus predicted, Xanthe regretted seeing Tim's empty chair at the tea house. She began to replay her part in the split and grudgingly owned some tiny fault could be hers.

Tim's landlady, Chantel Cheron, still believed him to be gay. Not privy to the blackmail video Sebastian made, she had no idea Tim and Xanthe were in love.

Chatting while busily working, Chantel casually mentioned Tim had given a months notice on renting the cheap flat. Xanthe did not welcome the news.

"Tim's leaving?"

"Apparently he is and we're sorry to see him go. He's been an excellent tenant."

"Did he say why?"

"Just said he is moving on. He's smart enough to get promoted. Maybe he took a better job offer in the city or overseas. He expressed interest in travelling before he got mugged."

Chantel prattled on while Xanthe's world fell apart. Suddenly her tiny admission of fault grew into a monster.

NO! I've lost him! I blabbed that he's a virgin then I called him a stuffy old book nerd. I argued with him in front of my parents! How could I be so stupid and insensitive.

Xanthe managed to get through her day in a state of numbed shock. The twins heard all about the altercation. Their older sister kept them awake at night with her anguished crying.

"I wish I never said all that stuff now."

"Maybe you can say you had your period?" Lirah suggested.

"Too late for excuses. I've lost him." she sobbed.

"No Xanthe. Tim loves you. It's just a storm in a teacup." Kinta sympathised.

"He's leaving the flat. Chantel thinks he took a promotion and maybe it's overseas."

"Dad hasn't said anything about that."

"No but he's been going around whistling and seems pretty happy." Lirah said.

"Bet he knows Tim is going away and that solves one problem."

"We could ask Mum. They seem to be talking again. He'd tell her if Tim applied for a transfer."

"Mum is going to go on and on lecturing me." Xanthe mourned.

"We'll ask her so you don't have to." Kinta offered.

The twins tackled their mother when she drove them in to the school bus stop.

"Mum. Xanthe says Tim is moving away overseas. Is that right?"

"First I heard of it." Opal replied. "Hurry up, here comes the bus."

That night Xanthe analysed the result.

"Mum and Dad might want to keep it from me." Xanthe said.

"Why would they?"

"In case I run to him and do something before he gets away. Actually maybe I will!"

"Uh oh. But it looks like he has dumped you Xanthe. Are you sure you still want to do that?"

"I've never been surer."

Xanthe marched down the footpath towards Tim's flat and caught a glimpse of his car turning into the esplanade. Sebastian's bicycle remained in the back of the tea house. Xanthe borrowed it to cycle after Tim, knowing he couldn't have gone far since the road he took ended in a cul-de-sac.

Tim had kept his new apartment purchase secret, wanting the place to be totally finished before showing Xanthe around. He had basic furniture and appliances installed and arranged to meet an interior designer to advise on window coverings and final touches.

The decorator he hired via email, arrived soon after he opened the patio doors to air the place out. The professional turned out to be an elegant woman in her forties. They exchanged polite greetings.

"My husband would have come too but he had another appointment. Anyway, I've brought a lot of ideas and product samples."

Stopping opposite Tim's car parked on the roadside, Xanthe could see Tim and the attractive woman inside the home unit. Their voices could be heard off and on as they wandered around the rooms. The woman spoke with enthusiasm and Tim's answers sounded agreeable. He'd stocked his fridge with refreshments in preparation for this visit.

"Would you like a cold drink? I have sparkling water or iced tea."

"Iced tea would be lovely, thank you. It's so hot out isn't it? These wide glass doors are lovely for the view, but I would consider block out blinds for times when you need to keep the temperature at a comfortable level indoors."

"That's a good idea."

The woman expounded keenly over more practical and artistic ideas.

Xanthe believed Tim to be entertained in a beautiful woman's up-market apartment. Furthermore, he seemed very familiar with the place. The open plan allowed a view through to the kitchen, where she spied Tim helping himself to something from the fridge.

Broken hearted, Xanthe forced her leaden legs to cycle back to the tea parlour.

Xanthe bawled it all out to the twins in their bedroom that night.

"They were acting really chummy. He's obviously been there before."

"So, you're not going to do it with him now?"

"There's no point even trying. He's going for this woman who looks like a fashion model."

"You're beautiful too Xanthe." Kinta said kindly.

"I know. But I called Timmy a stuffy old book nerd and he said I was immature."

"Too bad Xanthe. Now he's set his sights on a more mature woman." Lirah said unnecessarily.

Tim hungered for Xanthe's love so desperately he requested *Unchained Melody* be played on local radio. He bit the bullet by asking for it to be dedicated to Xanthe from Tim. No one heard it except her parents who had the radio in their bedroom tuned in.

"Tim has declared publicly!" Angus exclaimed.

"The poor boy. He is so lovesick." Opal felt sorry for Tim.

"Do you think Xanthe heard it?"

"No. I can hear them nattering as usual. By the way, the girls seem to think Tim might be moving overseas. Could that be right?"

"Not that I know of. Maybe he's just planning a holiday cruise."

"I guess he'd need to get away. Xanthe has broken his heart."

"I reckon they'll mend their fences. We always do." Angus kissed his wife.

"But you're a pushover my darling."

"According to you I'm a big dick too."

"Mmm. There is that."

When Tim moved into his new home, he hadn't seen Xanthe for over three weeks. He imagined showing her around. Perhaps he'd carry her over the threshold as practice for when they married…IF they married. Plagued by doubts, Tim now felt insecure about Xanthe even wanting to see him again.

Every night, Xanthe poured out her grief to her sisters who tried to make her feel better. Kinta was better at it than Lirah.

"He isn't serious about that model if he is going overseas." Kinta argued.

"She might travel with him. By the looks of her apartment, she is well off." Xanthe replied.

The sensitive gene skipped Lirah:

"Don't blame yourself for losing him Xanthe. A gorgeous rich bitch is a hard act to follow."

"Tim has only taken her on the rebound anyway. You're his true love Xanthe." Kinta sympathised.

Xanthe considered which twin might be closer to the truth.

"I so wanted to be Timmy's first. I really hate that model sheila for taking advantage of his innocence. Maybe I should just go and give her a piece of my mind. I'll tell her I am his first love, and he is just using her to get over me."

"Do you want us to come as back up?" Lirah hoped to be invited.

"No. I will face her woman to woman."

When Xanthe set her jaw and blazed her eyes, she looked exactly like her mother.

34

Having Fun

Howling at the Moon

Xanthe chose to confront the *other woman* very early on a Sunday in order to catch her at home. Planning ahead, she'd ridden Sebastian's bicycle home the day before.

"Where did this bike come from?" her police sergeant father asked.

"It belongs to Sebastian. I'm borrowing it."

"Well, he won't be needing it for a long time." Angus shrugged. *The bastard owes her anyway.*

Xanthe cycled to the apartment with the wind in her hair. Her lips moved rehearsing the scathing speech she'd make to the despised *boyfriend thief.*

Leaving the bike propped against the front of the building, Xanthe entered via an open ground floor foyer and climbed the stairs to the door of Number One The Esplanade. Xanthe psyched herself up:

She thinks she is number one. Well she isn't. I saw Tim first. I will always be number one.

Tim had just rolled from his bed ready to hit the surf when he heard the knock on his door. He couldn't be more surprised or pleased to see who stood outside.

"Xanthe!"

"Tim! What are you doing here? No don't tell me. So where is the she?"

"Who? How did you find this place?"

"Think you're so smart don't you Tim Fun. Well I've seen you in there with that old tart."

"What old tart? I don't know who or what you're talking about."

Tim's blatant denial and early morning presence in the woman's home mocked what Xanthe planned to say. Thwarted in her quest, she could only choke out a last goodbye:

"So that's it. You've made your choice. Goodbye forever Tim Fun."

Xanthe turned to run but Tim grasped her wrist and held on firmly. He had an idea her wires were somehow crossed, and he wasn't prepared to let her go.

"Xanthe Bridcombe. I'm arresting you." he said sternly.

"You are not! On what charge?" she cried.

"Stealing."

Tim picked her up bodily, slung her over his shoulder and carried her inside. He deftly kicked the door shut with his foot, the only part of the threshold crossing that went as he'd envisaged. The rest of the act didn't go exactly to plan either, since Xanthe struggled and beat his bare back with her fists.

"I haven't stolen anything. That bike is borrowed."

"You've stolen my heart Xanthe."

For want of a better place, he dumped her on his rumpled bed and straddled her body until she calmed her wild cat act down.

"Let me go! This makes me sick being in HER bed where you've been with HER."

"It's MY bed Xanthe. I haven't shared it with anyone."

"YOUR bed? So you even have your own room here?"

"This is my apartment."

His apartment? But...

"Anyway no matter whose apartment this is, I saw you with that conniving female." she added lamely.

"When."

"I saw you drive down this way so I followed you."

"The only female who's been here is an interior decorator. If you want to expand your detective skills Xanthe, you'll find her hefty invoice on the kitchen bench. I wanted this place to be perfect before you saw it."

Xanthe's heart overflowed. For once she didn't mind being wrong.

"I stole your heart?"

"Yes Xanthe. I guess you didn't hear the song I had played for you on the radio."

"No. I didn't. What was it?"

"Unchained Melody."

"I love that melody and the lyrics of that song. Have you really hungered for my touch Timmy?"

"Yes really. I've been starving to have you Xanthe."

"Me too. I yearn to be with you Timmy. I've missed you so much."

"This place will never feel complete without you in it Xanthe."

They kissed greedily, very aware of being on the big bed together. Tim pushed her t-shirt up and squeezed her breasts. She flicked the button open on her front opening bra.

"Xanthe my darling. You are so beautiful." he kissed her erect nipples.

"Oh I love you doing that." she crooned. "But please don't start anything you don't intend to finish."

"Finish? How?"

"Here and now Timmy."

Tim didn't need telling twice. This was it. He couldn't hold back with Xanthe under him, in his bed, in his private apartment that no one knew about.

"Hell. I don't have any condoms." he groaned.

"I'm on the pill Timmy."

"You are? Since when?"

"Since before I decided to get you. Getting a script from a pharmacist was the one useful thing I learnt during sex-ed at school. I didn't need parental consent for it. No one else knows."

"And...would it be effective by now?"

"Well and truly. I began just wanting you to be my first, but now I want you to be my first and last. I love you Timmy."

"And I truly love you Xanthe."

Tim pulled her clothes off and got rid of his shorts in record time. They paused drinking in the sight of each other naked. Xanthe ran her hands down his chest admiring his firm muscled torso. He wished she would touch his erection. He craved it enough to ask.

"Xanthe, will you kiss me down there like you did that other time?"

"I thought you didn't like that."

"I liked it too much, but I didn't want it to be the main event. That's still how I feel. I want to be inside you. Let me know when you feel ready."

"Timmy, I've felt ready ever since we first met."

Tim's maleness intrigued Xanthe as the perfect yang to her yin. She fondled every vein and ridge of his fascinating member wanting to know him completely.

"Oh my god," he moaned, "please kiss me there."

Xanthe kissed the end of his throbbing penis and tickled it with her tongue. Watching and feeling her do it, peaked Tim's anticipation to the point of no return. He had to have her.

"Does that feel good Timmy?"

"Unbelievably good. Xanthe, I could show you how it feels, if you allow me."

She lay back and writhed to the sensation of his tongue. He took the opportunity to spread her apart and slip a finger inside her warmth.

"You feel absolutely ready Xanthe. I know I am."

Mounting, careful not to put his whole weight on her, his penis found its way home like a heat seeking missile. Tim exulted in gaining smooth entry. His great concern had been fumbling for it ineptly. They began their initiations together to the sound of waves crashing on the nearby shore.

Every fibre of his being urged Tim to bash out his pent up frustrations. Overcome with desire, his first rock hard thrust went deep. Xanthe cried out in pain, wincing and biting her bottom lip.

Full penetration hurt far more than she expected. The invader driven inside her felt impossibly enormous. She believed this part was supposed to feel wonderful, but it was like being impaled by a stinger. She could only hope it got better.

Tim felt her tension and cursed himself for being too rough and ready. Xanthe had always been so uninhibited and forward, he had only worried about his own performance being too weak.

"Does it hurt?"

"Yes. In a good way." she fibbed.

"I can stop if you want. I mean slow down. Not stop."

After getting this far, withdrawal was not in Tim's game plan.

"Maybe go easy so I can gradually adjust to your size. I want to contain you all the way Timmy."

Pride for his manhood prompted Tim to fish for compliments.

"Am I too big?"

"You are perfect Timmy."

Euphoric for being described as perfect, Tim rocked Xanthe gently to the rhythm of life.

"You feel amazing." he said. "Relax my darling and I promise it will get better."

Tim hoped he was right because he revelled in ecstatic pleasure greater than he'd thought possible.

Xanthe only began to enjoy it as Tim climaxed. His warm juices anointed her internal discomfort as the best possible balm. She loved hearing his high pitched cry of pleasure on his ultimate release.

Their first coupling culminated too quickly and therefore been bitter sweet. They lay panting in the afterglow, reliving the event, already looking forward to a rerun.

"Now you're mine Xanthe. Forever. Are you okay?"

She smiled and nodded. *Yes.*

"I thought I'd be showing you around this place well before that ever happened."

"Is this place really yours? Aren't you moving overseas?"

"Yes it is mine, and the banks of course. Why would you think I'm moving overseas?"

"Just something Chantel said when you gave notice on the flat."

"Chantel? I don't know how Chantel got that idea. You do know she still thinks I'm gay."

"We've kept our secrets Timmy."

Tim changed the soiled bed linen while Xanthe went to the bathroom. The blood stained sheet, stark evidence of a dream come true, but also of his failure to honour her parents' wishes. Yet, taking Xanthe had been so worth it. Despite his guilt, Tim had no remorse.

"What now?" Xanthe asked.

"Now we can try out the walk-in shower. I might even wash your back."

"Oh. Yes please."

Tim made tea and poached eggs on toast while Xanthe admired the well-appointed kitchen. She loved the sliding drawers and pull out shelving.

"Does the kitchen meet with your approval? I know you're doing a culinary course this year."

"The whole apartment is amazing. Everything is finished to the nth degree."

"As I said, this place will never feel complete without you Xanthe. I want you here with me."

"You mean when I'm old enough to marry?"

"No I mean from now on. By hook or by crook. If I can't have you in my bed tonight and every night, I'll be howling at the moon again."

They decided to front Xanthe's parents and plead their case.

Angus, Opal and the twins were watching a movie together when the lovers arrived at the Bridcombe residence.

"So you've made up your differences. Knew you would." Angus remarked mildly.

"Have you had lunch? There's a roast in the oven."

"Thanks Mum. Better wait until you hear our news. You might disown me."

Uh oh.

"What news would that be?"

Tim put his hand up. Drawing on Dulcy's advice to Angus about keeping statements simple, he chose to drop the bombshell all in one short sentence:

"I have taken Xanthe as my own and I want her to move in with me. Today."

The four other Bridcombe's stared, astonished by Tim's unexpected announcement. Bolstered by being head over heels in love, the couple stood their ground. No one doubted what Tim meant, yet Xanthe explained further:

"We have made love at last and want to be together now and forever."

"I'm sorry I failed to honour your wishes, but I can't be sorry for loving Xanthe."

Tim had answers prepared for the onslaught and uproar:

"What about..." Opal began.

"We used contraception."

"But where..."

"I bought a large home unit. It's at Number One The Esplanade."

"So you planned this behind our backs." Angus growled.

"Xanthe. Did you know Tim bought that unit?" Opal exclaimed.

"No Mum. I only found out today."

Tim attempted to explain further:

"I acquired the apartment with a view to the future, living in hope Xanthe might share it with me some day. I hadn't told anyone about it."

"But Xanthe has shared it with you now." Angus snarled.

"Yes, but it wasn't supposed to happen this way. I respected your advice and stayed completely away from her for weeks. But this morning the situation...um...changed. I missed Xanthe so much. I found myself unable to resist temptation."

"He's been howling at the moon Mummy." Xanthe added.

"I'd like to see that." Lirah said.

"How romantic!" Kinta sighed.

"Romantic! Is that all you girls think about?"

"Daddy. I always planned to be Timmy's girl. I think that has been pretty obvious."

"It was obvious to me." Lirah said.

"Me too." Kinta added, "So Tim, does this mean you're not moving overseas?"

"No. Like many rumours about me, that one is wildly exaggerated."

"I went to that apartment this morning ready to fight for my Timmy. You see, I followed him one day and saw him with another woman there. I thought it was her place."

"What! You had another girlfriend on the side Tim?" Opal cried.

"No no no. The woman Xanthe saw is a decorator. She's a married woman who runs a local interior design business with her husband. They're in the high street."

"That posh shop with all the fancy stuff in the window and no prices?"

"Yes. That's the one."

"Bet they saw you coming." Angus said.

"Coming and going Angus." Tim agreed.

"I saw the bill. It's enough to buy a decent car. But the apartment looks fabulous." Xanthe added.

"How did you get there Xanthe?" Opal asked.

"I borrowed a bicycle."

"I knew about the bicycle." Angus admitted.

"You didn't tell me about her borrowing any bicycle." Opal riled.

"Why would I? It wasn't important. Geez."

"Xanthe was going to biff that other woman." Lirah butted in.

"I wasn't going to biff her Lirah. I was going to tell her off in a dignified manner."

"Xanthe's been crying all night about Tim being with that beautiful model." Kinta added.

Xanthe took Tim's hand.

"Timmy is all mine now. I jumped to the wrong conclusion."

"I told you Xanthe. Tim always loved you." Kinta smiled.

"Even if you called him a stuffy old book nerd." Lirah offered.

"Thanks for bringing that up."

"You're welcome."

"Timmy did a ring-in request for *Unchained Melody*." Xanthe said.

"Yes we heard it." Angus replied dourly.

"I love that song!" Kinta clasped her hands to her heart. "I hope I get someone handsome and brave and romantic like Tim for my first lover."

"How many lovers do you plan to get Kinta?" Lirah teased.

"Just one would do if he were anything like Tim."

"Yep. I agree. Great body. Good job. Nice new apartment. Great body."

"You said great body twice, Lirah."

Tim practice his deadpan face almost perfectly apart from a slight twitch to his mouth. Xanthe caught it.

"Stop talking about my guy like he isn't here." she scolded.

Opal put her foot down:

"That's enough of that carry-on. This is a serious family matter. You girls can set the table for six and serve the roast while we discuss this in private. Angus! In the bedroom."

Angus obediently followed his wife.

"Angus. It can't have been easy for Tim to be straight up-front with us." Opal began.

"He is brave. I'd actually be relieved to get one of them settled." Angus admitted.

"Tim is worthy of her. She really could do worse."

"True. Alright. But let's make him sweat it out for a while."

"You've got a mean streak Angus."

"Had a good teacher." he replied.

Opal and Angus took their places at the dining table without a word. Everyone began eating. On tenterhooks, Tim broke the silence.

"This is delicious."

"Roast dinners are Mum's speciality. I can't wait to start our cooking classes together."

"You'd still want to do that if you move out?" Opal asked.

"Of course! We would see each other all the time. And I'd still work at *Chantel's* too."

"I'll miss Xanthe." Kinta began to cry.

Unconcerned, Lirah mopped up her gravy with bread and stuffed it in her mouth.

"But Tim would be a great brother." she mumbled.

"Don't speak with your mouth full Lirah."

"I wasn't."

"You're doing it now."

Tim put them back on track with an earnest promise:

"I'd take my family duties very seriously and protect all of you with my life."

Opal eyed Angus. She wanted him to be the boss in saying their sixteen year old daughter could live with a twenty-nine year old lover.

"Alright Tim Fun. You jumped the gun with Xanthe. But you jumped in once before and saved my life, or I wouldn't be here. This has come about sooner than ideal. However, Opal and I choose to give our blessings. Plus, I need all the help I can get looking out for the other two."

"Yay! We get a third more wardrobe space." Lirah cheered.

35

Alright?

I'll Live

After leaving the Bridcombe family home, with her parents' blessings, Tim and Xanthe spent their first night living together as a couple.

Xanthe chose to shower and change alone in the bathroom so she could use a vaginal lubricant and inspect any damage to her person. No more bleeding showed on a white tissue. She felt good to go.

Tim's breath caught when his beautiful girlfriend entered the bedroom. A shadow of dark pubic hair and a hint of pink nipples showed through her flimsy nightgown. He reclined against a stack of pillows, his eagerness on full display since he never wore clothes to bed.

Xanthe grinned but kept him waiting while she attended to her bedtime beauty rituals.

She sat at the dressing table and diligently applied moisturiser to her face and hands before taking up her hairbrush. Tim waited and waited.

He knew nothing of the hundred brush strokes needed to maintain such lovely long tresses. In his impatience he imagined Xanthe delayed joining him in bed on purpose. He thought perhaps she did not feel as keen as he did.

Tim reminded himself of the bloodstained sheets that morning and how he'd lustily plunged into her like a rampant beast. As much as he yearned for their second time, he considered how his young lover might be feeling.

"Xanthe, perhaps our first time was better for me than it was for you."

She only smiled vaguely because she didn't want to lose count of the steady brush strokes through her long brown hair...*48, 49, 50*...

Tim waited for her to say something. When she didn't speak, he pulled the top sheet up to hide his keen expectations. Xanthe noticed he did so and wondered why. She'd been enjoying his naked reflection in the dressing table mirror...*67, 68, 69*...

Tim soldiered on, trying to keep any disappointment out of his voice:

"Darling, we could just cuddle tonight. Okay?"

Xanthe paused plying her hairbrush.

"You don't want to have sex?"

"I always want to have sex, except if there are issues with soreness and exhaustion."

Xanthe understood it had been a long and gruelling day. She didn't want to overtax her Timmy, but she had very looked forward to their second bout. Having him cry off for just a cuddle irked her no end. She put her head down and threw her mass of hair over to brush from the nape upwards.

"Now I've lost count." she huffed.

"It's only been once Xanthe."

Once? Surely he didn't want her to start over.

"No Timmy. I was nearly up to 90 strokes."

"I meant only once for real. The whole way. Like this morning. Only I'd do better."

"Right. I'll just do five more and call it done. 1,2,3,4,5." she mumbled aloud as she brushed.

Being a canny detective, Tim twigged his girl had been counting her brush strokes.

Xanthe slid in beside Tim and pecked a sweet little kiss on his cheek. No pressure.

"I'm up for a nice cuddle." she said.

"A few *proper* goodnight kisses wouldn't go astray." he replied.

"Okay. If you're sure you can handle it. I aim to please."

Xanthe peeped under the sheet. His upright willy did not seem exhausted. Nevertheless, she began her proper goodnight kisses very softly where he liked it most. Tim groaned.

Poor Timmy. Xanthe wasn't surprised he felt sore after the vigorous innings of that morning.

"Sorry darling Timmy. I'll make it up to you."

To save him exerting too much energy, she carefully straddled his waist and kissed his mouth. Again, Tim smelt his masculine scent on her lips. It drove him mad. He flipped her nightdress off over her head.

"I want to look at you."

"You like my titties hey."

"I adore your titties."

Xanthe rose on her knees, offering a breast to his mouth. He grasped a nipple in his lips and sucked.

"Is that nice Xanthe? Can I do the other one?"

"Oh yes please. It's the best feeling. I love it."

Transported by waves of pleasure, Xanthe instinctively slid her body down onto Tim's rigid erection. Slow massaging gyrations eased him in where she ached for fulfilment. The cuddle session progressed better than Tim expected. He had no objections.

"I'll do all the work Timmy. If it hurts too much I'll stop."

"I wouldn't want it to hurt." he panted his desire.

"Don't worry. I'll be very gentle."

Xanthe forgot to be gentle as she experienced her first ever orgasm. Tim exulted in her cries of delight and the satisfaction on her face. He rolled her over and took his turn on top, revelling in shared joy. Finally, they collapsed fully sated. Neither were able to raise the energy to utter flowery endearments.

"Alright?" she asked unnecessarily.

"I'll live." he replied.

They fell asleep smiling in each other's arms.

When Tim gave Xanthe a diamond ring for her seventeenth birthday, he only had one question:

"You can be known as Mrs. Fun or Mrs. Funicular. Officially you will be Mrs. Anwei Timothy Funicular of course. What do you want?"

"I love the long version. But I want to be known as Mrs. Fun so there is no mistake that I am your wife Tim Fun." Xanthe laughed happily.

They planned to marry within six weeks.

"It has to be by the sea because it's where we first met."

"You're my siren mermaid Xanthe."

Tim's wedding celebrant aunt, Francis Funicular, officiated.

Despite ceremonies held on the beach, Tim chose to wear a suit, and Xanthe wore a beautiful but simple pale blue wedding dress overlaid with white lace. Lirah and Kinta as bridesmaids wore matching dresses in ocean colours of pale green and deep blue. Opal forbade them wearing bikinis which had been their fondest wish.

Angus wore his best police uniform to give Xanthe away. As mother of the bride, Opal chose an elegant silk ensemble in pale pink.

Indoors at the surf club, the only formal table setting had been reserved for the bride and groom, the Bridcombes, Francis Funicular, the Grimslades plus Jarrah and Warragul.

The four Birdwhistles sat with Chantel Chiron, David Dubois and their wayward sons, Davy and Dominic.

"Isn't Tim Fun supposed to be gay?" David whispered.

Chantel replied with her fingers crossed behind her back.

"Apparently, Xanthe converted him."

She finally appreciated Tim's little white lie and imagined he only did it so she could save face.

An informal breakfast catered by the surf club had all the lifeguards and other members welcomed to attend. The nastier surfer girls did what they did best: Cashed in on the free nosh and bitched.

"Well at least he's made one of those Bridcombe girls an honest woman."

"Girl. Not woman. She's barely seventeen."

"Makes me sick. Guess where they'll be living...Number One *The Esplanade* no less."

More than one of Tim Fun's past failed dates regretted letting him get away.

Ribald speeches from the lifeguards got the party going, and everyone enjoyed the festivities. Angus made a quiet remark to his wife.

"One down, two to go."

Opal took the cue to ask the twins what they wanted to do after leaving school.

"I mean as serious viable careers, not pie in the sky."

Kinta replied first.

"Okay. Seriously. I am going to join the police force."

The unexpected choice from the meeker twin surprised her parents.

"Why the police force Kinta?" her father asked.

"Well, Dad, I was totally impressed seeing you take control when we found Tim. I realised what amazing work you do and that it is really worthwhile. If I could become half as good as you, it would be a great achievement, and I would make you both proud." Kinta replied earnestly.

Angus had something in his eye and couldn't reply.

"How about you Lirah?" Opal asked.

"Me? I will join the police force too."

"And why?"

"To snag a great bloke like Tim Fun of course." Lirah laughed.

The End

Credits

Quotes & Songs

"Some people are nobody's enemies but their own" ~ Charles Dickens 1867 "The Adventures of Oliver Twist".

"We never tire of the friendships we form with books."~ Charles Dickens 1914 " A Charles Dickens Birthday Book".

"New thoughts and hopes were whirling through my mind, and all the colours of my life were changing." ~ Charles Dickens "David Copperfield".

"Put Your Head on My Shoulder" ~ a song written by Canadian-born singer-songwriter Paul Anka, recorded in August 1958 at Bell Sound Studios in New York City ~ lyrics available online.

"Unchained Melody" ~ is a 1955 song by Alex North with lyrics by Hy Zaret. One of the most recorded songs of the 20th century, with the version recorded by the Righteous Brothers in 1965 notable in its own right.

Also By Jo Milanne

Other Titles

A FAIR CRACK ~ And a Walk-in Wardrobe ~ a feisty newspaper reporter invents a fake boyfriend to ward off attentions from her boss.

THE BRUISER ~ Bad to the Core ~ a man with a damaged personality goes on a crime spree across Australia.

THE PECKISH ~ A bored supermarket check-out girl secretly engages in matchmaking customers with each other.

LEMON TANGO ~ A woman loves two men. One is her best friend. The other is her obsession.

THE WHODUNIT THING ~ The love life of a lady detective from childhood through puberty to maturity.